RANDOM HOUSE

HOUSE

LARGE

PRINT

TEN BIG
ONES

Also by Janet Evanovich
available from Random House Large Print

To the Nines
Visions of Sugar Plums
Hard Eight
Seven Up

TEN BIG
ONES

Janet Evanovich

RANDOM HOUSE
LARGE PRINT

Copyright © 2004 by Evanovich, Inc.

All rights reserved under International and Pan-American Copyright Conventions. Published in the United States of America by Random House Large Print in association with St. Martin's Press, New York, and simultaneously in Canada by Random House of Canada Limited, Toronto. Distributed by Random House, Inc., New York.

The Library of Congress has established a Cataloging-in-Publication record for this title.

ISBN 0-375-43203-5

www.randomlargeprint.com

FIRST LARGE PRINT EDITION

10   9   8   7   6   5   4   3   2   1

This Large Print edition published in accord with the standards of the N.A.V.H.

*This book is an Evanovich/Enderlin
publishing adventure. Thanks to SuperJen,
AKA SuperEditor!*

*Thanks to Mitch Adelman for suggesting the title
for this book.*

ONE

THE WAY I see it, life is a jelly doughnut. You don't really know what it's about until you bite into it. And then, just when you decide it's good, you drop a big glob of jelly on your best T-shirt.

My name is Stephanie Plum, and I drop a lot of jelly globs, figuratively and literally. Like the time I accidentally burned down a funeral home. That was the mother of all jelly globs. I got my picture in the paper for that one. I'd walk down the street and people would recognize me.

"You're famous now," my mother said when the paper came out. "You have to set an example. You have to exercise, eat good food, and be nice to old people."

Okay, so my mother was probably right, but I'm from Jersey and truth is, I have a hard time getting a grip on the good example thing. A good example in Jersey isn't exactly the national ideal. Not to mention, I inherited a lot of unmanageable brown hair and rude hand gestures from my father's Italian side of the family. What am I supposed to do with that?

My mother's side is Hungarian and from this I get blue eyes and the ability to eat birthday cake and still button the top snap on my jeans. I'm told the good Hungarian metabolism lasts only until I'm forty, so I'm counting down. The Hungarian genes also carry a certain amount of luck and gypsy intuition, both of which I need in my present job. I'm a Bond Enforcement Agent, working for my cousin Vincent Plum, and I run down bad guys. I'm not the best BEA in the world, and I'm not the worst. An incredibly hot guy with the street name Ranger is the best. And my sometimes partner, Lula, is possibly the worst.

Maybe it's not fair to have Lula in the running for worst bounty hunter of all time. To begin with, there are some really bad bounty hunters out there. And more to the point, Lula isn't actually a bounty hunter. Lula is a former hooker who was hired to do the filing for the bail bonds office but spends a lot of her day trailing after me.

At the moment, Lula and I were standing in the parking lot of a deli-mart on Hamilton Avenue. We were about a half mile from the office and we were leaning against my yellow Ford Escape, trying to make a lunch choice. We were debating nachos at the deli-mart against a sub at Giovichinni's.

"Hey," I said to Lula. "What happened to the filing job? Who does the filing now?"

"I do the filing. I file the ass out of that office."

"You're never in the office."

"The hell I am. I was in the office when you showed up this morning."

"Yeah, but you weren't filing. You were doing your nails."

"I was thinking about filing. And if you hadn't needed my help going to look for that loser Roger Banker, I'd still be filing."

Roger was accused of grand theft auto and possession of controlled substances. In layman's terms, Roger got high and went joy riding.

"So you're still officially a file clerk?"

"Heck no," Lula said. "That's so-o-o boring. Do I look like a file clerk to you?"

Actually, Lula still looked like a hooker. Lula's a full-bodied black woman who favors animal print spandex enhanced with sequins. I figured Lula didn't want to hear my fashion opinion, so I didn't say anything. I just raised an eyebrow.

"The job title is tricky since I do a lot of this here bounty hunter stuff but I've never really been given any of my own cases," Lula said. "I suppose I could be your bodyguard."

"Omigod."

Lula narrowed her eyes at me. "You got a problem with that?"

"It seems a little . . . Hollywood."

"Yeah, but sometimes you need some extra firepower, right? And there I am. Hell, you don't even carry a gun half the time. I always got a gun. I got a gun now. Just in case."

And Lula pulled a 40-caliber Glock out of her purse.

"I don't mind using it either. I'm good with a gun. I got an eye for it. Watch me hit that bottle next to the bike."

Someone had leaned a fancy red mountain bike against the big plate glass window in the front of the deli-mart. There was a quart bottle next to the bike. The bottle had a rag stuffed into it.

"No," I said. "No shooting!"

Too late. Lula squeezed off a shot, missed the bottle, and destroyed the bike's rear tire.

"Oops," Lula said, doing a grimace and immediately returning the gun to her purse.

A moment later, a guy ran out of the store. He was wearing a mechanic's jumpsuit and a red devil mask. He had a small backpack slung over one shoulder and he had a gun in his right hand. His skin tone was darker than mine but lighter than Lula's. He grabbed the bottle off the ground, lit the rag with a flick of his Bic, and threw the bottle into the store. He turned to get onto the bike and realized his tire was blown to smithereens.

"Fuck," the guy said. "FUCK!"

"I didn't do it," Lula said. "Wasn't me. Someone came along and shot up your tire. You must not be popular."

There was a lot of shouting inside the store, the guy in the devil mask turned to flee, and Victor, the Pakistani day manager, rushed out the door. "I am done! Do you hear me?" Victor yelled. "This is the fourth robbery this month and I won't stand for any more. You are dog excrement!" he shouted at the guy in the mask. "Dog excrement."

Lula had her hand back in her purse. "Hold on. I got a gun!" she said. "Where the hell is it? Why can't you ever find the damn gun when you need it?"

Victor threw the still lit but clearly unbroken bottle at the guy in the devil mask, hitting him in the back of the head. The bottle bounced off the devil's head and smashed against my driver's side door. The devil staggered, and instinctively pulled the mask off. Maybe he couldn't breathe, or maybe he went to feel for blood, or maybe he just wasn't thinking. Whatever the reason, the mask was only off for a second, before being yanked back over the guy's head. He turned and looked directly at me, and then he ran across the street and disappeared into the alley between two buildings.

The bottle instantly ignited when it hit my car, and flames raced along the side and the undercarriage of the Escape.

"Holy crap," Lula said, looking up from her purse. "Damn."

"Why me?" I shrieked. "Why does this always happen to me? I can't believe this car is on fire. My cars are always getting exploded. How many cars have I lost like this since you've known me?"

"A lot," Lula said.

"It's embarrassing. What am I going to tell my insurance company?"

"It wasn't your fault," Lula said.

"It's never my fault. Do they care? I don't think they care!"

"You got bad car karma," Lula said. "But at least you're lucky at love."

For the last couple months I've been living with Joe Morelli. Morelli's a very sexy, very handsome Trenton cop. Morelli and I have a long history and possibly a long future. Mostly we take it day by day, neither of us feeling the need for documented commitment right now. The good thing about living with a cop is that you never have to call home when disaster strikes. As you might suspect, that's also the bad part. Seconds after the emergency call goes in on the robbery and car fire, describing my yellow Escape, at least forty different cops, EMTs, and fire fighters will track Morelli down and tell him his girlfriend's done it again.

Lula and I moved farther from the fire, knowing from experience that an explosion was a possibility. We stood patiently waiting, listening to the sirens whining in the distance, getting closer by the second. Morelli's unmarked cop car would be minutes behind the sirens. And somewhere in the mix of emergency vehicles my professional mentor and man of mystery, Ranger, would slide in to check things out.

"Maybe I should leave," Lula said. "There's all that filing back at the office. And cops give me the runs."

Not to mention she was illegally carrying a concealed weapon that was instrumental in this whole fiasco.

"Did you see the guy's face when he pulled his mask off?" I asked her.

"No. I was looking for my gun. I missed that."

"Then leaving might be a good idea," I said. "Get me a sub on the way back to the office. I don't think they'll be making nachos here for a while."

"I'd rather have the sub anyways. A car fire always gives me an appetite."

And Lula took off power walking.

Victor was on the other side of the car,

stomping around and pulling at his hair. He stopped stomping and fixed his attention on me. "Why didn't you shoot him? I know you. You are a bounty hunter. You should have shot him."

"I'm not carrying a gun," I told Victor.

"Not carrying a gun? What kind of bounty hunter are you? I watch television. I know about these things. Bounty hunters always have many guns."

"Actually, shooting people is a no-no in bond enforcement."

Victor shook his head. "I don't know what this world is coming to when bounty hunters don't shoot people."

A blue-and-white patrol car arrived and two uniforms got out and stood hands on hips, taking it all in. I knew both cops. Andy Zajak and Robin Russell.

Andy Zajak was riding shotgun. Two months ago he'd been plainclothes, but he'd asked a local politician some embarrassing questions during a robbery investigation and had gotten busted back to uniform. It could have been worse. Zajak could have been assigned to a desk in the tower of Irrelevance. Sometimes things could get tricky in the Trenton police department.

Zajak waved when he saw me. He said something to Russell, and they both smiled. No doubt enjoying the continuing calamitous exploits of Stephanie Plum.

I'd gone to school with Robin Russell. She was a year behind me, so we weren't the closest of friends, but I liked her. She wasn't especially athletic when she was in high school. She was one of the quiet brainy kids. And she surprised everyone when she joined Trenton P.D. two years ago.

A fire truck followed Zajak and Russell. Plus two more cop cars and an EMT truck. By the time Morelli arrived, the hoses and chemical extinguishers were already out and in use.

Morelli angled his car behind Robin Russell's and walked across to me. Morelli was lean and hard muscled with wary cop eyes that softened in the bedroom. His hair was almost black, falling in waves over his forehead, brushing his collar. He was wearing a slightly oversize blue shirt with the sleeves rolled, black jeans, and black boots with a Vibram sole. He had his gun on his hip and, with or without the gun, he didn't look like someone you'd want to mess with. There was a tilt to his mouth that could pass for a smile. Then again, it could just as easily be a grimace. "Are you okay?"

"It wasn't my fault," I told him.

This got a genuine smile from him. "Cupcake, it's never your fault." His eyes traveled to the red mountain bike with the destroyed tire. "What's with the bike?"

"Lula accidentally shot the tire. Then a guy wearing a red devil mask ran out of the store, took a look at the bike, tossed a Molotov cocktail into the store, and set off on foot. The bottle didn't break, so Victor pitched it at the devil. The bottle bounced off the devil's head and crashed against my car."

"I didn't hear the part about Lula shooting the tire."

"Yeah, I figured it wasn't necessary to mention that in the official statement."

I looked past Morelli, as a black Porsche 911 Turbo pulled to the curb. There weren't a lot of people in Trenton who could afford the car. Mostly high-level drug dealers . . . and Ranger.

I watched as Ranger angled out from behind the wheel and ambled over. He was about the same height as Morelli, but he had more bulk to his muscle. Morelli was a cat. Ranger was Rambo meets Batman. Ranger was in SWAT black cargo pants and T-shirt. His hair was dark, and his eyes were dark, and his skin reflected his Cuban ancestry. No one knew Ranger's age, but I'd guess it was close to mine. Late twenties to early thirties. No one knew where Ranger lived or where his cars and cash originated. Probably it was best not to know.

Ranger nodded to Morelli and locked eyes with me. Sometimes it felt like Ranger could look you in the eye and know all the stuff that was inside your head. It was a little unnerving, but it saved a lot of time since talk wasn't necessary.

"Babe," Ranger said. And he left.

Morelli watched Ranger get into his Porsche and take off. "Half the time I'm happy to have him watching over you. And half the time it scares the hell out of me. He's always in black, the address on his driver's license is a vacant lot, and he never says anything."

"Maybe he has a dark history . . . like Batman. A tortured soul."

"Tortured soul? Ranger? Cupcake, the guy's a mercenary." Morelli playfully twirled a strand of my hair around his finger. "You've been watching Dr. Phil again, right? Oprah? Geraldo? *Crossing Over* with John Edward?"

"*Crossing Over* with John Edward. And Ranger's not a mercenary. At least not officially in Trenton. He's a bounty hunter . . . like me."

"Yeah, and I really hate that you're a bounty hunter."

Okay. I know I have a crappy job. The money isn't all that great and sometimes people shoot at me. Still, someone's got to make sure the accused show up in court. "I do a service for the community," I told Morelli. "If it wasn't for people like me the police would have to track these guys. The taxpayer would have to foot the bill for a larger police force."

"I'm not disputing the job. I just don't want *you* doing it."

There was a loud *phooonf* sound from the underside of my car, flames shot out, and a steaming tire popped off and rolled across the lot.

"This is the fourteenth Red Devil robbery," Morelli said. "The routine is always the same. Rob the store at gunpoint. Get

away on a bike. Cover your getaway with
a bottle bomb. No one's ever seen enough
to ID him."

"Until now," I said. "I saw the guy's face.
I didn't recognize him, but I think I could
pick him out of a lineup."

AN HOUR LATER, Morelli dropped me
off at the bond office. He snagged me by
the back of my shirt as I was leaving his
unmarked seen-better-days Crown Vic
cop car. "You're going to be careful,
right?"

"Right."

"And you're not going to let Lula do any
more shooting."

I did a mental sigh. He was asking the
impossible. "Sometimes it's hard to control Lula."

"Then get a different partner."

"Ranger?"

"Very funny," Morelli said.

He French-kissed me good-bye, and I
thought probably I could control Lula.
When Morelli kissed me, I thought anything was possible. Morelli was a terrific
kisser.

His pager buzzed and he pulled away to

check the readout. "I have to go," he said, shoving me out the door.

I leaned in the window at him. "Remember, we promised my mom we'd come for dinner tonight."

"No way. You promised. I didn't promise. I had dinner at your parents' house three days ago and once a week is my limit. Valerie and the kids will be there, right? And Kloughn? I'm getting heartburn just thinking about it. Anybody who eats with that crew should get combat pay."

He was right. I had no comeback. A little over a year ago my sister's husband took off for parts unknown with the babysitter. Valerie immediately moved back home with her two kids and took a job with a struggling lawyer, Albert Kloughn. Somehow, Kloughn managed to get Val pregnant and in nine months' time my parents' small three-bedroom, one-bathroom house in the Chambersburg section of Trenton was home to my mom, my dad, Grandma Mazur, Valerie, Albert Kloughn, Val's two little girls and newborn baby.

As a short-term fix to my sister's housing dilemma I volunteered the use of my apartment. I was spending most of my nights with Morelli anyway, so it wasn't a total sacrifice on my part. It's now three months down the road and Valerie is still in my apartment, returning to my parents' house every night for dinner. Once in a while something fun happens at dinner . . . like Grandma setting the table-cloth on fire or Kloughn choking on a chicken bone. But usually it's just flat-out migraine-inducing bedlam.

"Boy, too bad you'll miss the roast chicken with gravy and mashed potatoes," I told Morelli in a last-ditch effort. "Probably pineapple upside-down cake for dessert."

"Not gonna work. You're going to have to come up with something better than roast chicken to get me over to your parents' house tonight."

"What, like wild gorilla sex?"

"Not even wild gorilla sex. It would have to be an orgy with identical Japanese triplets."

I gave Morelli an eye roll, and I left for the bond office.

"Your sub's filed under S," Lula said when I swung through the door. "I got you capicolla and provolone and turkey and pepperoni with some hot peppers."

I opened the file and retrieved my sub. "There's only half a sandwich here."

"Well, yeah," Lula said. "Me and Connie decided you wouldn't want to get fat by eating that whole sub all yourself. So we helped you out."

Vincent Plum Bail Bonds is a small storefront office on Hamilton Avenue. Ordinarily a more lucrative location for a bonds office would be across from the courts or the lockup. Vinnie's office is across from the Burg, and a lot of Vinnie's repeat customers are local. Not that the Burg is a bad neighborhood. Truth is, the Burg is possibly the safest place to live if you have to live in Trenton. There's a lot of low-level mob in the Burg and if you misbehave in the Burg you could quietly disappear for a very long time . . . like forever.

It's even possible that some of Connie's relatives might assist in the disappearance. Connie is Vinnie's office manager. She's five foot four and looks like Betty Boop with a mustache. Her desk is positioned in front of Vinnie's small inner office, preventing the unsuspecting from walking in on Vinnie while he's on the phone with his bookie, taking a snooze, or having a private conversation with his johnson. Also behind Connie's desk is a bank of file cabinets. And behind the file cabinets is a small stockroom packed with guns and ammo, office supplies, bathroom supplies, and assorted confiscated booty that mostly runs to computers, fake Rolex watches, and fake Louis Vuitton handbags.

I slouched onto the scarred dung-brown fake leather couch that was positioned against a side wall of the outer office and unwrapped the sub.

"Big day in court yesterday," Connie said, waving a handful of manila folders at me. "We had three guys fail to appear. The bad news is they're all chump change. The good news is none of them have killed or raped in the last two years."

I took the folders from Connie and returned to the couch. "I suppose you want me to find these guys," I said to Connie.

"Yeah," Connie said. "Finding them would be good. Dragging their asses back to jail would be even better."

I flipped through the folders. Harold

Pancek. Wanted for indecent exposure and destruction of personal property.

"What's the deal on Harold?" I asked Connie.

"He's local. Moved to the Burg three years ago from Newark. Lives in one of the row houses on Canter Street. Got drunk two weeks ago and tried to take a leak on Mrs. Gooding's cat, Ben. Ben was a moving target and Pancek mostly got the side of Gooding's house and Gooding's favorite rosebush. Killed the rosebush and took the paint off the house. And Gooding says she washed the cat three times and he still smells like asparagus."

Lula and I had our faces frozen in curled-lip grimaces.

"He doesn't sound like much of a threat," Connie said. "Just make sure you stand back if he whips it out to relieve himself."

I took a quick look at the two remaining files. Carol Cantell, wanted for holding up a Frito-Lay truck. This brought an instant smile to my face. Carol Cantell was a woman after my own heart.

The smile turned to raised eyebrows when I saw the name on the last file. Salvatore Sweet, charged with assault. "Omigod," I said to Connie. "It's Sally. I haven't seen him in ages." When I first met Salvatore Sweet he was playing lead guitar for a transvestite rock band. He helped me solve a crime and then disappeared into the night.

"Hey, I remember Sally Sweet," Lula said. "He was the shit. What's he doing now besides beating on people?"

"Driving a school bus," Connie said. "Guess the rock career didn't work out. He's living on Fenton Street, over by the button factory."

Sally Sweet was an MTV car crash. He was a nice guy but he couldn't get through a sentence without using the "f" word fourteen times. The kids on Sally's bus probably had the most inventive vocabularies in the school.

"Have you tried calling him?" I asked Connie.

"Yeah. No answer. And no answering machine."

"How about Cantell?"

"I talked to her earlier. She said she'd kill herself before she'd go to jail. She said you were going to have to come over there and shoot her and then drag her dead body out of the house."

"It says here she held up a Frito-Lay truck?"

"Apparently she was on that no-carbohydrate diet, got her period and snapped when she saw the truck parked in front of a convenience store. Just got whacked out at the thought of all those chips. She threatened the driver with a nail file, filled her car with bags of Fritos, and took off, leaving the driver standing there in front of his empty truck. The police asked him why he didn't stop her, and he said she was a woman on the edge. He said his wife got to looking like that sometimes, and he didn't go near her when she was like that, either."

"I've been on that diet and this crime makes perfect sense to me," Lula said. "Especially if she had her period. You don't want to go through your period without Fritos. Where you gonna get your salt from? And what about cramps? What are you supposed to take for cramps?"

"Midol?" Connie said.

"Well, yeah, but you gotta have some Fritos while you're waiting for the Midol to kick in. Fritos have a calming influence on a woman."

Vinnie stuck his head out the door of his inner office and glared at me. "What are you sitting around for? We got three FTAs in this morning and you already had one in your possession. Four FTAs! Christ, I'm not running a charity here."

Vinnie is my cousin on my father's side of the family and sole owner of Vincent Plum Bail Bonds. He's an oily little guy with slicked-back black hair, pointy-toed shoes, and a bunch of gold chains hanging around his scrawny tanning salon–tanned neck. It's rumored that he once had a romantic relationship with a duck. He drives a Cadillac Seville. And he's married to Harry the Hammer's only daughter. Vinnie's rating as a human being would be in the vicinity of pond slime. His rating as a bonds agent would be considerably higher. Vinnie understood human weakness.

"I haven't got a car," I told Vinnie. "My car got firebombed."

"What's your point? Your cars are always getting firebombed. Have Lula drive you. She doesn't do anything around here anyway."

"Your ass," Lula said.

Vinnie pulled his head back into his office, and he slammed and locked the door.

Connie rolled her eyes. And Lula flipped Vinnie the finger.

"I saw that," Vinnie yelled from behind his closed door.

"I hate when he's right," Lula said, "but there's no reason we can't use my car. I just don't want to pick up the drunken leaker. If he takes paint off a house, I'm not letting him near my upholstery."

"Try Cantell," Connie said. "She should still be at home."

FIFTEEN MINUTES LATER we were in front of Cantell's house in Hamilton Township. It was a trim little ranch on a small lot, in a neighborhood of similar houses. The grass was neatly cut, but it was patchy with crabgrass and parched from a hot, dry August. Young azaleas bordered the front of the house. A blue Honda Civic was parked in the driveway.

"Don't look like the home of a hijacker," Lula said. "No garage."

"Sounds like this was a once-in-a-lifetime experience."

We approached the front door and knocked. And Cantell answered.

"Oh God," Cantell said. "Don't tell me you're from the bond agency. I told the woman on the phone I didn't want to go to jail."

"This is just a rebooking process," I told her. "We bring you in and then Vinnie bonds you out again."

"No way. I'm not going back to that jail. It's too embarrassing. I'd rather you shoot me and kill me."

"We wouldn't shoot you," Lula said. "Unless, of course, you drew a gun. What we'd do is gas you. We got pepper spray. Or we could zap you with the stun gun. My choice would be the stun gun on account of we're using my car and there's a lot of snot produced if we give you a face full of pepper spray. I just had my car detailed. I don't want the backseat full of snot."

Cantell's mouth dropped open and her eyes glazed over. "I just took a couple bags of chips," she said. "It's not like I'm a criminal."

Lula looked around. "You wouldn't have any of them chips left over, would you?"

"I gave them all back. Except for the ones I ate."

Cantell had short brown hair and a pleasant round face. She was dressed in jeans and an extra-roomy T-shirt. Her age was listed as thirty-two.

"You should have kept your court date," I said to Cantell. "You might have only gotten community service."

"I didn't have anything to wear," she wailed. "Look at me. I'm a house! Nothing fits. I ate a truck full of Fritos!"

"You're not as big as me," Lula said. "And I got a lot of stuff to wear. You just gotta know how to shop. We should go out shopping together some day. My secret is I only buy spandex and I buy it too small. That way it sucks everything in. Not that I'm fat or anything. It's just I got a lot of muscle."

Lula was currently in athletic gear mode, wearing hot pink stretch pants, matching halter top, and serious running shoes. The strain on the spandex was frightening. I was heading for cover at the first sign of a seam unraveling.

"Here's the plan," I said to Cantell. "I'm going to call Vinnie and have him meet us at the courthouse. That way you can get bonded out immediately, and you won't have to sit around in a holding cell."

"I guess that would be okay," Cantell said. "But you have to get me back here before my kids get off the school bus."

"Sure," I said, "but just in case, maybe you want to make alternative arrangements."

"And maybe I can lose some weight before I have to go to court," Cantell said.

"Be a good idea not to hold up any more snack food trucks," Lula said.

"I had my period! I needed those chips."

"Hey, I hear you," Lula said.

AFTER WE GOT Cantell rebooked and rebonded and returned to her house, Lula drove me across town, back to the Burg.

"That wasn't so bad," Lula said. "She seemed like a real nice person. Do you think she's going to show up for court this time?"

"No. We're going to have to go over to her house and drag her to court, kicking and screaming."

"Yeah, that's what I think, too."

Lula pulled to the curb and idled in front of my parents' house. Lula drove a red

Firebird that had a sound system capable of broadcasting rap over a five-mile radius. Lula had the sound on low but the bass at capacity, and I could feel my fillings vibrating.

"Thanks for the ride," I told Lula. "See you tomorrow."

"Yo," Lula said. And she took off.

My Grandma Mazur was at the front door, waiting for me. Grandma Mazur rooms with my parents now that Grandpa Mazur is living *la vida loca* everlasting. Grandma Mazur has a body like a soup chicken and a mind that defies description. She keeps her steel gray hair cut short and tightly permed. She prefers pastel polyester pantsuits and white tennis shoes. And she watches wrestling. Grandma doesn't care if wrestling's fake or real. Grandma likes to look at big men in little spandex panties.

"Hurry up," Grandma said. "Your mother won't start serving drinks until you're at the table, and I need one real bad. I had the day from heck. I traipsed all the way over to Stiva's Funeral Parlor for Lorraine Schnagle's viewing, and she turned out to have a closed casket. I heard she looked real bad at the end, but that's

still no reason to deprive people from seeing the deceased. People count on getting
a look. I made an effort to get there, dressing up and everything. And now I'm not
going to have anything to talk about when
I get my hair done tomorrow. I was
counting on Lorraine Schnagle."

"You didn't try to open the casket, did
you?"

"Me? Of course not. I wouldn't do such
a thing. And anyway, it was locked up real
tight."

"Is Valerie here?"

"Valerie's always here," Grandma said.
"That's another reason I'm having the day
from heck. I was all tired after the big disappointment at the funeral parlor, and I
couldn't take a nap on account of your
niece is back to being a horse and won't
stop the galloping. And she whinnies all
the time. Between the baby crying and the
horse thing, I'm pooped. I bet I got bags
under my eyes. If this keeps up I'm going
to lose my looks." Grandma squinted up
and down the street. "Where's your car?"

"It sort of caught fire."

"Did the tires pop off? Was there an
explosion?"

"Yep."

"Darn! I wish I'd seen that. I always miss the good stuff. How'd it catch fire this time?"

"It happened at a crime scene."

"I'm telling you this town's going to hell in a handbasket. We never had so much crime. It's getting to where you don't want to go out of the neighborhood."

Grandma was right about the crime. I saw it escalating at the bond office. More robberies. More drugs on the street. More murders. Most of it drug and gang related. And now I had seen the Red Devil's face, so I was sucked into it.

TWO

I FOUND MY mom at the kitchen sink, peeling potatoes. My sister Valerie was in the kitchen, too. Valerie was seated at the small wood table, and she was nursing the baby. It seemed to me Valerie was always nursing the baby. There were times when I looked at the baby and felt the pull of maternal yearnings, but mostly I was glad I had a hamster.

Grandma followed me into the kitchen, anxious to tell everyone the news. "She blew up her car again," Grandma announced.

My mother stopped peeling. "Was anyone hurt?"

"No," I said. "Just the car. It was totaled."

My mother made the sign of the cross and took a white-knuckled grip on the paring knife. "I hate when you blow up cars!" she said. "How am I supposed to sleep at night knowing I have a daughter who blows up cars?"

"You could try drinking," Grandma said. "That always works for me. Nothing like a good healthy snort before bedtime."

My cell phone chirped, and everyone paused while I answered.

"Are you having fun yet?" Morelli wanted to know.

"Yeah. I just got to my parents' house and it's lots of fun. Too bad you're missing it."

"Bad news. You're going to have to miss it, too. One of the guys just brought in a suspect, and you're going to have to ID him."

"Now?"

"Yeah. Now. Do you need a ride?"

"No. I'll borrow the Buick."

When my Great Uncle Sandor went into the nursing home, he gave his '53 powder blue-and-white Buick Roadmaster to Grandma Mazur. Since Grandma

Mazur doesn't drive (at least not legally), the car mostly sits in my father's garage. It gets five miles to a gallon of gas. It drives like a refrigerator on wheels. And it doesn't fit my self-image. I see myself more as a Lexus SC430. My budget sees me as a secondhand Honda Civic. My bank was willing to stretch to a Ford Escape.

"That was Joe," I told everyone. "I have to meet him at the police station. They think they might have the guy who set fire to my car."

"Will you be back for the chicken?" my mother wanted to know. "And what about dessert?"

"Don't wait dinner. I'll get back if I can, and if not I'll take leftovers." I turned to Grandma. "I'm going to have to commandeer the Buick until I can replace the Escape."

"Help yourself," Grandma said. "And I'll ride with you to the police station. I could use to get out of the house. And on the way home we could stop at Stiva's to see if they got the lid up for the evening viewing. I'd hate to miss out on seeing Lorraine."

———

TWENTY MINUTES LATER, Grandma and I cruised into the public parking lot across the street from the cop shop. The Trenton police are housed in a no-nonsense chunk of brick and mortar in a no-nonsense part of town that gives the cops easy access to crime. The building is half cop shop and half courthouse. The courthouse half has a guard and a metal detector. The cop half has an elevator decorated with bullet holes.

I looked at Grandma's big black patent leather purse. Grandma was known to, from time to time, carry a .45 long barrel. "You don't have a gun in there, do you?" I asked.

"Who, me?"

"If they catch you taking a concealed weapon into the building they'll lock you up and throw the key away."

"How would they know I got a concealed weapon if it's concealed? They better not search me. I'm an old lady. I got certain rights."

"Carrying a concealed weapon isn't one of them."

Grandma pulled the gun out of her purse and shoved it under her seat. "I don't know what this country's coming to when an old lady can't keep a gun in her purse. We got a rule for everything these days. What about the bill of health? It says I can bear arms!"

"That's the Bill of Rights, and I don't think it specifically addresses guns in purses." I locked the Buick and called Joe on my cell. "I'm across the street," I told him. "And I've got Grandma with me."

"She isn't armed, is she?"

"Not anymore."

I could feel Joe smile across the phone line. "I'll meet you downstairs."

Civilian traffic in the building was minimal at this time of day. The courts were closed, and police business was shifting from front door inquiries to back door arrests. A lone cop sat in a bulletproof cage at the end of the hall, struggling to stay awake on his shift.

Morelli stepped out of the elevator just as Grandma and I swung through the front entrance doors.

Grandma looked at Morelli and gave a snort. "He's wearing a gun," she said.

"He's a cop."

"Maybe I should be a cop," Grandma said. "Do you think I'm too short?"

THIRTY MINUTES LATER, Grandma and I were back in the Buick.

"That didn't take long," Grandma said. "I hardly had a chance to look around."

"I couldn't make an ID. They picked up a guy who was carrying the backpack, but it wasn't the guy who ran out of the store. He said he found the backpack discarded in an alley."

"Bummer. This doesn't mean we're going to have to go back to the house, does it? I can't take any more of the galloping and the baby talk."

"Valerie talks baby talk to the baby?"

"No, she talks it to Kloughn. I don't like to make judgments on people, but after a couple hours of listening to 'honey pie smoochie bear cuddle umpkins' I'm ready to smack someone."

Okay, so I was glad I'd never been there when Valerie called Kloughn cuddle umpkins because I would have wanted to smack someone, too. And my self-restraint isn't as well honed as Grandma's.

"It's too early to go to the viewing," I

said to Grandma. "I guess I could stop in on Sally Sweet. He turned up Failure To Appear today on an assault charge."

"No kidding? I remember him. He was a nice young man. Sometimes he was a nice young woman. He had a plaid skirt I always admired."

I pulled out of the lot, right-turned onto North Clinton, and followed the road for almost a quarter mile. At one time in Trenton's history this was a thriving industrial area. The industry had all vacated or drastically downsized and the rotting carcasses of factories and warehouses produced an ambience similar to what you might find in postwar Bosnia.

I left Clinton and wove my way through a neighborhood of small bleak single-story row houses. Originally designed to contain the factory workers, the row houses were now occupied by hardworking people who lived one step above welfare . . . plus there were a few oddballs like Sally Sweet.

I found Fenton and parked in front of Sweet's house. "Wait in the car until I find out what's going on," I said to Grandma.

"Sure," Grandma said, her hands gripping her purse in excited anticipation, her eyes glued to Sweet's front door. The

Buick was a car designed for a man, and Grandma seemed swallowed up by the monster. Her feet barely touched the floor, her face was barely visible over the dash. A timid woman might feel overwhelmed by Big Blue. Grandma was a little shrunken, but she wasn't timid, and there wasn't a whole lot that overwhelmed Grandma. Thirty seconds after Grandma agreed to wait in the car, she was on the sidewalk, following me to Sweet's front door.

"I thought you were going to wait in the car?" I said.

"I changed my mind. I thought you might need help."

"Okay, but let me do the talking. I don't want to alarm him."

"Sure," Grandma said.

I knocked on Sweet's front door, and the door opened on the third knock. Sally Sweet looked out at me, recognition kicked in, and his face creased into a grin. "Long time no see," he said. "What brings you to my *casa*?"

"We're here to drag your behind back to jail," Grandma said.

"*Fuck*," Sally said. And he slammed the door shut.

"What was that?" I asked Grandma.

"I don't know. It just popped out."

I gave another rap on the door. "Open the door," I said. "I just want to talk to you."

Sally cracked the door and peeked at me. "I can't go to jail. I'll lose my job."

"Maybe I can help."

The door opened wide, Sally stepped to the side to allow us entry, and I gave Grandma a warning glare.

"My mouth is zipped," she said, making a zipping gesture. "And look, I'm locking the zipper and throwing away the key. See me throw away the key?"

Sally and I stared at Grandma.

"Mmmmf, mmmf, mmf," Grandma said.

"So what's new?" I asked Sally.

"I get band gigs on weekends," he said. "Weekdays I drive a school bus. It's not like the glory days when I was with the Lovelies, but it's pretty cool."

"What's with the assault charge?"

"It's bogus, man. I was having a discussion with this dude and all of a sudden he started coming on to me. And I was 'Hey, man, that's not where I live,' you know. I mean, okay, so I was wearing a dress, but that's my professional persona. Wearing a dress is my thing. It's my trademark now. Sure, I was playing support for a rap group, but people still expect me to be in a pretty dress. I'm Sally Sweet, you know? I got a reputation."

"I could see where it might be confusing," Grandma said.

I was trying hard not to look appalled. "So you hit him?"

"Only once . . . with my guitar. Knocked him on his keister."

"Holy cow," I said. "Was he hurt bad?"

"No. But I broke his glasses. The guy was such a pussy. He started it all, and then he reported it to the police. He said I hit him for no reason. Called me a drugged-out guitar player."

"Were you drugged out?"

"No way. Sure, I smoke weed between sets, but everybody knows weed doesn't count as drugs if you're a guitar player. And I'm real careful. I buy organic. I only do natural drugs, you know. It's okay if they're natural. Natural weed, natural 'shrooms . . ."

"I didn't know that," Grandma said.

"It's a fact," Sally told her. "I think it might even be union rules that guitar players have to do weed between sets."

"That makes sense," Grandma said.

"Yeah," I said. "That would explain a lot."

Sally was out of costume, wearing jeans and ratty sneakers and a faded Black Sabbath T-shirt. He was over six feet tall in flats and close to seven in heels. He had a large hook nose, and he had a lot of black hair . . . everywhere. He was an okay guy, but he was without a shadow of a doubt the ugliest drag queen in the tristate area. I couldn't imagine any man in his right mind coming on to Sally.

"Why didn't you show up for your court date?" I asked Sally.

"I had to drive the little dudes. It was a school day. I take this job very seriously."

"And you forgot?"

"Yeah," he said. "I fucking forgot." He closed his eyes and smacked his head with the heel of his hand. "Darn." He was wearing a thick elastic band around his left wrist. He snapped the elastic against his wrist and yelped. "Ow!"

Grandma and I both did raised eyebrows.

"I'm trying to quit cussing," Sally said. "The little dudes were getting detention for talking trash mouth after getting off my bus. So my boss gave me this elastic band, and I have to snap it every time I cuss."

I looked down at his wrist. It was solid red welts. "Maybe you should think about getting a different job."

"No fucking way. Oh shit! Damn."

Snap, snap, snap.

"That's gotta hurt," Grandma said.

"Yeah, it hurts like a bitch," Sally said.

Snap.

If I brought Sally in now he'd have to overnight and wait for the courts to open before Vinnie could bond him out again. He didn't look like much of a threat to flee, so I decided to give him a break and bring him in during business hours. "I have to get you rebonded," I said to Sally. "We can arrange a time between bus runs."

"Wow, that would be awesome. I always have a couple hours off in the middle of the day."

Grandma looked at her watch. "We better get a move on if we want to get to the funeral home on time."

"Hey, rock on," Sally said. "Who's laid out?"

"Lorraine Schnagle. I went earlier today but they had the lid down on the casket."

Sally made a sympathetic sound. *Tsk.* "Don't you hate that?"

"Drives me nuts," Grandma said. "So I'm going back, hoping the lid will be up for the night viewing."

Sally had his hands in his pockets, and he was nodding his head like a bobble-head doll. "I hear you. Give my best to Lorraine."

Grandma's face lit. "Maybe you want to come with us. Even with the lid down it should be a good viewing. Lorraine was real popular. The place will be packed. And Stiva always puts out cookies."

"I could do that," Sally said, still bobbing. "Just give me a second to get more dressed up."

Sally disappeared into the bedroom, and I made a deal with God that I'd try to be a nicer person if only Sally didn't return in sling-back heels and a gown.

When Sally reappeared he was still wearing the faded T-shirt, jeans, and ratty sneakers but he'd added dangly rhinestone earrings and a vintage tuxedo jacket. I felt like God hadn't totally come through for me, but I was willing to take a shot at honoring the deal anyway.

We all piled into the Buick and headed across town to Stiva's.

"I'm hungry," Grandma said. "I wouldn't mind having a burger. We haven't got a lot of time, though, so maybe we could do a drive-by."

A quarter mile later I swung into the drive-thru lane of a McDonald's and ordered a bag of food. A Big Mac, fries, and a chocolate shake for Grandma. Cheeseburger and Coke for me. A chicken Caesar salad and Diet Coke for Sally.

"I have to watch my weight," Sally said. "I have this to-die-for red gown, and I'd be pissed if I fucking grew out of it." He grimaced. "Oh shit." *Snap, snap, snap.*

"Maybe you should try not to talk," Grandma said. "You're gonna give yourself a blood clot with all that snapping."

I handed the bag of food over to Grandma for distribution and pulled forward. A guy dressed out in a black do-rag, homeboy jeans, new basketball shoes, and a lot of gold jewelry that flashed in the overhead streetlight exited the McDonald's and headed for a car with a high bling rating. It was a brand-new black Lincoln Navigator with gleaming chrome wheel covers and black tinted windows. I rolled closer to get a better look and confirmed my suspicion. It was Red Devil. He was carrying a huge bag of food plus a drink holder with four cups.

Now I know the Red Devil's held up fourteen deli-marts, and I personally saw him toss a flaming Molotov cocktail into a store. So on the one hand, I had to think that this was a bad guy. Problem was, it was hard to take someone seriously when he was going around doing his robbing wearing a cheap rubber mask, riding on a mountain bike.

"Hey!" I shouted at him. "Wait a minute. I want to talk to you."

When I got close enough to talk, I was going to reach out and choke him until he turned blue. I didn't care all that much about his deli-mart robbing career, but I was really unhappy about my yellow Escape.

He stopped and stared at me and suddenly placed me. "You!" he said. "You're one of the dumb bitches who trashed my bike."

"You're calling *me* dumb?" I yelled back at him. "You're the one going around robbing stores dressed up in a stupid mask, riding a kid's bike. I bet you're too dumb to get a driver's license."

"Dumb bitch," he said again. "Dumb punk-ass bitch."

The passenger side door opened on the Navigator, and I could hear guys laughing inside the car. Red Devil got in, slammed the door shut, and the car came to life.

I was itching to jump out of the Buick, run over to the SUV, wrench the door open, and drag the devil guy out of the car. Since, by my cup tally, there most likely were at least three other people in the Lincoln, and they might all have guns, and they might be cranky about me ruining their dinner, I decided to go with the more conservative plan of getting the license plate number and following at a respectful distance.

"Was that the devil bandit?" Grandma wanted to know.

"Yes."

Grandma sucked in some air. "Let's get

him! Ram him from behind, and then when he stops we'll drag him out of the car."

"I can't do that. I have no authority to capture him."

"Okay, so we don't capture him. How about we just kick him a couple times after we get him out of the car?"

"That would be assault," Sally said. "And it turns out it's illegal."

I hit the speed dial for Morelli's number on my cell phone.

"Is this about the Japanese triplets?" Morelli wanted to know.

"No. It's about Red Devil. I'm in the Buick with Grandma and Sally Sweet, and I'm following the devil guy. We're on State, heading south. I just passed Olden. He's in a new black Lincoln Navigator."

"I'll put it out. Don't approach him."

"No *problemo*." I gave Morelli the license number and put my phone on the seat, next to my leg. I followed the SUV for three blocks and saw a blue-and-white come up behind me. I pulled to the side, the blue-and-white sped past and put his lights on.

Grandma and Sally were mouths open,

eyes glued to the cop car in front of me.

"That guy in the SUV isn't stopping," Grandma said.

The SUV ran a light and we all followed. I knew the cop in front of me. It was Eddie Gazarra, riding alone. He was a likeable blond-haired Polish chunk. And he was married to my cousin Shirley-the-Whiner. He was probably looking in his rearview mirror, wishing I'd go away.

The SUV suddenly made a right turn and then a quick left. Eddie stuck to his bumper, and I struggled to stay with Eddie, using my whole body to help muscle the Buick around corners. I was sweating from the exertion. Probably some of the sweat was from fear. I was at the brink of losing control of the car. And I was worried about Gazarra, all by himself, in front of me.

My cell was still on, still connected to Morelli. "We're chasing these guys," I yelled down at the phone, giving Morelli cross streets, telling him Gazarra was in front of me.

"*We?*" Morelli yelled back. "There's no *we*. This is a police chase. Go home."

Sally had himself braced in the backseat, his rhinestone earrings reflecting in my rearview mirror. "He could be right, you know. Maybe we should split."

"Don't listen to him," Grandma said, her blue-veined, bony hands gripping the shoulder strap. "Keep the pedal to the metal! You could be a little careful on the turns, though," she added. "I'm an old lady. My neck could snap like a twig if you whip around a corner too fast."

Not much chance of taking a corner that fast in the Buick. Motoring the Buick around was like steering a cruise ship.

Without warning, the SUV went into a turn in the middle of the road and skidded to a stop. Eddie laid some rubber and pulled up a couple car lengths from the SUV. I two-footed the brake pedal and stopped about a foot from Eddie's back bumper.

The rear side window slid down on the SUV, and there was a flash of rapid gunfire from inside the car. Grandma and Sally hit the floor, but I was too stunned to move. The blue-and-white's windshield crumbled, and I saw Eddie jerk to the side and slump.

"I think Eddie's shot!" I yelled at my phone.

"Fuck," Sally said from the backseat. *Snap.*

The SUV took off, wheels spinning, and was out of sight within seconds. I shoved my door open and ran to check on Gazarra. He was hit twice. A bullet had grazed the side of his head. And he had a shoulder wound.

"Shit," I said to Gazarra. "Don't die."

Gazarra looked at me through narrowed eyes. "Do I look like I'm going to die?"

"No. But I'm not an expert."

"Cripes, what happened? It was like World War III broke out."

"Seemed like the gentlemen in the SUV didn't want to chat with you."

I was being glib, hoping it would keep me from bursting into tears. I'd stripped my T-shirt off and had it pressed to Gazarra's shoulder wound. Thank goodness I was wearing a sports bra, because I'd feel conspicuous if I was wearing my lacy Victoria's Secret Wonderbra when the cops got here. There was undoubtedly a first aid kit in the squad car, but I wasn't thinking that clearly. The T-shirt seemed easier and faster. I was pressing hard enough that my hands weren't visibly shaking, but my heart was racing and my breathing was ragged. Grandma and Sally were standing huddled together in silence by the Buick.

"Is there anything we can do?" Grandma asked.

"Talk to Joe. He's on the cell phone. Tell him Gazarra needs help."

Sirens were screaming in the distance, and I could see the flash of police strobes a block away.

"Shirley's gonna be pissed," Gazarra said. "She hates when I get shot." To my recollection, the only other time Gazarra was shot was when he was playing quick draw in the police station elevator, and his gun accidentally discharged. The bullet ricocheted off the elevator wall and lodged in Gazarra's right buttock.

The first cop car angled in. It was followed by a second blue-and-white and Morelli in his SUV. I took a step back to allow the men access to Eddie.

Morelli looked first to me and then glanced over at Gazarra. "Are you okay?" he asked.

I was covered with blood, but it wasn't mine. "I didn't get hit. Eddie's been shot twice, but I think he's going to be all right."

I guess there are places in this country where cops are always perfectly pressed. Trenton wasn't one of those places. Trenton cops worked hard and worried a lot. Every cop on the scene had a sweat-soaked shirt and grim set to his mouth, including Morelli.

"They opened fire with an automatic weapon from the backseat," I told Morelli. "We were coming out of the McDonald's drive-thru on State, and I saw the devil guy cross the lot and get into the Lincoln. The devil guy got into the front passenger seat, so he wasn't the shooter. He had four drinks with him, so there were probably three other guys in the car. I followed him out of the lot and called you. You know the rest."

Morelli slid an arm around me and pulled me close, resting his cheek on mine. "I don't want to get mushy here in front of the guys, but there was a moment back there when I heard shots fired over the phone . . . and I didn't care a lot about the triplets."

"Nice to know," I said, slumping against him, happy to have someone holding me up. "It happened so fast. No one got out of a car. Eddie was still buckled into his seat belt. They shot him through the windshield."

"The Lincoln was stolen. They probably thought Gazarra was going to bust them."

"No, it was me," I said. "This is all my fault. The Red Devil knew I recognized him."

An EMT truck arrived and parked next to Gazarra. Cops were directing traffic, securing the area, shouting over the static and chatter of the dispatch radio.

"It's uncanny the way you stumble into this stuff," Morelli said. "It's creepy."

Grandma was standing behind us. "Two disasters in one day," she said. "I bet it's a personal record."

"Not even close," Morelli said. His eyes settled on my sports bra. "I like the new look."

"I used my T-shirt as a compress."

Morelli removed his shirt and draped it around my shoulders. "You feel cold."

"That's because my heart stopped pumping blood about ten minutes ago." My skin was pale and clammy, and my forearms were goose-bumpy. "I need to get back to my parents' house and have some dessert."

"I could use some dessert, too," Grandma said. "Probably they don't have the lid up on Lorraine, anyway." She turned to Sally. "I know I promised you a good time at the funeral parlor, but it didn't work out. How about some dessert instead? We got chocolate cake and ice cream. And then we can send you home in a cab. My son-in-law drives a cab sometimes, so we get a break on the rates."

"I guess I could eat some cake," Sally said. "I probably burned off a couple hundred calories just now from fright."

Morelli buttoned me into his shirt. "Are you going to be okay to drive?"

"Yeah. I don't even feel like throwing up anymore."

"I need to check on a few things here, and then I'll follow you over."

MY MOTHER WAS on the front porch when we arrived. She was rigid with her arms crossed over her chest and her lips pressed tight together.

"She knows," Grandma said. "I bet the phone's been ringing off the hook."

"How could she know?" Sally asked. "We were way across town, and it's been less than an hour, start to finish."

"The first call always comes from Traci Wenke and Myron Flatt on account of they listen to the police band on their radios," Grandma said. "And then Elsa Downing probably called. She finds out early because her daughter works as a dispatcher. And I bet Shirley called to see if she could drop the kids off so she could go to the hospital."

I parked the Buick, and by the time I got to my mother her face was white, and I expected steam to begin curling out of her ears at any moment. "Don't start," I said. "I'm not talking about it until I've had some cake."

My mother wheeled around without a word, marched to the kitchen, and sliced me a wedge of cake.

I followed after her. "Ice cream," I said.

She scooped half a tub of ice cream onto my plate. She stepped back and looked at me. "Blood," she said.

"Not mine."

She made the sign of the cross.

"And I'm pretty sure Eddie's going to be okay."

Another cross.

There'd been places left at the table for Grandma and me. I took my place and shoveled in cake. Grandma brought an extra chair from the kitchen for Sally and bustled around filling plates. The rest of the family was silent at the dining room table. Only my father was active, head down, forking up chicken and mashed potatoes. Everyone else was frozen in their seats, mouths open, eyes wide, not sure what to make of me with the blood on my shirt . . . and Sally in his earrings.

"You all remember Sally, don't you?" Grandma asked as introduction. "He's a famous musician, and he's a girl sometimes. He's got a whole bunch of pretty dresses and high heel shoes and makeup. He's even got one of them black leather bustier things with pointy ice cream cone breasts. You don't even hardly notice his chest hair when he's got that bustier thing on."

THREE

"HOW CAN HE be a girl sometimes?" Mary Alice wanted to know.

Mary Alice is in second grade and is two years younger than her sister, Angie. Mary Alice can ride a bike, play Monopoly if someone helps her read the Chance cards, and can recite the names of all of Santa's reindeer. She's in the dark on gender crossing.

"I just dress up like a girl," Sally said. "It's part of my on-stage persona."

"I'd want to dress up like a horse," Mary Alice said.

Angie looked at Sally's wrist. "Why are you wearing an elastic band?"

"I'm trying to quit cussing," Sally said. "Every time I cuss I snap the elastic band.

It's supposed to make me not want to cuss anymore."

"You should just say a different word than the cuss word," Angie said. "Something that sounds like the cuss word."

"I've got it!" Grandma said. "Fudge. That's what you should say."

"Fudge," Sally repeated. "I don't know . . . I feel silly saying fudge."

"What's the red stuff all over Aunt Stephanie?" Mary Alice wanted to know.

"Blood," Grandma said. "We were in a shoot-out. None of us got hurt, but Stephanie was helping out Eddie Gazarra. He was shot twice, and he had blood spurting all over the place."

"Eeeuw," Angie said.

Valerie's live-in boyfriend, Albert Kloughn, was seated next to me. He looked down at my blood-spattered arm and fainted. *Crash.* Right off his chair.

"He fucking fainted," Sally said. "Oh f-f-fudge." *Snap.*

I was done with my cake, so I went to the kitchen and tried to clean up. Probably I should have cleaned up before coming to the table but I really needed the cake.

When I got back to the table Albert was sitting in his seat. "I'm not squeamish or anything," he said. "I just slipped. It was one of those freak accidents."

Albert Kloughn was about five foot seven, had sandy blond hair showing the beginnings of male pattern baldness, and the chubby face and body of a twelve-year-old. He was a lawyer, of sorts, and he was the father of Valerie's baby. He was a sweet guy, but he felt more like a pet than a future brother-in-law. His office was located next to a laundromat, and he dispensed more quarters than legal advice.

There was a light rap on the front door, the door opened, and Joe walked in. My mother was immediately running for an extra plate, not sure where she was going to put it. Even with the leaf in, the table could only accommodate eight, and Joe made ten.

"Here," Kloughn said, jumping to his feet, "you can have my place. I'm done eating. I don't mind. Honest."

"Isn't he a cuddle umpkins?" Valerie said.

Grandma hid behind her napkin and made a gagging gesture. Morelli held his response to a benign smile. My father kept eating. And it occurred to me that cuddle umpkins fit Kloughn perfectly. How awful is that?

"Now that everyone's here, I have an announcement to make," Valerie said. "Albert and I have set a date to get married."

This was an important announcement because when Valerie was pregnant she was thinking she might hold out for Ranger or Indiana Jones. This was a worrisome situation since it was unlikely either of those guys would be interested in marrying Valerie. Valerie's opinion of Albert Kloughn improved with the birth of the baby, but until this moment my mother harbored the fear that she'd be saddled with Valerie gossip for the rest of her life. Unwed mothers, horrific painful deaths, and cheating husbands were the favorite topics of the Burg gossipmongers.

"That's wonderful!" my mother said, clapping a hand to her mouth, her eyes filling with tears. "I'm so happy for you."

"A wedding!" Grandma said. "I'll need a new dress. And we need a hall for the reception." She dabbed at her eyes. "Look at me . . . I'm all teary."

Valerie was crying, too. She was laughing and sniffling back sobs. "I'm going to marry my snuggy wuggums," she said.

Morelli paused, his fork halfway to the roast chicken platter. He slid his eyes to me and leaned close. "If you ever call me snuggy wuggums in public I'll lock you in the cellar and chain you to the furnace."

Kloughn was standing at the end of the table with a glass of wine in his hand. "I have to make a toast," he said. "To the future Mrs. Kloughn!"

My mother went still as stone. She hadn't totally thought through the consequences of Valerie's marriage to Albert. "Valerie Kloughn," she said, trying not to show her horror.

"Holy crap," my father said.

I leaned close to Morelli. "Now I'm not the only clown in the family," I whispered.

Morelli raised his glass. "To Valerie Kloughn," he said.

Kloughn drained his glass and refilled it. "And to me! Because I'm the luckiest man ever. I found my lovey pumpkin, my one true lovey dovey, my big fat sweetie pie."

"Hey, wait a minute . . ." Valerie said. "Big fat sweetie pie?"

Grandma refilled her wineglass. "Somebody stun-gun him," she said. "I can't take no more."

Kloughn rushed on. His face was flushed, and he'd started to sweat. "I've even got a baby," he said. "I don't know how that happened. Well, I mean, I guess I know how it happened. I think it happened on the couch in there . . ."

Everyone but Joe sucked in some air. Joe was smiling. "And to think, I almost missed this," he whispered to me.

My mother looked like tomorrow she'd be shopping for a new couch. And my father was studying his butter knife . . . undoubtedly wondering how much damage he could do. Good thing the carving knife was in the kitchen.

"It usually takes Kloughns years to get pregnant," Albert said. "Historically we have a low mobility. Our guys can't swim. That's what my father always said. He said, Albert, don't expect to be a father, because Kloughns can't swim. And look at this. My guys could swim! It's not like I was even trying. I just couldn't figure out how to get the thingy on. And then once I got it on, but I think it had a hole in it, because it seemed like it was leaking. Wouldn't it be something if that was the time? Wouldn't it be something if my guys could swim through the thingy? Like I had Superman guys!"

Poor Snuggy Uggums was motoring down the road to doom, gaining momentum, out of control with no idea how to stop.

"Do something," I said to Joe. "He's dying."

Morelli was still wearing his gun. He took it off his hip and pointed it at Kloughn. "Albert," he said, very calmly. "Shut up."

"Thank you," Kloughn said. And then he wiped the sweat off his forehead with his shirttail.

"What about dessert?" my father wanted to know. "Isn't anyone going to serve dessert?"

IT WAS CLOSE to nine when Morelli and I staggered through the front door to his town house. Bob-the-Dog came galloping from the kitchen to greet us, attempted a sliding stop on Morelli's polished wood floor, and slammed into Morelli. This was Bob's usual opening act, and Morelli had been braced for the hit. Bob was a big

goofy orange-haired beast who ate everything that wasn't nailed down and had
more enthusiasm than brains. He shoved
past us and bounced out the door, in a
rush to tinkle on Morelli's minuscule front
yard. This was always Bob's first choice of
bathroom, and as a result the grass was
scorched brown. Bob returned to the
house, Morelli closed and locked the front
door, and we stood there for a moment
sucking in the silence.

"This wasn't one of my better days," I
said to Morelli. "My car was destroyed, I
was involved in a shooting, and I just sat
through the dinner from hell."

Morelli slung an arm around me. "Dinner wasn't that bad."

"My sister talked cuddle umpkins to
Kloughn for two hours, my mother and
grandmother cried every time someone
mentioned the wedding, Mary Alice
whinnied nonstop, and the baby threw up
on you."

"Yeah, but aside from that . . ."

"Not to mention, Grandma got completely snookered and passed out at the
table."

"She was the smart one," Morelli said.

"You were the hero."

"I wouldn't actually have shot him," Morelli said. "Not to kill, anyway."

"My family is a disaster!"

Morelli grinned. "I've called you Cupcake for as long as I can remember, but I'm rethinking it after listening to the two hours of cuddle umpkins."

"Just exactly what is a human-type cupcake?"

"It's like a cream puff but not as squishy. It's dessert. It's soft and sweet . . . and it's good to eat."

The eating part gave me a rush that went straight to my doodah.

Morelli kissed me just below my earlobe and told me a few things about the right way to eat a cupcake. When he got to the part about licking the icing off the top, my nipples shrunk to the size and hardness of steel ball bearings.

"Boy, I'm really tired," I said. "Maybe we should be thinking about going to bed."

"Good idea, Cupcake."

I'VE BEEN LIVING with Morelli for several months now, and it's been surprisingly easy. We still like each other, and the magic hasn't gone out of the sex. Hard to imagine it ever would with Morelli. He's nice to my hamster, Rex. He doesn't expect me to make him breakfast. He's neat without being freaky about it. And he remembers to close the lid on the toilet . . . most of the time. What more can you ask from a man?

Morelli lives on a quiet street in a small, pleasant house he inherited from his Aunt Rose. The house mirrors my parents' house and every other house on Morelli's street. When I look out his bedroom window I see neatly parked cars and two-story redbrick attached town houses with clean windows. There are small trees and small shrubs in small yards. And behind the front doors are frequently large people. Food is good in Trenton.

The bedroom window in my apartment looks out at a blacktop parking lot. The apartment building was constructed in the seventies and is totally lacking in charm and amenities. My interior decorating style is one step away from college dorm. Decorating takes time and money. And I have neither.

So it's a mystery why I would miss my apartment, but the truth is, sometimes I felt homesick for the depressing mustard and olive green bathroom, the hook in the entrance area where I hang my jacket, the cooking smells and television noise from the neighboring apartments.

It was nine in the morning and Morelli was off, ridding the city of bad guys, protecting the populace. I rinsed my coffee cup and set it in the dish drain. I tapped on Rex's cage and told him I'd be back. I hugged Bob and told him to be good and not eat any chairs. After I hugged Bob I had to use the lint roller on my jeans. I was rollering my jeans when the doorbell bonged.

"Howdy," Grandma Mazur said when I answered the door. "I was out for a walk, and I was in the neighborhood, so I thought I'd stop by for a cup of coffee."

"That's a long walk."

"Your sister came over first thing with her laundry, and the house got real crowded."

"I was just going out," I told Grandma. "I have some people to pick up this morning."

"I could help! I could be your assistant. I'd be good at it. I can be real scary when I try."

I grabbed my shoulder bag and denim jacket. "I don't actually need anybody scary, but you can ride along if you want. My plan is to stop at the office to say hello. And then I'm going to get Sally so he can reschedule."

Grandma followed me out the front door, to the curb. "This sure is a pip of a car," Grandma said, taking the Buick in. "I feel like one of them old-time gangsters when I ride in this car."

I feel poor when I ride in the car, since I'm the one buying the gas. No car in the history of the world guzzled gas better than the Buick.

LULA WAS AT the door when I parked in front of the bonds office. "Don't bother trying to get that boat docked just right," she said. "We got an emergency call. Remember the chip lady? Well, she's having some kind of a breakdown. Connie just got off the phone with the chip lady's sister, and Connie said we should go over there and see what's happening."

Sometimes part of my job falls under the category of preventive care. If you know something's going wrong in a bondee's life it's best to check in with him from time to time rather than wait for him to flee.

"Hell-*o*," Lula said, peeking in the car window. "We got Grandma on board."

"I'm helping Stephanie this morning," Grandma said. "What's a chip lady?"

"It's some woman held up a Frito-Lay truck," Lula said. "And then she ate the chips."

"Good for her," Grandma said. "I've always wanted to do that."

Lula climbed into the backseat. "Me, too. You read those adult magazines and they're always talking about sex fantasies, but I say chip fantasies are where it's at."

"I wouldn't mind combining them," Grandma said. "Suppose you had some good-looking naked man feeding you the chips."

"No way," Lula said. "I don't want to be distracted by no man when I'm eating chips. I'd rather have dip. Just get out of my way when I see the chips and dip."

"It's good you have priorities," Grandma said.

"Know thyself," Lula replied. "Someone famous said that. I don't remember who."

I took Hamilton to Klockner, passed the

high school in Hamilton Township, and turned into Cantell's neighborhood. A woman was standing on Cantell's front porch. She took a startled step back when she saw the three of us emerge from Big Blue.

"Guess she's never seen a '53 Buick before," Grandma said.

"Yeah," Lula said, hitching up her fuchsia and black animal print spandex pants. "I'm sure that's it."

I approached the porch and handed the woman my business card. "Stephanie Plum."

"I remember you," the woman said. "You had your picture in the paper when you burned the funeral home down."

"It wasn't my fault."

"It wasn't my fault either," Grandma said.

"I'm Cindy, Carol's sister. I know she's been having a hard time so I called her this morning. Just checking in, you know? And as soon as I heard her I knew something was wrong. She didn't want to talk on the phone, and she was real secretive. So I came over here. I only live two blocks away. She wouldn't answer her door when I knocked, so I went around back and that door was locked, too. And the shades are all drawn. You can't see into the house at all."

"Maybe she just wants to be alone," Lula said. "Maybe she thinks you're nosey."

"Put your ear to the window," Cindy said.

Lula put her ear to the front window.

"Listen real close. What do you hear?"

"Uh oh," Lula said. "I hear the crinkle of a chip bag. I hear crunching."

"I'm afraid she's held up another truck!" Cindy said. "I didn't want to call the police. And I didn't want to call her ex-husband. He's a real jerk. If I'd been married to him, I'd be a little nutty, too. Anyway, I remembered Carol saying how nice you all were, so I thought maybe you could help."

I rapped on the front door. "Carol. It's Stephanie Plum. Open the door."

"Go away."

"I need to talk to you."

"I'm busy."

"She's going to jail," Cindy wailed. "She's a habitual offender. They're going to lock her up and throw away the key. She's a chip junky. My sister's an addict!"

"We don't want to get carried away with this," Lula said. "Last I looked, Fritos weren't on the list of controlled substances."

"Maybe we should shoot the lock off the door," Grandma said.

"Hey, Carol," I yelled through the door. "Did you rob another Frito-Lay truck?"

"Don't worry," Cindy called out. "We'll get you a good lawyer. Maybe you can plead insanity."

The door flew open and Carol stood in the doorway, holding a bag of Cheez Doodles. Her hair was smudged with orange doodle dust and stood out from her scalp like an explosion had gone off inside her head. Her mascara was smudged, her lipstick eaten off, replaced with orange doodle stain. She was dressed in a night-gown, sneakers, and a warm-up jacket. Doodle crumbs stuck to the jacket and sparkled in the morning sunlight.

"Whoa," Lula said. "It's fright night."

"What is it with you people?" Carol screeched. "Don't you have lives? Go away. Can't you see I'm having breakfast?"

"What should we do?" Cindy asked. "Should we call 911?"

"Forget 911," Lula said. "Call an exorcist."

"What's the deal with the Cheez Doodles?" I asked Carol.

"I slipped. I fell off the wagon."

"You didn't rob another truck, did you?"

"No."

"A store?"

"Absolutely not. I paid for these. Okay, maybe a couple bags got stuck in my jacket, but I don't know how that happened. I don't have any memory of it, I swear."

"You're a nut," Lula said, prowling through the house, gathering up stashed bags of chips. "You got no self-control. You need Chips Anonymous." Lula opened a bag of Doritos and scarfed a few.

Grandma held out a grocery bag. "I found this in the kitchen. We can put the chips in it and take them with us so she isn't tempted to eat any more."

"Put the chips in the bag and give them to Cindy," I told Grandma.

"I thought it might be a good idea if *we* took them," Grandma said.

"Yeah," Lula said. "That's a much better

idea than making poor Cindy cart them off."

I wasn't great in the willpower department. Even as I was standing there, I could feel the Cheez Doodles calling my name. I didn't want a whole grocery bag of doodles and chips in the car with me. I didn't want to end up looking like Carol.

"Give all the chips to Cindy," I said. "The chips should stay in the family."

Grandma looked over at Carol. "Are you gonna be okay if we give her *all* the chips? You aren't gonna flip out, are you?"

"I'm okay now," Carol said. "Actually, I feel kind of sick. I think I'm going to lie down for a while."

We filled the grocery bag with the remaining chips and left Carol standing at the door, the pallor of her skin looking slightly green under the orange doodle dust. Cindy drove off with the chips. And Grandma and Lula and I stuffed ourselves into the Buick.

"Hunh," Lula said, settling in. "We could have taken a few bags with us."

"I had my eye on that bag of barbecue chips," Grandma said. "It's gonna be hard for me to keep up my strength without some chips."

"Uh oh," Lula said. "Look at this, a couple of bags of chips somehow got in my big ol' purse . . . just like what happened to Carol."

"Chips are devilish like that," Grandma said.

"Yeah," Lula said. "Guess we should eat them so they don't go to waste."

"How many bags do you have?" I asked her.

"Three. You want one?"

I blew out a sigh, and Lula handed me a bag of Fritos. Not only was I going to eat them . . . I was secretly glad she snitched them.

"Now what?" Lula wanted to know. "I'm not going to have to go back to the filing, am I?"

"Sally Sweet's next up," I said.

"I'm in," Lula said.

Sally lived on the opposite side of town. By the time we got there, he'd be done with his morning bus run, and it'd be a good time to bring him in and get him re-bonded.

I called Morelli on the way over to get a report on Eddie Gazarra.

"He's going to be okay," Morelli said. "He'll probably get released from the hospital tomorrow."

"Anything new going on?"

"There was another devil holdup last night. This time the firebomb worked and the store burned down."

"Anyone hurt?"

"No. It was late at night, and the store was empty. The night manager got out the back door. The word on the street is that the Comstock Street Slayers are bragging about the cop shooting."

"I didn't realize we had Slayers in Trenton."

"We've got everything in Trenton."

"If you rounded up all the Slayers, I might be able to identify the Red Devil," I said to Morelli.

"To the best of our knowledge there are twenty-eight active Slayers, and they're about as easy to round up as smoke. And probably the twenty-eight figure is low."

"Okay, suppose I rode around in their neighborhood, looking for the guy?"

"Honey, even *I* don't ride around in that neighborhood."

I disconnected and turned onto Fenton Street. It was easy to find Sally's house. A big yellow school bus was parked at the curb. I pulled up behind the bus, and we all trooped out.

Sally opened the door with the security chain still in place. "I've changed my mind," he said. "I don't want to go."

"You have to go," I told him. "It's the law."

"The law's bogus. I didn't do anything wrong. And now if I go with you I'm going to have to pay more money, right? Vinnie's gonna have to write another bond, right?"

"Uh . . . yeah."

"I haven't got more money. And anyway, I'm not even the one who should have been arrested. They should have arrested that jerk Marty Sklar. He's the one who started all this."

I felt my eyebrows shoot halfway up my forehead. "Marty Sklar is the guy who made a pass at you?"

"Do you know him?" Sally asked.

"I went to school with him. He was a big macho football player. And he married Barbara Jean Biabloki, the pom-pom queen." It was a perfect match. They deserved each other. Sklar was a bully, and Barbara Jean thought she could walk on water because she grew perfect breasts. Last I heard, Sklar was working in his father-in-law's Toyota dealership, and Barbara Jean had porked up to biblical proportions. "Was Sklar drunk?"

"Fuckin' A. Oh crap!" *Snap, snap.*

"You gotta remember about fudge," Grandma said.

Sally nodded. "Fudgin' A."

We all did a mental *eeyeuuw*. Fudgin' A didn't sound tasty coming out of Sally's mouth.

"Maybe fudge don't work for that one time," Grandma said.

If I could get Sklar to drop the charges against Sally, and we had a sympathetic judge, I could save Sally the expense of a second bond. "You're not going anywhere," I said to Sally. "I don't need to bring you in today. I'll talk to Sklar and see what I can do about getting the charges dropped."

"No shit!" *Snap.*

"You better clean up your mouth, or you're gonna lose that hand," Lula said to Sally. "You're gonna amputate yourself."

"F-f-fudge," Sally said.

Grandma looked down at her watch. "You're going to have to take me home now. I have a beauty parlor appointment this afternoon, and I don't want to be late. I got a lot of ground to cover today what with the shooting and all."

This was a good deal for me because the negotiation with Marty Sklar would go better without Grandma present. In fact, I'd prefer to do it without Lula but I didn't think that was going to happen. I pointed the Buick toward the Burg and motored across town. I dropped Grandma off in front of my parents' house. My sister's car was still in the driveway.

"They're planning the wedding," Grandma said. "Ordinarily I'd be right there, but it looks to me like this is going on for days. They spent two hours this morning talking about what kind of suit Mr. Cutie Uggums was going to wear. I don't know how your mother does it. That woman has the patience of a saint."

"Who's Mr. Cutie Uggums?" Lula wanted to know.

"Albert Kloughn. He and Valerie are getting married."

"That's scary," Lula said.

MELVIN BIABLOKI'S TOYOTA dealership took up half a block on South Broad

Street. It wasn't the biggest or the best dealership in the state, but according to Burg gossip it made enough money to send Melvin and his wife on a cruise every February and to give a job to his son-in-law.

I parked in the area reserved for customers, and Lula and I went searching for Sklar.

"This here's a butt-ugly showroom," Lula said. "They should buy some new carpet. And what's with the nasty plastic chairs? For a minute there I thought I was back at the office."

A guy in a sports coat ambled over, and it took me a moment to realize it was Marty Sklar. He was shorter than I remembered. His hair was balding. He was wearing glasses. And his six-pack stomach had turned to a keg. Marty wasn't aging well.

"Stephanie Plum," Marty said. "I remember you. Joe Morelli used to write poems on bathroom walls about you."

"Yeah. I'm living with him now."

Sklar touched his index finger to my lip. "Then all those things he said must be true."

He'd caught me flat-footed. I wasn't expecting the touch. I slapped his hand away, but it was too late. I had Marty Sklar cooties on my lip. Yuk. I needed mouthwash. Disinfectant. I was going to rush home and take a shower. Maybe two showers.

"Hey," Lula said. "Don't you touch her. Did she say you could touch her? I don't think so. I didn't hear her give you permission. You keep your nasty-ass hands to yourself."

Sklar cut his eyes to Lula. "Who the hell are you?"

"I'm Lula. Who the hell are you?"

"I'm Marty Sklar."

"Hunh," Lula said.

I tried not to think about the lip cooties and pushed forward. "Here's the thing, Marty. I want to talk to you about Sally Sweet."

"What about him?"

"I thought you might want to drop the charges. It turns out he's hired a really good lawyer. And the lawyer's found a bunch of witnesses who've officially stated you came on to Sweet."

"He hit me with his guitar."

"That's true, but I thought you might not want it to go public about the sex thing."

"What sex thing?"

"The witnesses said you wanted to have sex with Sally."

"That's a lie. I was just busting his balls."

"It's not going to sound like that at the trial."

"Trial?"

"Well, he's got this lawyer now. And all the witnesses . . ."

"Shit."

I looked at my watch. "If you move fast and make a phone call you can stop the process before it gets out of control. Probably your father-in-law would be upset to learn that you propositioned a transvestite."

"Yeah," Lula said. "That's like a double cheat. You were gonna cheat with a guy in a dress. Father-in-laws hate that."

"What's the name of this hotshot lawyer?" Sklar asked.

"Albert Kloughn."

"And he's supposed to be good? I never heard of him."

"He's a shark," I said. "He's new to the area."

"So what's your interest in this?" Sklar asked me.

"Just being a friend, Marty. Since we went to school together and all."

And I left the showroom.

Lula and I didn't say anything until we were out of the lot.

"Girl, you can lie!" Lula yelled when I turned the Buick onto Broad. "You are the shit. I almost gave myself a hemorrhoid trying not to laugh back there. I can't believe how good you can lie. I mean I've seen you lie before, but this was like Satan lying. It was inspired lying."

FOUR

I DROVE TWO blocks up Broad and pulled into a Subway shop.

"This is a good place to eat lunch," Lula said. "They got them low-carb sandwiches. And they got them low-fat sandwiches. You could lose a lot of weight eating here. The more you eat, the more you lose."

"Actually, I chose Subway because it was next to Dunkin' Donuts."

"Friggin' A," Lula said.

We each got a sub. And then we each got six doughnuts. We sat in the car and ate the sub and the doughnuts in silence.

I crumpled my wrappers and shoved them into the doughnut bag.

"Do you know anything about the Slayers?" I asked Lula.

"I know they're bad news. There's a whole bunch of gangs in Trenton. The Comstock Street Slayers and the Bad Killer Cuts are the two big ones. Used to be you only heard about Slayers on the West Coast, but they're everywhere now. Kids join up in prison, and then they bring it back to the street. Comstock Street is gangland these days."

"I talked to Morelli a while ago. He said the Slayers are bragging about shooting Eddie Gazarra."

"Bummer. You better watch out on account of you disrespected Red Devil, and he was hanging with those guys. You don't want to get on the bad side of a Slayer. I'd be real careful of that if I was you."

"You're the one who shot up the devil guy's tire!"

"Yeah, but he didn't know it was me. He probably thought it was you. You're the big-deal bounty hunter. I'm just a file clerk."

"Speaking of file clerk, I should get you back to the office so you can do some filing."

"Yeah, but who's gonna watch out for

your ass then? Who's gonna help catch the bad guys? You know what we should do? We should go take a look around Comstock Street. Maybe we could get the Red Devil."

"I don't want to get the Red Devil. He shoots at people. He's a police problem."

"Boy, what's with you? Everything's a police problem these days."

"I enforce bail bond requirements. That's the extent of my authority."

"Well, we don't have to actually get him. We could just do some investigating. You know, like we could ride around in the neighborhood. Maybe talk to a couple people. I bet we could find out who the devil guy is. You're the only one who knows what he looks like."

Lucky me. "To begin with, I don't know where the devil guy lives, so it would be hard to ride around in his neighborhood. And if that isn't enough, even if we found his neighborhood and went asking questions, no one would talk to me."

"Yeah, but they'd talk to me. Everyone talks to me. I got a winning personality. And I look like I belong in a gang-infested neighborhood." Lula scrounged in her big black leather purse, found her cell phone, and punched in a number.

"Hey," she said when the connection was made. "It's Lula, and I need some information." Pause. "Your ass," she said. "I'm not doing that no more." Another pause. "I'm not doing that either. And I'm especially not doing that last thing. That's disgusting. Are you gonna listen to me, or what?"

There were about three more minutes of conversation, and Lula dropped her phone back into her bag.

"Okay, I got some gang boundaries now. The Slayers are between Third and Eighth Streets on Comstock. And Comstock's one block over from Stark," Lula said. "I used to work part of that area. My corner was on Stark, but I got a lot of customers from the south side. It wasn't so bad back then. That was before the gangs moved in. I figure we just mosey on over there and take a look around."

"I don't think that's a good idea."

"How bad could it be? We're in a car. We're just driving through. It's not like we're in Baghdad, or something. And anyway, the gangs aren't out during the day. They're like vampires. They only come out at night. So during the day the streets are real safe."

"That's not true."

"Are you calling me a fibber?"

"Yeah."

"Well, okay, maybe they aren't *real* safe. But they're safe enough in a car. What could happen to you in a car?"

Problem was, Lula and I were sort of the Abbott and Costello of law enforcement. Things happened to us all the time. Things that weren't normal.

"Give me a break," Lula said. "I don't want to go back and file. I'd rather ride through hell than file."

"Okay," I said on a sigh. "We'll do a drive-through." Abbott and Costello weren't all that bright. They were always doing stupid things like this. And more to the point, I felt guilty about Eddie Gazarra. I felt like he got shot because I'd acted impulsively. I felt like I owed him. Anyway, Lula was probably right. It was daytime. It was probably reasonably safe. I could do a simple ride through the Slayer's neighborhood and maybe I'd get lucky. If

I could find the Red Devil, the police might have a chance at getting the guy who shot Eddie.

I cut through the center of the city and turned up Stark Street. Stark Street started out bad and got worse. The gang graffiti increased with each block. By the time we were at Third the buildings were solid slogans and signs. The sidewalks were spray-painted. The street signs were spray-painted. First-floor windows were laced with iron security bars, and the bars and pawn shops were behind partially closed security gates.

I turned right at Third and drove one block to Comstock. Once off Stark there were fewer businesses and the streets narrowed. Cars were parked on both sides of Comstock, reducing the road to barely two lanes. We passed a couple guys on a corner. They were young, dressed in baggy jeans and white T-shirts. Their arms and hands were tattooed. Their expressions were sullen and watchful.

"Not a lot of people out," Lula said. "Except for the two sentries we just passed."

"It's the middle of the day. People are working."

"Not in this neighborhood," Lula said. "Most of these people don't got jobs unless you count holding up liquor stores as a profession."

I checked my rearview mirror and saw one of the corner watchers put a cell phone to his ear.

"I'm getting a bad feeling," I said.

"That's because you're a minority here."

"You mean being white?"

"No. I mean you're the only one for blocks not packin' a gun."

I cruised past Fifth and started looking for a way out. I didn't want to go deeper into the 'hood. I wanted to get back to Stark and head for city center. I turned left onto Sixth and realized the truck in front of me wasn't moving. It was double-parked. No one at the wheel. I put the Buick into reverse and inched back. I was about to pull onto Comstock when a kid appeared from out of nowhere. He was in his late teens, and he looked like a clone of the guys on the corner.

He approached the car and rapped on the driver-side window. "Hey," he said.

"You might want to ignore him," Lula said. "And it might not be a bad idea to back up a little faster."

"I'd like to back up faster, but there are a couple really nasty-looking guys at my bumper. If I back up I'll run over them."

"So what's your point?"

"I know you," the kid at my window said, his face inches from the glass. "You're a fucking bounty hunter. You busted my uncle. You were with some Rambo guy. And you're the one fingered Red Devil."

The car started to rock, and I realized the guys in the back were on the bumper. More faces pressed against the side windows.

"Step on the freaking gas," Lula said. "It don't matter if you run these clowns over. They've been run over lots of times. Look at them. Don't they look like they've been run over?"

"The guy at your window is saying something. What's he saying?"

"How would I know," Lula said. "It's gangsta talk shit. Something about kill the bitches. And now he's licking the glass. You're gonna have to Clorox this car if we ever get outa here."

All right, I have three options. I can call Joe and have him send the police. That would be really embarrassing, and they might not get here in time to stop the bitch killing. The second choice is that I call Ranger. Equally embarrassing. And there might be bloodshed. Not mine, probably. Or I could run over a couple of these fine, upstanding young men.

"I'm getting real nervous about this," Lula said. "I think you might have made a bad decision to come into this neighborhood."

I felt my blood pressure edge up a notch. "This was your idea."

"Well, it was a bad idea. I'm willing to admit that now."

The Buick bounced around a little, and I could hear scraping, thumping sounds overhead. The idiots were jumping up and down on the roof.

"Your grandma's not gonna like it one bit if they scratch her car," Lula said. "This here's a classic."

"Hey," I yelled to the guy with his face pressed against my window. "Back off from the car. It's a classic."

"Classic this, bitch," he said. And he pulled a gun out of his baggy pants and aimed it at me, the barrel about an inch from the window glass.

"Holy shit," Lula said, eyes the size of duck eggs. "Get me the fudge out of here."

Option number three, I thought. And I mashed the accelerator down to the floorboard. The car sucked gas and roared back like a freight train. I didn't feel any bumps under the tires indicating that I'd run over a body. I took that as a good sign. I wheeled backward onto Comstock and screeched to a stop to change gears. Three guys flew off my roof. Two bounced off the right front fender onto the road. And one smacked onto the hood and grabbed hold of a windshield wiper.

"Don't stop now," Lula yelled. "And don't worry about the hood ornament. You'll lose him on the next turn."

I rammed the car into drive and took off. I could hear a lot of noise behind me. A lunatic mix of yelling and gunfire and laughter. The guy on the hood stared in at me, the pupils of his eyes dilated to the size of nickels.

"Think he got a pharmaceutical problem going," Lula said.

I leaned on the horn, but the hood rider didn't blink.

"This here's like having an insect stuck on

your windshield," Lula said. "A big ugly drugged-out praying mantis."

I hauled the Buick around into a looping left turn onto Seventh, and the insect silently sailed off into space and crashed into a rusted-out van that was parked at the curb. I resumed breathing when I got to Stark.

"See, that worked out okay," Lula said. "Too bad we didn't find the devil guy, though."

I gave her a sideways glance. "Maybe you want to go back tomorrow and try again?"

"Maybe not tomorrow."

I called Connie and told her we were on our way back to the office and asked her to run a search for me.

"If I give you some street boundaries can you check our files for guys in that neighborhood?" I asked her.

"I can search by zip code, and I can search by street. As long as the area isn't too big, I can do the *by street* search."

I felt a responsibility to Eddie, and I thought chances were decent that the devil guy had a record. I'd declined to go through mug shots at police headquarters. I'd done that drill for other crimes and found it to be spectacularly unhelpful. After looking at a hundred head shots, I tended to forget the face of the perp. A search by neighborhood would produce a much smaller pool of potentials.

CONNIE WAS PULLING files when Lula and I swung through the front door. "I got seventeen hits for the boundaries you gave me," she said. "None are outstanding. It's not really our neighborhood."

Lula looked through the pile of files on Connie's desk. "Hey, this is the guy who was stuck to the hood of your car," Lula said, holding a photo for me to see.

Connie grabbed a file and closed the drawer with her foot. "That's Eugene Brown. He's been arrested so many times we have a personal relationship. Never been convicted of anything but possession."

"Looks like we bonded him out for armed robbery and vehicular manslaughter," Lula said.

"Eyewitnesses have a way of disappearing when Eugene's involved," Connie said. "And there's a lot of sworn testimony recanting. What was he doing on the hood of your car?"

"We were sort of cruising up Comstock Street . . ." Lula said.

Connie's eyes got wide. "Where on Comstock?"

"Third."

"Do you have a death wish? That's Slayerland."

"We were just riding through," Lula said.

"The two of you? In what car? The Buick? The powder blue-and-white Buick? You can't go past Third on Comstock in a powder blue car! That's Cut's colors. You don't go into gang territory with another gang color."

"Well, yeah, but I didn't think it counted for cars. I just thought it counted for clothes. For, like, do-rags and shirts and shit," Lula said. "And it's hard to believe anybody'd take Cut serious with a color like powder blue. Powder blue is a sissy color."

I took the files from Lula and shuffled through them. No devil guy. Connie handed me the remaining four files. No devil guy there either. This left me with

three possibilities. The devil guy didn't
have a record. Or the devil guy used a different bond agent. Les Sebring, maybe.
Or the devil guy gave an address outside
of Slayerland.

I saw Connie and Lula go still and fix
their eyes on the door behind me. Either
someone walked in with a gun in his hand
or else Ranger was here. Since no one
ducked for cover, I was betting it was
Ranger.

A warm hand settled at the base of my
neck, and I felt Ranger lean into me.
"Babe," he said, softly, his right arm
snaking around me to take the file from
my hand. "Eugene Brown," he read. "You
might not want to spend a lot of time with
Eugene. He's not a fun guy."

"I sort of bounced him off the hood of
the Buick today," I told Ranger. "But it
wasn't my fault."

Ranger tightened his hold on my neck.
"You want to be careful with Eugene. He
hasn't got much of a sense of humor,
Babe."

"I don't suppose you know the identity
of the devil guy who's robbing all the deli-
marts?"

"Don't suppose I do," Ranger said. "But

it's not Eugene. There'd be more bodies on the floor if it was Eugene."

Vinnie's inner office door opened, and Vinnie stuck his head out. "What's up?"

"I'm going out of town for a couple weeks," Ranger said. "Tank will be on the job, if you need him." Ranger dropped the Brown file on Connie's desk and turned to me. "I want to talk to you . . . outside."

It was late afternoon and the sky was overcast, but the autumn air was still warm in spite of the gloom. Ranger's customized black Ford F-150 FX4 was parked curbside. A black SUV with tinted windows was parked behind the truck. The SUV had its motor running.

I followed Ranger out of the office, glancing first at the SUV and then at the heavy traffic on Hamilton. Rush hour in Trenton.

"What if *I* need something?" I asked Ranger, doing a little flirting, feeling brave because I was on a public street. "Should I call Tank?"

He ran a fingertip along my hairline and tucked a stray curl behind my ear. "It depends what you need. Did you have anything special in mind?"

Our eyes held, and I felt the first licks of panic. I should know better than to play with Ranger. He never got rattled, and he never backed down. I, on the other hand, frequently got rattled with Ranger and almost always backed down.

"How about if I need a car?" I asked, searching for something legitimate to change the tone. There'd been times past when I'd needed a car, and Ranger had provided one.

Ranger pulled a set of keys from his pocket and dropped them into my hand. "You can take my truck. I can get a ride back with Tank."

A narrow alley separated Vinnie's office from the neighboring business. Ranger nudged me into the shadow of the alley, pressed me against the brick wall, and kissed me. When his tongue touched mine my fingers curled into his shirt, and I think I might have momentarily lost consciousness.

"Hey," I said, when consciousness returned. "You're poaching."

"And?"

"Stop it."

"You don't mean that," Ranger said, smiling.

He was right. A woman would have to be dead not to want to kiss Ranger. And I wasn't even close to dead.

I gave the keys back to him. "Nice gesture but I can't take the truck."

"Call Tank if you change your mind. And be careful. Don't try to play with Eugene."

And he was gone.

Lula and Connie were shuffling papers, trying to look busy, when I returned to the office.

"Is he gone?" Lula wanted to know.

"Yeah."

"Lord, he makes me nervous. He is so hot. I got flashes. Look at me. I'm having a flash. I'm not even in menopause, and I'm hot flashing."

Connie rolled back in her chair. "Did he tell you where he was going? How long he'd be away?"

"No."

Connie had a problem. When Ranger was gone she was left with me and a couple part-time BEAs. If a high-stakes bond went south, she'd be in a bind. The case would have to go to me. At least temporarily. I was okay at my job, but I wasn't Ranger. Ranger had skills that went way beyond the normal parameters of human ability.

"I hate when he does this," Connie said.

"I been noticing the last two times he took off there was a coup in Central America," Lula said. "I'm going home, and I'm watching CNN."

I left the office and headed home to Joe's house. Somehow I'd managed to keep busy all day, but it didn't feel like I'd accomplished much. I stopped at Giovichinni's deli on Hamilton and picked up some lunch meat, sliced provolone, a medium container of potato salad, and a loaf of bread. I added a couple tomatoes and a small tub of chocolate ice cream.

It was a bad time to stop at Giovichinni's, but it was my only option if I wanted to eat. St. Francis Hospital was a block away, and half the hospital emptied out into Giovichinni's at this hour.

Mrs. Wexler came up to me while I was standing in line. "My goodness," she said, "I haven't seen you in an age. I understand your sister is getting married. Isn't that nice for her, but it must be a very stressful time for you. Is that a cold sore on your lip, dear?"

My hand immediately flew to my lip. I

didn't have anything on my lip when I left the house this morning, but yes, there was definitely something erupting on my mouth. I dug in my purse for a mirror. "I've never had a cold sore," I told Mrs. Wexler. "I swear to God."

"Well, it does look like a cold sore," Mrs. Wexler said.

I squinted into my mirror. Yikes! There it was . . . big and red and angry looking. How did this happen? And then it hit me. Marty Sklar and his cooties! I studied my lip. No. Wait a minute, it wasn't a cold sore. It was a boo-boo.

I'd gnawed a hole into my lip on the way across town, worrying about Eugene Brown and God knows what else. Okay, and the fact that I was attracted to two men didn't help. Probably I loved both of them. How sick is that?

"It's a cut," I said to Mrs. Wexler. "I got it this afternoon."

"Of course," Mrs. Wexler said. "I can see that now."

My mother called on my cell phone. "Mrs. Rogers just called," my mother said. "She said you're in Giovichinni's, and you have a cold sore."

"It's not a cold sore. It's a cut."

"Well, that's a relief. Could you pick up a couple things for me while you're there at Giovichinni's? I need a pound of olive loaf, an Entenmann's raspberry swirl coffee cake, and a quarter pound of Swiss. Make sure they don't slice the Swiss too thin. It all sticks together if it's too thin."

I scurried off to the deli counter, got my mother's stuff, and got back into line.

Leslie Giovichinni was working the register. "Gosh," she said, when I stepped in front of her. "You poor thing. You've got a big herpes!"

"*It's not a herpes,*" I said. "It's a *cut.* I got it this afternoon."

"You should put ice on it," she said. "It looks real painful."

I paid Leslie and slunk out of the store. I hunched behind the wheel of the Buick and turned into the Burg. I had to park in the driveway when I got to my parents' house because there was a big yellow school bus at the curb.

Grandma was at the door, waiting for me. "Guess who's here?" she said.

"Sally?"

"He came over because he was so excited that the charges were dropped. And he's been real helpful on account of Valerie's still here, and we've been discussing the bridesmaids' dresses. Valerie wants pink, but Sally thinks they should be a fall color since it's fall."

Valerie was in the kitchen, sitting at the table with the baby hanging from her neck in a kind of sling apparatus. My mother was at the stove, stirring a pot of marinara.

Sally was sitting across from Valerie. His long black curly hair was Medusa meets Howard Stern. He was wearing a Mötley Crüe T-shirt, jeans with the knees torn out, and red lizard cowboy boots.

"Hey, man, thanks for getting the charges dropped," Sally said. "I got a call from the court. And then Sklar called me just to make sure I wasn't gonna go ahead with the lawyer. I didn't know what to say at first, but I just went with it. It was real good."

I put the cheese and lunch meat in the fridge, and I set the coffee cake on the table. "Glad it worked out."

"So what do you think of the dresses?" Valerie wanted to know.

"Are you sure you want to have a big wedding?" I asked Valerie. "It seems like a lot of work and expense. And who will you have for bridesmaids?"

"You'll be my maid of honor. And then there's Loretta Stonehouser. And Rita Metzger. And Margaret Durski as bridesmaids. And the girls can be junior bridesmaids."

"I'm thinking pumpkin would be a good color for the bridesmaids' gowns," Sally said.

I cut myself a large wedge of coffee cake. It was going to take a lot of cake to improve my mood on the pumpkin gown.

"You know what we need?" Grandma said. "We need a wedding planner. Like that movie. Remember where Jennifer Lopez is the wedding planner?"

"I could use help," Valerie said. "It's hard to find the time for everything, but I don't think I can afford a wedding planner."

"Maybe I could help plan the wedding," Sally said. "I have extra time between my bus runs."

"You'd be a perfect wedding planner," Grandma said. "You have a real eye for color, and you got ideas about all that seasonal stuff. I would never have thought to have pumpkin gowns."

"It's settled then. You're the wedding planner," Valerie said.

My mother's attention wandered to the pantry. She might have been taking a mental inventory, but more likely, she was contemplating the whiskey bottle hidden behind the olive oil.

"How's the house search going?" I asked Valerie. "Any luck?"

"I haven't had a lot of time to put to it," she said. "But I promise to start looking."

"I sort of miss my apartment."

"I know," Val said. "I'm really sorry this is taking so long. Maybe we should move back here with Mom and Dad."

My mother's back went rigid at the stove. First the wedding planner and now this.

I cut another piece of cake and headed out. "I have to go. Joe's waiting."

JOE AND BOB were on the couch, watching television. I dropped my purse on the small hall table and took the grocery bag into the kitchen. I made sandwiches and spooned out the potato salad.

"I'm thinking about getting a cookbook," I told Morelli when I handed him his plate.

"Wow," he said. "What's that all about?"

"I'm getting tired of sandwiches and pizza."

"A cookbook sounds like a big commitment."

"It's not a commitment," I said. "It's a stupid cookbook. I could learn how to cook a chicken or a cow, or something."

"Would we have to get married?"

"No." Jeez.

Bob finished his sandwich and looked first to me and then to Morelli. He knew from past experience that it wasn't likely we'd share, so he put his head down on his paw and went back to watching *Seinfeld*.

"So-o-o," I said. "Did you hear about Eugene Brown?"

"What about him?"

"I bounced him off my car today."

Morelli took a forkful of potato salad. "Am I going to hate the rest of this story?"

"It's possible. It was sort of a hit-and-run."

"So this falls under the category of making an official police report?"

"Unofficial police report."

"Did you kill him?"

"I don't think so. He was latched on to the hood of the Buick, hanging on to the windshield wiper, and he got pitched off when I turned the corner. I was at Seventh and Comstock, and I didn't think it was a good idea to get out of the car to check his vital signs."

Morelli collected the three plates and stood to take them to the kitchen. "Dessert?"

"Chocolate ice cream." I followed after him and watched while he scooped. "That was too easy," I said. "You didn't yell or tell me I was stupid, or anything."

"I'm pacing myself."

I ROLLED OUT of bed with Morelli at the crack of dawn.

"This is getting scary," Morelli said. "First you're thinking about buying a cookbook. And now you're getting up with me. Next thing you'll be inviting my grandmother over for dinner."

Not likely. His Grandma Bella was nuts. She had this Italian voodoo thing going that she called the eye. I'm not saying the eye worked, but I've known people who got the eye to coincidentally lose their hair, or skip their period, or break out in an unexplained rash. I was half Italian, but none of my relatives could give the eye. Mostly, my relatives gave the finger.

We showered together. And that involved some fooling around. So before Morelli even had breakfast he was already a half hour late.

I had coffee going by the time he came downstairs. He chugged a cup while he did the gun and badge routine. He dropped a blueberry into Rex's cage. And he dumped two cups of dog crunchies into Bob's bowl.

"What's the reason for the early start?" he asked. "You aren't going back to Comstock Street, are you?"

"I'm checking out real estate. Valerie isn't doing anything about finding her own place, so I thought I'd do some searching for her."

Morelli looked over his cup at me. "I thought you were all settled in here. What about the cookbook?"

"I like living with you, but sometimes I miss my independence."

"Like when?"

"Okay, maybe independence is the wrong word. Maybe I just miss my own bathroom."

Morelli grabbed me and kissed me. "I

love you, but not enough to add a second bathroom. I'm not budgeted for any more renovations." He set his cup on the counter and headed for the front of the house. Bob ran with him, woofing, jumping around like a rabbit.

"Bob needs to go out," I said.

"Your turn," Morelli said. "I'm late, and besides, you owe me for the shower."

"What? What do you mean I owe you for the shower?"

He shrugged into a jacket. "I did your favorite thing today. Almost drowned doing it, too. And I think I got a bruise on my knee."

"Excuse me? What about that thing I did for you last night? I was just getting payback this morning."

Morelli was grinning. "They're not nearly equal, Cupcake. Especially since I did it in the shower." He took his keys off the hall table. "Come on. Be a sport. I'm really late."

"Fine! Go. I'll walk the dog. Yeesh."

Morelli opened the front door and stopped. "Shit."

"What?"

"We had visitors last night."

FIVE

I TIGHTENED MY robe and peeked around Morelli. There was graffiti on the sidewalk and graffiti on the Buick. We both stepped out onto the small porch. The graffiti was on the front door.

"What are these marks?" I asked. "They look like little kitty paws."

"These are gang symbols. The Comstock Street Slayers are affiliated with Crud and Guts. Sometimes Crud and Guts is known as Cat Guts. So you have CSS with a paw print." Morelli was pointing as he was talking. "The GKC on the door would stand for Gangsta Killer Cruds."

I moved off the porch, over to the Buick. Every square inch of the car was spray-painted. "Slay the bitch" and "Crud

Money" were prevalent themes. Morelli's SUV had been left untouched.

"Seems like there's a message here," I said to Morelli. I wasn't all that fond of the Buick but I hated seeing it defaced. The Buick had from time to time saved my butt. And probably this is a weird thing to say, but sometimes I had the feeling there was more there than just a car. Not to mention, the slogans seemed directed at me. And I suspected they weren't indicators of affection.

" 'Slay the bitch' is self-explanatory," Morelli said. His no-expression cop face was in place with only the tight corners of his mouth giving him away. Morelli wasn't happy. " 'Crud Money' describes the gangster lifestyle of extortion and drug sales. In this case, it could be putting you on notice that you're marked for retribution."

"What does that mean? Retribution?"

Morelli turned to me and our eyes held. "Could be anything," he said. "Could be death."

A greasy wave of undefined emotion slid through me. I suspected fear was heavy in the mix. I didn't know a lot about gangs, but I was coming up to speed fast. I hadn't felt especially threatened by gang-related crime three days ago. Now it was sitting at my curb, and it didn't feel good.

"You're exaggerating, right?" I asked.

"Executions are a part of gang culture. Gangs have been steadily on the rise in Trenton, and the murder rate has been rising with them. It used to be that the gangs were small and composed of kids looking to have a local identity. Now the gangs have their roots in the prison system and have national affiliations. They control the drug sales and territories. They're violent. They're unpredictable. They're feared in their communities."

"I knew there was a problem. I didn't know it was that bad."

"It's not something we like to talk about since we're at a loss how to fix it." Morelli pushed me into the house and closed the door. "I want you to stay here today until I get some intel on this. I'm going to have the Buick picked up and impounded in the police garage, so someone from the street gangs task force can take a look at it."

"You can't take the Buick. How will I get to work?"

Morelli tapped me gently on the forehead with his index finger. "Anybody home in there? Look at that car. Do you want to drive that car around?"

"I've driven around in worse." And that was the honest-to-God sad truth. How pathetic is that?

"Humor me, okay? Stay in the house. You should be safe here. To my knowledge, the Slayers have never burned down a house."

"Just a deli," I said.

"Yeah. A deli."

We both thought about that for a moment.

Morelli took my car keys from my purse and left. I locked the front door and went to the living room window to watch Morelli pull away in his SUV.

"How are we going to go for a walk?" I asked Bob. "How am I going to do my job? What will I do all day?"

Bob was pacing in front of the door, looking desperate.

"You're going to have to do it in the backyard today," I said, not all that unhappy about missing the walk. Bob pooped *everywhere* in the morning, and I got the privilege of carting it home. It's hard to enjoy a walk when you've got a big bag of poop in your hand.

I hooked Bob up to his backyard leash and tidied the kitchen. By one o'clock the bed was made, the floors were clean, the toaster was polished, the laundry was washed, dried, and folded, and I was cleaning out the fridge. At some point when my back was turned, the Buick disappeared from the curb.

"Now what?" I said to Bob.

Bob looked thoughtful, but he didn't come up with anything, so I called Morelli. "Now what?" I said to Morelli.

"It's only one o'clock," he said. "Give me a break. We're working on it."

"I polished the toaster."

"Un hunh. Listen, I have to go now."

"I'm going nuts here!"

There was a disconnect and then a dial tone.

I still had the phone in my hand when it rang.

"What's going on?" Connie wanted to know. "Are you sick? You always check in at the office by now."

"I have a car problem."

"And? You want me to send Lula?"

"Sure. Send Lula."

Ten minutes later, Lula's red Firebird was idling in front of Morelli's house.

"Looks like Morelli got his house decorated," Lula said.

"It appears Eugene Brown didn't enjoy getting flipped off my hood."

"I didn't get none of this gang crap on my house, so it looks like you're the only one he's holding a grudge against. I guess that's on account of I was just an innocent passenger."

I gave Lula the squinty-eyed death glare.

"Don't you look at me like that," Lula said. "You should be happy for me that I'm not involved in this. Anyways, Vinnie's not happy either. He said there's just five days left to get Roger Banker's ass hauled into court, or he's gonna be out the bond."

If I had a quarter for every time I tried to snag Roger Banker, I could go to Bermuda for a week. Banker was as slippery as they come. He was a repeat offender, so he knew the drill. I couldn't feed him a load of baloney about just going down to the court to reschedule. He knew once the cuffs were on him, he was going to jail. He was unemployed, living off an indeterminate number of loser girlfriends and loser relatives. And he was hard to spot. Banker had no memorable features. Banker was like the invisible man. I once stood next to him at a bar and didn't recognize him. Lula and I had been collecting photographs of him and committing the photographs to memory with hopes that would help.

"Okay," I said, "let's make the rounds. Maybe we'll get lucky."

The rounds consisted of Lowanda Jones, Beverly Barber, Chermaine Williamson, and Marjorie Best. There were other people and places to include in the Banker hunt, but Lowanda, Beverly, Chermaine, and Marjorie were my top picks. They all lived in the projects just north of the police station. Lowanda and Beverly were sisters. They lived four blocks apart, and they were a car crash.

Lula cruised into the projects. "Who's first up?" Lula asked.

"Lowanda."

The projects covered a large chunk of Trenton real estate that was less than prime. *A lot* less than prime. The buildings were redbrick, government-issue low rise. The fencing was industrial chain-link. The cars at the curb were junkers.

"Good thing for the gang graffiti or this would be real drab," Lula said. "Wouldn't you think they could grow grass? Hell, plant a bush."

I suspected even God would have a hard time landscaping the projects. The ground was as hard and as blighted as the lives of the people who lived here.

Lula turned onto Kendall Street and parked two doors down from Lowanda's garden apartment. The term *garden* being used loosely. We'd been here before so we knew the layout. It was a ground-floor unit with one bedroom and seven dogs. The dogs were of varying sizes and ages. All of indeterminate breed. All of them horny buggers willing to hump anything that moved.

We got out of the car cautiously, on the lookout for the pack of beasts.

"I don't see any of Lowanda's dogs," Lula said.

"Maybe they're locked up in the house."

"Well, I'm not going in if they're in the house. I hate those dogs. Nasty-assed humpers. What's she thinking, anyway, to keep a pack of pervert dogs like that?"

We knocked once. No answer.

"I know she's in there," Lula said. "I can hear her talking, doing business."

Lowanda did phone sex. She didn't look like she was rolling in money, so I was guessing she wasn't all that good at the job. Or maybe she just spent her money on beer, cigarettes, and chicken nuggets. Lowanda ate a lot of chicken nuggets. Lowanda ate chicken nuggets like Carol Cantell ate Cheez Doodles.

I knocked again and tried the doorknob. The door wasn't locked. I held the door open a crack, and Lula and I peeked in. No dogs in sight.

"Not likely Banker's in here," Lula said, following me through the front door. "The door would be locked up. And anyway, jail would look good compared to this pigpen."

We stepped over a suspicious stain on the rug and stared into the jumbled mess that passed for Lowanda's home. There was a mattress on the floor in the far corner of the living room. The mattress was covered with a tattered yellow chenille spread. An open, empty pizza delivery box was on the floor by the mattress. Clothes and shoes were scattered everywhere. A couple rickety folding chairs had been set up in the living room. The backs of the chairs said "Morten's Funeral Parlor." A big brown leather recliner had been placed in front of the television. The recliner had a gash in one arm and in the seat, and some of the stuffing was spilling out.

Lowanda was in the recliner with her back to us, a phone to her ear and a bucket of chicken nuggets balanced on the roll of fat that circled her waist. She was wearing gray sweats decorated with ketchup stains.

"Yeah, honey," she said into the phone. "That's good, baby. Oh yeah. Oh-h-h-h yeah. I just got myself all naked for you. An' I got love oil on myself 'cause I'm gonna get hot."

"*Hey!*" Lula said. "Lowanda, you paying attention here?"

Lowanda jumped in her seat and whipped around to look at us. "What the hell?" she said. "What are you doing scaring me like that when I'm trying to earn a honest living?" She returned to the phone. "Excuse me, sugar. Lowanda's got a small problem. Could you just work on yourself some? I be right back." She covered the phone with her hand and got up, some of the chair stuffing sticking to her double-wide ass. "What?"

"We're looking for Roger Banker," Lula said.

"Well, he isn't here. Does it look like he's here?"

"Maybe he's hiding in the other room," Lula said.

"You got a search warrant?"

"We don't need a search warrant," Lula said. "We're bounty hunters."

"Whatever," Lowanda said. "Just do your search and get out. I gotta get back to my caller. Soon as you stop talking to Mr. Stiffy he turns into Mr. Softy. And I get paid by the job. I do a volume business here."

Lula moved through the house while I stayed with Lowanda.

"I'm willing to pay for information," I told Lowanda. "Do you have any information?"

"How much you paying?"

"Depends on the information," I said.

"I got an address. I know where he's at if you hurry over there." She handed the phone over to me. "You talk to this guy, and I'll write down the address."

"Wait a minute . . ."

"Hello?" Mr. Stiffy said. "Who's this?"

"None of your business."

"I like that," he said. "Spunky. I bet you'd like to spank me."

"Wait a minute. I know your voice. Vinnie?"

"Stephanie? Christ." Disconnect.

Lowanda came back with the paper. "Here it is," she said. "This is where he's staying."

I looked at the paper. "This is your sister's address."

"And? What happened to my caller?"

"He hung up. He was done."

Lula returned to the living room. "Lowanda," she said, "you better do something about your kitchen. You got a cockroach as big as a cow in there."

I gave Lowanda a twenty.

"This is it? This is all I get?" Lowanda said.

"If Banker's at Beverly's house, I'll be back with the rest of the money."

"Where's the dogs?" Lula wanted to know.

"Out," Lowanda said. "They like to go out when the weather's nice."

Lula opened Lowanda's door and looked around. "How far out do they go?"

"How the hell do I know? They go *out*. And they stay out all day. *Out* is *out*."

"Just asking," Lula said. "No need to get touchy. You don't exactly have the best-mannered dogs, Lowanda."

Lowanda had her hands on her hips, lower lip stuck out, eyes narrowed. "You dissin' on my dogs?"

"Yeah," Lula said. "I *hate* your dogs. Your dogs are rude. Those dogs hump everything."

"Wasn't so long ago people was saying that about *you*," Lowanda said. "You got some nerve coming around here asking for information and then dissin' my dogs. I got a mind to never give you no more information."

I grabbed Lula before she removed Lowanda's eyes from her eye sockets, and I shoved Lula out the door.

"Don't provoke her," I said to Lula. "She's probably got guns."

"I got a gun," Lula said. "And I got a mind to use it."

"No guns! And get moving. I don't like standing out here in the open where the dogs can find us."

"I think she insulted me," Lula said. "I'm

not ashamed of my past. I was a damn good ho. But I didn't like the tone of her voice just now. It was an insulting tone."

"I don't care what tone she had . . . move your butt to the car before the dogs get us."

"What's with you and the dogs? Here I just been insulted, and all you can think about is the dogs."

"Do you want to be standing here when those dogs come running around the corner of the building?"

"Hunh. I could take care of those dogs if I had to. It's not like I'm *afraid* of those dogs."

"Well, *I'm* afraid of those dogs, so haul ass."

And that was when we heard them. Yipping, yipping, yipping in the distance. On the move. Getting closer. Somewhere out of sight, to the side of the building.

"*Oh shit,*" Lula said. And Lula started running for the car, knees up, arms pumping.

I was two steps in front of her, running for all I was worth. I could hear the dogs round the corner. I turned to look, and I saw them galloping after us, eyes wild, mouths open, tongues and ears catching wind. They were closing ground fast, the biggest of them in the lead.

Lula let out a shriek. "Lord help me!"

I guess the Lord was listening because they ran past Lula and took me down. The first dog hit me square in the back, sending me to my knees. Not a good position to be in when you're attacked by a pack of humpers. I tried to regain my footing, but the dogs were on me, and I couldn't get up. I had humpers on both legs, and a bulldog that looked like Winston Churchill humping my head. There was a humper on a humper.

"Keep going. Save yourself!" I yelled to Lula. "Tell my mother I love her."

"Get up!" Lula yelled at me. "You gotta get up! Those dogs'll hump you to death."

She was right. The pack was vicious. It was in a humping frenzy. Dogs in inferior humping positions were snarling and nipping, jockeying for better locations. The leg humpers held tight, grimly determined to finish the job, but the head humper kept losing his grip. The head humper was drooling and panting hot dog breath in my face. He'd hump some and slide off, and then he'd come scrambling back, trying to hump again.

"I can't get up!" I said. "I've got seven humping dogs on me. *Seven.* Do something!"

Lula was running around, hands in the air. "I don't know what to do. I don't know what to do."

"Get the dog off my head," I yelled. "I don't care about the leg humpers. *Just get the dog off my head!*"

"Maybe you should let them have their way with you," Lula said. "They'll go away as soon as they're done. That's the way it is with male humping."

"Maybe you should goddamn grab this horny humping bulldog and get him the hell off my freaking head!"

The door to Lowanda's apartment crashed open, and Lowanda yelled out to us. "Hey!" she said. "What are you doing to my dogs?"

"We aren't doing nothing," Lula said. "They're humping Stephanie."

Lowanda had a bag of dog kibble in her hand. She shook the bag and the dogs stopped humping and looked around. Lowanda shook the bag some more and the dogs gave a couple last halfhearted humps and took off for the kibble.

"Dumb-ass bounty hunters," Lowanda said, disappearing into the house with the dogs, slamming and locking the door behind her.

"I thought you were a goner," Lula said to me.

I was on my back, breathing heavy, eyes closed. "Give me a minute."

"You're a mess," Lula said. "Those dogs humped all over you. And you got something in your hair from that bulldog."

I got to my feet. "I'm going with drool. It looks like drool, right?"

"If you say so."

Lula and I moved to the safety of the car, and Lula drove the distance to Beverly's apartment. Beverly's apartment looked a lot like Lowanda's, except Beverly didn't have a recliner. Beverly had a couch hauled up to her television. The couch was partially covered with a blue sheet, and I feared there was a gross stain under the sheet, too terrible for even Beverly to overlook.

"You can't come in here now," Beverly said, when she opened the door. "I'm busy. I got my honey here, and we were just getting it on."

"More information than I need," Lula said. "I just watched a pack of dogs hump Stephanie. I about reached my humping limit for the day."

"Those must be Lowanda's dogs," Beverly said. "I don't know what the deal is with those dogs. I never seen anything like it. And three of them is female."

"We're looking for an FTA," I said to Beverly.

"Yeah, that's what you're always doing here," Beverly said. "But I'm not FTA. I didn't do nothing wrong. Swear to God."

"It's not you," I said. "I'm looking for Roger Banker."

"Hunh," Beverley said. "That's inconvenient. You gonna arrest him?"

"We're going to take him to the station to get rebonded."

"Then what? Then you gonna let him go?"

"Do you want us to let him go?" Lula asked.

"Well, yeah."

"Then that's what we'll do," Lula told her. "He'll be in and out. And on top of that, we'll give you a twenty if we get to take him in."

Lowanda and Beverly would give their mother up for spare change.

"Okay, I guess I could tell you then," Beverly said. "He's the honey in the back room. And he might be a little indisposed."

"Roger," Beverly called out. "I got a couple ladies out here want to see you."

"Bring them back," Roger said. "I can handle them. More is better when it comes to ladies."

Lula and I looked at each other and did some eye rolling.

"Tell him to get dressed and come out here to meet us," I said to Beverly.

"You should put some pants on and come out here," Beverly said. "They don't want to meet up with you in the back room."

We could hear some rustling and fumbling, and Banker strolled out. He was wearing khaki pants and sneakers. No socks, no shirt. I was betting on no underwear.

"Roger Banker," Lula said. "This here's your lucky day on account of we come to give you a free ride to the clink."

Banker blinked once at Lula and once at me. And then he whirled around and ran for the kitchen door.

"Cover the crappy car in the front," I yelled to Lula. "It's probably Banker's." And I took off after Banker, pushing around Beverly, following Banker out the back door. Banker was running fast, long legs gobbling up ground. He jumped a section of chain-link and disappeared around the end of the building. I scrambled to follow and got snagged on a piece of wire as I cleared the top of the fence. I ripped myself free and kept going. Banker was maybe half a block ahead of me, but I had him in view. He was on the street, doubling back, running toward his car. And he was slowing down. Good thing, too, because I was dying. I really needed to do more aerobics. The only time I actually worked out was when I was in bed with Morelli. And even then I spent a lot of time on my back.

Lula was between Banker and the car. She was in the road, looking like a big pissed-off bull about to charge. If I was Banker I would have thought long and hard about getting around Lula, but I guess Banker didn't feel like he had a lot of options, because he never broke stride. Banker ran straight on, into Lula. There was a sound like a basketball hitting against a brick wall. Lula went on her ass, and Banker bounced back about five feet.

I tackled him from behind, and we both went down. I had cuffs in my hand, and I was trying to grab a wrist, but Banker was flailing around.

"Help me!" I yelled to Lula. "Do something."

"Out of my way," Lula said.

I rolled free of Banker, and Lula sat down hard on him, simultaneously expelling every molecule of air out of both ends of Banker's body.

"*Oooff,*" Banker said. And then he went dead still, spread-eagled on his back, looking like roadkill.

I cuffed him, and stood free. His eyes were open but glazed, and he was breathing shallow.

"Blink if you're okay," I said.

"*Fuck,*" Banker whispered.

"Well, what were you thinking?" Lula asked down at him, hands on hips. "You don't just run into a woman like that. Didn't you see me standing there? I got a mind to sit on you again. I could squash you like a bug if I wanted."

"I think I messed myself," Banker said.

"Then you aren't riding in my car," Lula told him. "You can walk your sorry behind all the way to the police station."

I hauled Banker up onto his feet and searched his pockets for his car keys. I found the keys plus twenty dollars. "Give the money to Beverly," I told Lula. "I'll drive him to the station in his car, and you can follow."

"Sure," Lula said.

I dragged Banker to the crappy car parked curbside and turned to Lula. "You're going to wait for me at the police station, right?"

"Are you implying I don't always wait?"

"You never wait."

"I can't help it. I got a thing about police stations. It's from my troubled past."

AN HOUR LATER I had Banker securely behind bars, and I had the body receipt in my hand, guaranteeing that Vinnie wouldn't be out his bond money. I searched the parking lot, but I couldn't find Lula. Big surprise. I called her cell phone. No answer. I tried the office.

"Sorry," Connie said. "She's not here. She stopped in to say that you had Banker, but then she took off again."

Great. I had half the ass ripped out of my jeans, my shirt was covered with grass stains, and I didn't even want to think about the state of my hair. I was standing in the middle of the public parking lot across from the police station, and I had no car. I could call my father. I could call Morelli. I could call a cab. Problem was, they were all a temporary fix. When I woke up tomorrow I would be back to square one with no car.

Of course there was still one more choice available to me. Ranger's truck. It was big and black and brand new. It came fully loaded with all sorts of toys and customized options. And it smelled like expensive new leather and Ranger . . . an aroma second only to chocolate chip cookies baking in the oven. Too bad there were a lot of really good reasons not to use the truck. At the top of the list was the fact that Joe would be nuts.

My cell phone chirped in my bag. "It's me," Connie said. "Vinnie just left for the day, and his last directive was that you're responsible for Carol Cantell. He doesn't want any screw-ups."

"Sure," I said. "You can count on me." I disconnected, blew out a sigh, and dialed Ranger's man, Tank. The conversation with Tank was short. Yes, Ranger had given him instructions to turn the truck over to me. Delivery would take about twenty minutes.

I put the time to good use by rationalizing my actions. I had no choice. I had to take the truck, right? How else would I do my job? And if I didn't do my job I wouldn't get paid. And then I wouldn't be able to make my rent payment. True, my sister was paying the rent these days on my apartment, and I was living rent-free with Morelli. But that could change at any moment. Suppose Valerie suddenly moved out?

What then? And it wasn't as if I was married to Morelli. We could have a big fight, and I could be on my own again. In fact, now that I was getting the truck a big fight was almost a certainty. This was an exhausting thought. Life was fudging complicated.

The truck arrived exactly on time, followed by the black SUV. Tank got out of the truck and handed me the keys.

To say that Tank is a big guy is oversimplification. Tank is a tank. His freshly shaved head looks buffed up with Pledge. His body is perfectly toned and fat free. His ass is tight. It's rumored that his morals are loose. And his black T-shirt looks painted onto him. Hard to tell what Tank thinks of me. Or, for that matter, if Tank thinks at all.

"Call me if there's a problem," Tank said. Then he got into the SUV and took off.

Just like that . . . I had a truck. Not just any old truck, either. This was a wicked, bad-ass, four-door supercrew with over-sized cast aluminum wheels, a whole herd of horses under the hood, tinted windows, and GPS. Not to mention a slew of gadgets about which I was clueless.

I'd ridden with Ranger, and I knew he always had a gun tucked away, hidden from view. I climbed behind the wheel, felt under the seat, and found the gun. If it had been my truck and my gun, I'd have removed the gun. Ranger left it in place. Trusting.

I cautiously turned the key in the ignition and eased the truck into the flow of traffic. The Buick drove like a refrigerator with wheels. The truck drove like a monster Porsche. I decided if I was going to drive the truck I was going to need a whole new wardrobe. My clothes weren't cool enough. And I needed more basic black. And I should trade in my sneakers for boots. And probably I needed sexier underwear . . . a thong, maybe.

I crossed town, drove a couple blocks on Hamilton, and slipped into the Burg. I was taking the long way home to Joe's house. Always procrastinate the unpleasant. Morelli wouldn't be happy about me going off with Lula, but he'd understand. Going off with Lula when he'd asked me to stay in the house would generate the sort of anger that could be worked off with a half hour of vicious channel surfing. The truck was going to provoke a full-blown contest of wills.

I turned the corner onto Slater and felt my heart roll over in my chest. Morelli was home. His SUV was parked in front of the house. I lined up behind the SUV and told myself it might not be so bad. Morelli was a reasonable guy, right? He'd see that I had no choice. I had to take Ranger's truck. It was the sensible thing to do. And besides, it was my business. Just because you lived with someone didn't mean they ran your life. I didn't tell Morelli how to conduct his business, did I? Well, okay, maybe once in a while I stuck my nose in there. But he never listened to me! That's the important point here.

Problem was, it wasn't actually about the truck. It was about Ranger. Morelli knew he might not be able to help me if I was standing next to Ranger when Ranger was operating outside the law. And Morelli had enough of his own wild years to understand the feral side of Ranger's sexuality. Another good reason not to have me standing too close to Ranger.

I swung out of the truck, beeped it locked, and marched up to the house. I opened the door, and Bob rushed up to me and bounced around. I gave him some hugs and got some Bob slobber on my jeans. I didn't mind about the slobber. It seemed like a small price to pay for unconditional love. And besides, you could hardly notice the slobber mixed in with the grass and dirt stains and God knew what else. Bob sniffed at the God knew what else and backed off. Bob had standards.

Morelli didn't rush to greet me. He didn't bounce around or slobber or exude unconditional love. Morelli was slouched on the couch, watching the Three Stooges on television. "So," he said when I came into the room.

"So," I answered.

"What's with the truck?"

"What truck?"

He cut his eyes to me.

"Oh," I said. "That truck. That's Ranger's truck. He's letting me borrow it until I get the Buick back."

"Has the truck got a VIN?"

"Of course it has a VIN."

Is the VIN legitimate would have been a better question. Ranger has a seemingly inexhaustible supply of new black cars and trucks. The origin of these vehicles is unknown. The vehicle identification tag is almost always in place, but it seems possible the Bat Cave might contain a metal shop. Not that Ranger or any of his men would actually steal a car, but maybe they wouldn't ask too many questions upon delivery.

"You could have borrowed my SUV," Morelli said.

"You didn't offer it to me."

"Because I wanted you to stay in the house today. One day," Morelli said. "Was that too much to ask?"

"I stayed in the house for most of the day."

"Most of the day isn't all of the day."

"What about tomorrow?"

"It's going to be ugly," Morelli said. "You're going to be on a rant about women's equality and personal freedom. And I'm going to be waving my arms and yelling, because I'm an Italian cop, and that's what we do when women are irrational."

"It's not about women's equality and personal freedom. This isn't political. It's personal. I want you to support my career choice."

"You don't have a career," Morelli said. "You have a suicide mission. Most women try to avoid murderers and rapists. I have a girlfriend who goes out trying to find them. And if murderers and rapists weren't bad enough, now you've pissed off a gang."

"These gang people should get a grip.

The least little thing and they're all bent out of shape. What's the deal with them?"

"That's how they have fun," Morelli said.

"Maybe the police should try to get them involved in a hobby, like wood-working, or something."

"Yeah, maybe we could get it to replace all the drug dealing and killings they're doing now."

"Are they really that bad?"

"Yes. They're really that bad."

Morelli shut the television off and came over to me. "What the hell happened to you?" he said, looking more closely at my jeans.

"I had to run Roger Banker down."

"What's this in your hair?"

"I'm hoping it's dog drool."

"I don't get it," Morelli said. "Other women are happy to stay home. My sister stays home. My brothers' wives stay home. My mother stays home. My grand-mother stays home."

"Your grandmother is insane."

"You're right. My grandmother doesn't count."

"I'm sure there'll be a time in my life

when I want to stay home. This isn't it," I said.

"So I'm ahead of my time?"

I smiled at him and kissed him lightly on the lips. "Yeah."

He pulled me close to him. "You don't expect me to wait, do you?"

"Yep."

"I'm not good at waiting."

"Deal with it," I said, pushing away.

Morelli narrowed his eyes. "Deal with it? Excuse me?"

Okay, maybe I said it a little more authoritatively than I'd intended. But my day hadn't been all that great, plus I was feeling just a tad defensive over the foreign substance in my hair that might have been drool, but then maybe not. I could have ended the conversation there, but I didn't think it was smart to back down on the issue. And truth is, I was working my way out of Morelli's house.

"I'm not staying home. End of discussion."

"The hell this is the end," Morelli said.

"Oh yeah? Well end *this*." And I gave him the finger and headed for the stairs.

"Very adult," Morelli said. "Nice to

know you've thought this through and have it reduced to a hand gesture."

"I've thought it through, and I have a plan. I'm leaving."

Morelli followed me upstairs. "Leaving? That's a plan?"

"It's a temporary plan." I took the laundry basket from the closet and started putting clothes in it.

"I have a plan, too," Morelli said. "It's called you're staying."

"We'll do your plan next time." I emptied my lingerie drawer into the basket.

"What's this?" Morelli said, picking out lavender string bikini underpants. "I like these. You want to fool around?"

"No!" Actually, I sort of did, but it didn't seem in keeping with the current plan.

I gathered up some things from the bathroom, added them to the basket, and carted the basket downstairs. Then I lugged the hamster cage from the kitchen and put it on top of the clothes in the basket.

"You're serious about this," Morelli said.

"I'm not going to start every day off with an argument about hiding in the house."

"You don't have to hide in the house forever. Just lower your visibility for a few days. And it would be nice if you'd stop looking for trouble."

I hefted the laundry basket and pushed past him to the door. "On the surface that sounds reasonable, but the reality of it is that I give up my job and hide."

I was telling the truth. I didn't want to start every day off with an argument. But, I also didn't want to wake up to more graffiti on Joe's house. I didn't want a fire-bomb thrown through his front window. I didn't want a Slayer breaking in when I was alone and in the shower. I needed a place to stay that was unknown to the Slayers. Not Morelli's house. Not my parents' house. Not my apartment. I wouldn't feel completely safe in any of those places. And I didn't want to put any-one in danger. Maybe I was making a big thing out of nothing . . . but then, maybe not.

SO, HERE I was idling at the corner of Slater and Chambers with a pleasant, perfectly designed, color-coordinated Martha Stewart laundry basket on the seat beside me, filled with all the clean clothes I could find, a hamster cage wedged into the seat behind me . . . and no place to go.

I'd told Morelli I was going home to my parents' house, but it had been a fib. The truth was, I walked out without totally thinking the whole thing through.

My best friend Mary Lou was married and had a pack of kids. No room there. Lula lived in a closet. No room there either.

The sun was setting, and I was feeling panicky. I could sleep in Ranger's truck, but it didn't have a bathroom. I'd have to go to the Mobil station on the corner to use the toilet. And what about a shower? The Mobil station didn't have a shower. How was I going to get the drool out of my hair? And Rex? This was so pathetic, I thought. My hamster was homeless.

A flashy black Lexus SUV made its way up Slater. I slid low in the seat and held my breath as the Lexus rolled forward. Hard to see through the SUV's tinted windows. Could be anyone driving, I told myself. Could be a perfectly nice family in the Lexus. But in my gut I worried that they were Slayers.

The Lexus stopped in front of Morelli's

house. The bass from the SUV stereo thumped down the street and beat against my windshield. After a long moment the SUV moved off.

Looking for me, I thought. And then I burst into tears. I was in emotion overload, feeling sorry for myself. A bunch of gang guys were out to get me. The police had Big Blue. And I'd moved out on Morelli . . . for the umpteenth time.

Rex had come out of his soup can and was hunkered down on his wheel, myopically surveying his new surroundings.

"Look at me," I said to Rex. "I'm a mess. I'm hysterical. I need a doughnut."

Rex got all perky at that. Rex was always up for a doughnut.

I called Morelli on my cell and told him about the Lexus. "Just thought you should know," I said. "Be careful when you go out of the house. And maybe you shouldn't stand in front of any windows."

"They're not out for me," Morelli said.

I nodded agreement in the dark truck and disconnected. I drove a half mile down Hamilton and pulled into the drive-thru lane at Dunkin' Donuts. Is this a great country, or what? You don't even have to get out of your car to get a doughnut. Good thing, too, because I looked a wreck. Besides the grass-stained, ripped-up clothes, my eyes were all red and splotchy from crying. I got a dozen doughnuts, parked in the back of the lot, and dug in. I gave Rex part of a jelly doughnut and a piece from a pumpkin spice doughnut. I figured pumpkin was good for him.

After eating half the bag I was sick enough not to care about Morelli or the gang guys. "I ate too many doughnuts," I said to Rex. "I need to lie down or burp or something." I checked out my shirt. Big glob of jelly on my boob. Perfect.

The engine was off and the only diode blinking was for the antitheft system. I turned the key and the dash lit up like Christmas. I touched one of the buttons and the GPS screen slid into place. After a few seconds a map appeared, pinpointing my location. Very slick. I touched the screen and a series of commands appeared. One of the commands was return route. I touched the screen and a yellow line took me from Dunkin' Donuts back to Morelli's house.

Just for the hell of it I pulled out of the lot and followed the line. Minutes later, I was at Morelli's house. Interesting thing is, the line didn't stop there. I continued to follow the line and after a couple blocks I got really excited because I knew where I was going. The line was taking me to the police station. And if the line led me to the police station, maybe it would also retrace the route Tank took when he brought the truck to me. If the computer stored enough information there was the possibility that it might take me to the Bat Cave.

SIX

I REACHED THE police station and sure enough the yellow line kept going. I was moving back toward the river, into an area of renovated office buildings and street-level businesses. Now I had a new problem. The yellow line could go on forever. It could go right past the Bat Cave, and I'd never know. And just as I was thinking this, the yellow line stopped.

I was on Haywood Street. It was a side street with minimal traffic, two blocks away from the noise and frustration of city center rush-hour gridlock. A series of four-story town houses ran along the north side of the street. A couple office buildings occupied the south side. I had no idea where to go from here. None of the town houses had an attached garage and there was no

on-street parking. I circled the block, looking for an alley with rear-access parking.
None. This was a good central location,
and one of the town houses would make a
good Bat Cave, but I couldn't see Ranger
parking his truck any distance from his
house. I was idling in front of an office
building with underground parking.
Ranger could park in the underground
garage, but even then he'd have to cross the
street to get to the town house. Not a big
deal for an ordinary person. Seemed out of
character for Ranger. Ranger sat with his
back to the wall. Ranger never left himself
exposed.

The other possibilities weren't as much
fun. The computer could simply have run
out of allotted space, and Haywood Street
meant nothing. Or Tank could have taken
Ranger's truck and parked it convenient
to the Tank Cave.

Lights were on in most of the town
houses. The office buildings were mostly
dark. The building with parking was a relatively small seven-story structure. The
foyer plus floors six and five were lit. I
rolled back a couple feet, so I could see
through the large glass double door. The
foyer looked newly renovated. Elevators

to the rear. Reception desk to one side. There was a uniformed guy behind the reception desk.

A two-lane entrance to the underground parking garage sat like a black gap in the building façade. I pulled into the parking garage entrance, but I was stopped by a machine that demanded a passkey. A heavy iron gate barred my way. I squinted into the dark interior and got a rush. I was pretty sure I was looking at a black Porsche parked nose-in to the back wall.

I hit my high beams, but the angle of the truck didn't splash a lot of light around the garage. Fortunately, Ranger carried a full array of bounty hunter toys. I retrieved a three-pound Maglite from the backseat, swung out of the truck and played the light across the expanse of the garage. The back wall held a stairwell and elevator. There were four parking spaces in front of the elevator. The first two were empty. Ranger's Porsche Turbo filled the third. A Porsche Cayenne filled the fourth. His Mercedes was missing. And I had the truck. Two black SUVs were parked on the side wall.

"It's the Bat Cave," I said to Rex when I got back behind the wheel.

Kind of fun to finally have found it . . . but now what? Ranger was off somewhere, and I still didn't have a place to spend the night. I stared into the dark garage. I had no place to stay, and dollars to doughnuts, sitting in front of me was a building with a vacant apartment. Don't even think about it, I said to myself. That's like a death wish. This man is fanatical about protecting his privacy. He won't be happy to find you've broken into his apartment and done the Goldilocks thing.

There was a part of my brain that was in charge of stupid ideas. When I was seven it told me to jump off my parents' garage roof to see if I could fly. It also encouraged me to play Choo Choo with Joe Morelli when I was a kid. Morelli was the originator of Choo Choo. Morelli was the choo choo train, and I was the tunnel. And as it turned out it was necessary for the train to spend a lot of time under my skirt. Later in life the stupid idea part of my brain encouraged me to marry Dicky Orr. Orr was a slick talker who had a roving eye. Less than a year after the wedding, other body parts that belonged to Orr started roving as well. And that was the end of that marriage.

The stupid idea part of my brain was now telling me I might be able to break in and go undetected. Just for one night, it said. Do it for Rex's sake. Poor Rex needs a place to spend the night.

I backed out of the garage entrance and drove around the block, hoping the stupid idea department would shut down. Unfortunately, it was still up and running when I returned to Ranger's building. I had his truck. He hadn't bothered to remove his gun. Maybe he hadn't bothered to remove his passkey. I checked the visor and the console. I checked the side-door pockets and the glove box. I was looking for a plastic credit card–type key that would slide into the machine. I backed out a second time, drove to the corner, and parked under a streetlight so I could better see the interior of the truck. Still couldn't find the passkey.

I looked down at the key in the ignition. There was an extra key and two small black plastic devices attached to the key ring. One was a remote to unlock the truck. The second was also a remote of some sort. I circled the block, pulled into the garage entrance, pushed a button on the second remote, and the gate slid open.

Stephanie, I said to myself, if you have any sense at all, you'll turn tail and get out of here as fast as possible. Yeah, right. I'd gotten this far—how could I possibly not want to explore further? I mean this was the Bat Cave, for crying out loud.

There were two SUVs parked to the side. That meant Ranger wasn't the only person to use this garage. It would be awkward for Tank or one of Ranger's other men to discover Ranger's truck had wandered home, so I retreated from the driveway and parked on the next block. Then I walked back to the garage, let myself in, and remoted the iron gate closed. I stepped into the elevator and looked at the panel. Seven buttons plus garage. I bypassed the security guard at the desk on the first floor and pressed number two. The elevator rose two floors and the doors opened to a large darkened reception area that I assumed led to offices. Floors three and four were similar. I skipped five and six since these were the lighted and presumably occupied floors. And the seven button wouldn't work. The elevator would go down, but it wouldn't go all the way up to seven.

The penthouse, I thought. The dragon's

lair. It needed a passkey. Just for the hell of it, I aimed the garage remote at the panel and hit the remote button. The elevator silently rose to floor seven and opened. I stepped out to a small reception area with a patterned white-and-black marble floor and off-white walls. No windows, a breakfront on one of the walls, one door in front of me.

I'd like to say that I was very cool about all this, but the truth is, my heart was pounding so hard it was blurring my vision. If the door opened and Ranger looked out at me, I'd fall over dead on the spot. And what if he had a woman with him? What would I do? I wouldn't do anything, I reasoned, because I'd be dead, remember?

I held my breath and remoted the door. I turned the knob. Couldn't get in. I looked more closely at the door. It had a deadbolt. I inserted the extra key and the door opened. Now I had a real dilemma. Up to this point I wasn't feeling especially invasive. I'd discovered the location of Ranger's base of operations. In truth, not such a big deal. However, once I crossed the threshold in front of me, I was in Ranger's private space, and I was uninvited. This was officially breaking and entering. Not only was it illegal . . . it was rude.

The stupid part of my brain kicked in again. Yes, it said, but how about all those times Ranger let himself into *your* apartment? Half the time you were asleep, and he scared the bejeebers out of you. Can you ever remember one time that he knocked first?

Maybe one time, I answered. It stood to reason that he'd knocked at least once. But hard as I tried I couldn't recall him ever knocking. Ranger slipped in like smoke under the door.

I took a deep breath and stepped over the threshold. "Hello," I called softly. "Anybody home? Yoohoooo?"

Nothing. Not a sound. The reception area had been lit, but the apartment was dark. I was standing in a small hallway foyer. An antique wood sideboard was against the wall to my right. There was a tray on the sideboard that looked like it was supposed to hold keys, so I dropped Ranger's keys in the tray. I flipped the switch by the door and two side-by-side candlestick lamps, also on the sideboard, blinked on.

The foyer area was defined by an arch and beyond the arch the living room opened directly in front of me. Kitchen and dining area to the right of the living room. Bedroom suite to the left. The apartment was larger than mine and miles more opulent. Ranger had furniture. Expensive furniture. It was an eclectic mix of antique and modern. Lots of wood and black leather. Marble in the small powder room off the foyer.

Hard to imagine Ranger moving through these rooms dressed in SWAT black. The apartment felt masculine, but more like cashmere sweater and Italian loafers than bounty hunter fatigues. Okay, maybe jeans and boots and cashmere sweater but that was a stretch. The jeans would have to be excellent.

The kitchen was gourmet and stainless steel. I peeked in the refrigerator. Eggs, fat-free milk, four bottles of Corona, a plastic container of rustic olives, and the usual condiments. Apples, limes, and eating oranges in the crisper. Brie and cheddar in the dairy drawer. All jars and shelves were immaculate. Nothing but ice cubes in the freezer. Spartan, I thought. I looked through the cupboards. Organic unsweetened granola, a jar of honey, an unopened box of crackers, green tea, a foil bag of Kona coffee beans, a foil pack of smoked salmon, and a foil pack of tuna. Yeesh. No Cap'n Crunch, no peanut butter, no Entenmann's coffee cake. How could anyone live like this?

I prowled through the living room into the bedroom area.

There was a small sitting room with a comfy, clubby couch and large-screen plasma TV. The bedroom opened off the sitting room. King-size bed, perfectly made. Four king pillows in shams, matching the ivory sheets trimmed with three narrow ribbons of dark brown piping. All looked like they'd been ironed. A lightweight down comforter encased in a matching dark brown duvet covered the bed. No spread. Blanket chest at the foot of the bed. Brass lamps with black shades on tables. Fabrics on chairs and curtains were earth tones. Very subdued and classy. I'm not sure what I expected from Ranger, but it wasn't this.

In fact, I was having some doubts that he lived here. It was a great apartment, but there were no personal touches. No pho-

tographs in the living room. No book on
the nightstand next to the bed.

The master bath and dressing room attached to the bedroom. I stepped into
the bath and went momentarily breathless. The room very faintly smelled like
Ranger. I prowled around and discovered
the scent was from the soap. Again, as in
the rest of the house, nothing was out of
place. Towels were neatly stacked. Ivory
and dark brown, matching the sheets.
Very plush. The thought of them next to a
naked Ranger gave me a rush that buckled
my knees.

The double sink was soap scum–free and
set into a marble countertop. Toiletries
were displayed to the left. Straightedge
and electric razor to the right. No tub, but
there was a large marble-and-glass walk-in
shower. White terry robe on a hook by
the shower.

The dressing room was filled with
clothes. A mix of work and casual. I recognized the work clothes. The Ranger
who wore the casual hadn't been a part of
my life. Everything was neatly hung or
folded. No dirty socks on the floor.
Everything perfectly pressed. Thank God,

no ladies' lingerie. No birth control pills or box of tampons.

I decided there were two possibilities. Either Ranger lived with his mother, or else he had a housekeeper. I didn't see any evidence of a little Cuban lady in residence, so I was going with the housekeeper theory.

"So," I said to the empty apartment, "nobody'd mind if I stayed here tonight, right?"

Since no one objected, I took it as a positive sign. Ten minutes later, I was back in the apartment with Rex and a change of clothes. I set Rex's cage on a kitchen counter and gave him a chunk of apple. I ate the rest of the apple and wandered into the sitting room. I sunk into the comfy couch and picked up the remote for the television. Total space age. I hadn't a clue what to do with all the buttons. No wonder Ranger said he never watched television.

I gave up on the television and migrated into the bedroom. I was tired and the bed looked inviting, but the thought of sliding between Ranger's sheets had me in a cold sweat.

Get over it, I told myself. It's not like he's here.

Yes, I answered, but these are his sheets, for cripes' sake. His personal sheets. I did some chewing on my lower lip. On the other hand, they'd obviously been laundered since he'd slept in them. So it wasn't all that personal, right?

Problem number two: I didn't want to contaminate the sheets with the gunk in my hair. This meant I'd have to shower in Ranger's bathroom. A shower meant I'd have to get naked. And the thought of being naked in Ranger's bathroom brought back the cold sweat.

Just do it, I told myself. Be an adult. Unfortunately, being an adult was part of the dilemma. I was having a *very adult* reaction to getting naked in the shower. An uncomfortable mix of desire and acute embarrassment. I ordered myself to ignore it all. I squinched my eyes closed and took my clothes off. I opened my eyes, adjusted the water, and stepped under the spray. Serious. Down to business. Get the gunk out of my hair. Get out of the shower.

Halfway through lathering with Ranger's shower gel I was barely able to focus.

The scent seemed to swell around me. I was hot and slippery with shower gel, and I was surrounded by Essence of Ranger. Agony. Ecstasy. I was living a wet dream. *Yikes.* Next time I broke into Ranger's apartment I would bring my own soap.

I scrubbed my hair with a vengeance, rushed out of the shower, and toweled off. Yes, these were Ranger's towels and God only knows what they've touched, *so don't go there!* This was not exactly a silent thought. This was more of a mental shriek.

I got dressed in undies and T-shirt and marched off to bed. I slipped under the covers. I closed my eyes and groaned. It was heaven. Like floating on a seven-hundred-thread-count cloud. Total comfort, except for the uneasy feeling of impending doom.

THE ROOM WAS still dark when I awoke the next morning. Curtains were drawn throughout the apartment, and I wasn't about to open them. Didn't want to broadcast my presence. I rolled out of bed and went straight to the shower. It was daytime. I was feeling much more brave. And God help me, I was looking forward to Ranger's shower. I was a shower gel slut!

After the shower, I had an orange and some granola for breakfast. "I got through the night, and I survived the shower," I said to Rex, sharing a slice of orange with him, dropping some granola in his food dish. "I don't know why I was so worried. Probably Ranger wouldn't even mind that I was here. After all, he's slept in my bed and used my shower. Of course, I was in them at the time. Still, what's good for the gander is good for the goose, don't you think?" The apartment was quiet and comfortable, and I was feeling less like an intruder. "This isn't too different from living with Morelli," I told Rex. "I was a guest there. And I'm a guest here." The fact that Ranger didn't know I was a guest was starting to seem like a technicality. "Don't worry," I said. "I'm going to get our apartment back. All I have to do is find a place for Valerie. And hopefully the Slayer problem will go away."

I didn't expect Ranger would be home anytime soon, but I wrote a note of explanation, just in case, and propped it on Rex's cage. I closed Ranger's front door behind me and remoted it locked. Then I took the stairs, stopping periodically to listen for footfalls, keeping alert for the sound of a fire door opening above or below me.

I cracked the door to the garage and peeked out. Ranger's two cars were still in place. The SUVs had multiplied overnight. There were now four of them parked side by side. No humans walking around, so I scuttled across the garage, opened the gate, and hurried up the street to the truck.

I hauled myself up behind the wheel, locked the doors around me, and sat for a moment in the silence, inhaling the delicious aroma of leather seats and Ranger.

I sniffed my arm and groaned. The Ranger smell was coming from me. He'd given me his truck, and I'd moved into his home. I'd slept in his bed, and I'd showered with his shower gel. I couldn't imagine what would follow if he found out.

Ranger rarely showed emotion. He was more a man of action . . . throwing people against walls and out windows, never breaking a sweat, his face perfectly composed. Now you've made me mad, he'd calmly say. And then bodies would fly through the air. The bodies always belonged to scumbags who'd done really bad things, so the carnage wasn't totally unjustified. Still, it was a scary and awesome spectacle to watch.

I didn't think Ranger would throw me against a wall or out a window. My fear was more that we'd stop being friends. And there was also a small fear that retribution would be sexual. Ranger would never do anything that wasn't consensual. Problem was, once Ranger truly invaded my space there wasn't a lot I didn't eventually consent to. Ranger was very good in close.

Okay, so what's up for the day? Harold Pancek was my only outstanding case. I needed to work at finding Pancek. Probably I should check up on Carol Cantell. I should stay out of Slayerland. And I needed to find an apartment for Valerie.

A call to Morelli was in the number one slot.

"Hey," I said when he answered. "Just wanted to make sure you're okay."

"Where are you?"

"I'm in the truck on the way to work. Any new damage from the Slayers?"

"No. It was a quiet night . . . after you left. So what's the deal, are you coming back?"

"No. Never."

We both knew that was a big fib. I always came back.

"One of these days we should probably grow up," Morelli said.

"Yeah," I said, "but I don't think we should feel rushed into it."

"I'm thinking I might ask Joyce Barnhardt out on a date."

Joyce Barnhardt was a total skank and my archenemy. "That would be a definite detour off the road to maturity," I told him.

Morelli gave a snort of laughter and hung up.

Half an hour later, I was in the office, and Connie and Lula were standing noses pressed to the front window.

"That vehicle sitting at the curb looks like Ranger's personal truck," Lula said.

"It's a loaner," I told her.

"Yeah, but it's Ranger's, right?"

"Yep. It's Ranger's."

"Oh boy," Connie said.

"No strings attached," I told them.

Lula and Connie smiled. There were always strings attached.

They'd plotz if they knew about the Bat Cave. For that matter, I was having a hard time not plotzing when I thought about the Bat Cave.

"Today is Harold Pancek Day," I said.

"He's a no-brainer," Connie said. "I've been checking on him. He works at the multiplex. Shows up every day at two and works until ten. If you can't get him at home, you can get him at work."

"Have you tried calling him?"

"I reached him once, and he told me he'd come in for rescheduling. He was a no-show on that. And now I get a machine when I call."

"I vote we get him tonight at the multiplex," Lula said. "There's a movie I want to see. It's that one where the world gets blown up and there's only mutants left. I saw the ad on television, and one of those mutants is really fine. We could go to the movie and then snag ol' Harold on the way out." She was thumbing through the paper on Connie's desk, searching for the entertainment page. "Here it is. That movie starts at seven thirty."

The plan had a lot going for it. It would give me the entire day to try to find a place for Valerie. And it would take up some of my night. I didn't want to go back to Ranger's apartment until the building was in low-to-no traffic mode. Plus I'd seen those ads Lula was talking about and the mutant was extremely fine.

"Okey dokey," I said. "We'll go tonight. I'll pick you up at six thirty."

"You're gonna be in the Bat Truck, right?"

"It's all I've got."

"I bet you get a tingle when you sit in it," Lula said. "I can't wait. I want to try behind the wheel. I bet you feel like a real badass behind the wheel."

Mostly I felt like I was wearing someone else's underpants. Considering it was Ranger's underpants (figuratively speaking), the feeling wasn't entirely unpleasant.

"What are you doing for the rest of the day?" Lula wanted to know.

I took Connie's paper and turned to real estate. "I'm looking for an apartment for Valerie. She's not showing a lot of motivation to vacate mine, so I thought I'd help her out."

"I thought you were all settled in with Morelli," Lula said. "Uh oh, is there trouble in paradise?"

I started circling rentals. "No trouble. I just want my own space back."

I was concentrating on the paper, not looking up, not wanting to see Lula's and Connie's reactions.

I finished circling, folded the paper, and put it in my shoulder bag. "I'm taking the back end of your paper," I said to Connie. "And there's no trouble."

"Hunh," Lula said. She leaned forward and sniffed. "Damned if you don't smell good. You smell just like Ranger."

"Must be the truck," I said.

I'd barely gotten out the door when my cell phone rang.

"It's your mother," my mother said. As if I wouldn't know her voice. "Everybody's here, and we were wondering if you could stop by for just a second to take a look at some dress colors. We picked out a gown, but we need to make sure it's okay with you."

"Everybody?"

"Valerie and the wedding planner."

"The wedding planner? You mean Sally?"

"I never realized he knew so much about fabric and accessorizing," my mother said.

GRANDMA MAZUR WAS at the door, waiting for me, when I parked behind the big yellow school bus, in front of my parents' house.

"Now that's a truck," she said, eyeballing Ranger's Ford. "I wouldn't mind having a truck like that. I bet it's got leather seats and everything." She leaned forward and sniffed. "And don't you smell good. What is that, a new perfume?"

"It's soap. And it won't go away."

"It smells sort of . . . sexy."

Tell me about it. I was in love with myself.

"They're all in the kitchen," Grandma said. "If you want to sit you have to bring a chair from the dining room."

"Not necessary," I told her. "I can't stay long."

My mother, Valerie, and Sally were having coffee at the kitchen table. There were some fabric samples, next to the coffee cake, and Valerie had a couple pages torn from a magazine in front of her.

"Sit," my mother said. "Bring a chair."

"Can't. Got things to do."

Sally handed one of the pages to me. "This is a picture of the bridesmaids' dresses. Your dress will be the same, but a different color. I'm still thinking pumpkin."

"Sure," I said. "Pumpkin would be terrific." Anything would be okay at this point. I didn't want to be a party pooper, but I had other things on my mind.

"What things do you have to do?" Grandma wanted to know.

"Bounty hunter things."

My mother made the sign of the cross.

"You should see Stephanie's new truck," Grandma Mazur said. "It looks like a truck the devil himself would drive."

This got everyone's attention.

"It's a loaner from Ranger," I said. "I had some problems with the Buick, and I haven't got the insurance money from the Escape yet."

Another sign of the cross from my mother.

"What's sticking out of your bag?" Grandma asked me. "Looks like the want ads in the paper. Are you looking for a car? I could go with if you're looking for a car. I like cars."

"I'm not looking for a car today. Val's been too busy with the new baby to look for an apartment, so I thought I'd help her out. I saw a couple places in the paper that looked interesting."

Valerie reached out and took the paper from my bag. "No kidding? Wow, that's really nice of you. Is there anything good in here?"

My mother scooted around so she could look at the paper with Valerie.

"Here's one that's a house for rent. And it says it has a Burg location. That would be perfect," my mother said. "The girls could stay in the same school." She looked over at me. "Did you call the number? Do you know where this is?"

"I called on the way here. It's a duplex on Moffit Street. The house next to Gino's Tomato Pie. The owner lives in the other half. I told her I'd stop around this morning."

"I know that house," Grandma said. "It's pretty nice. Lois Krishewitz used to own that house. She sold it two years ago when she broke her hip and had to move into assisted living."

Valerie was on her feet. "Just give me a minute to get a few things together for the baby, and then we can go look at it. We wanted to buy, but we can't seem to scrape together a down payment. This would give us more space in the meantime."

"I'll get my purse," my mother said.

"I'll come, too," Sally said.

"Me, too," Grandma said.

"We can take my bus," Sally said. "We'll have more room."

"This is gonna be cool," Grandma said, starting for the door. "We're gonna be just like the Partridge family. Remember when they all traveled around in that bus?"

Don't panic, I told myself. We're just going a short distance. If you sit low in your seat no one will see you.

Valerie had the baby in a carrier on her back and the big patchwork quilt diaper bag over her shoulder. "Where's my purse?" she asked. "I need my purse."

Grandma handed Val her purse. And Val draped her big shoulder bag over her free shoulder.

"Jeez, Val," I said, "let me give you a hand with some of that."

"Thanks," she said, "but I'm balanced this way. I do this all the time."

I don't mean to sound cynical, but if Val ever needed fast cash we could probably get her a job as a pack animal. She could work alongside the mules that take people into the Grand Canyon.

"I've got my checkbook," my mother said, closing the door behind us. "Just in case we like the house."

Valerie lumbered down the porch steps, followed by Grandma.

"I want the front seat," Grandma said, hurrying along. "I don't want to miss anything."

It was a crisp blue-sky morning, and Sally's big hoop earring gleamed gold in the sunlight as he took the wheel. He was wearing a Buzz Lightyear T-shirt, his usual ratty sneakers, and ripped jeans. He had a shark tooth necklace around his neck, and the volume of his hair seemed to have increased since I saw him last. He settled little heart-shaped Lolita-type sunglasses on his big hook nose, and he started the bus.

"You gotta turn at the corner," Grandma

told him. "Then you go two blocks and make a right."

Sally took the first corner wide, and Grandma slid off her seat, onto the floor.

"Fuck," Sally said, looking down at Grandma. *Snap.*

"Don't worry about me," Grandma said, righting herself. "I just didn't remember to hold on. I don't know how all those little kids do it. These seats are slippery."

"The kids are all over the fucking bus all the time," Sally said. "Oh shit." *Snap, snap.*

"Sounds like you're having a relapse," Grandma said to Sally. "You were doing real good for a while there."

"I have to concentrate," Sally told her. "It's hard to stop doing something that took me years to perfect."

"I can see that," Grandma said. "And it's a shame you have to give up something you're so good at."

"Yeah, but it's for a good cause," Sally said. "It's for the little dudes."

Sally eased the bus up to the curb in front of the rental house and opened the door with a *whoosh* of the hydraulic. "Here we are," he said. "Everybody out."

I tagged along after my mother, Grandma Mazur, Valerie and the baby, and Sally as they all hustled up to the front porch.

My mother knocked on the landlord's door, and everyone quieted down for a moment. My mother knocked a second time. Still, no one opened the door.

"That's odd," Grandma said. "I thought she was supposed to be home."

Sally put his ear to the door. "I think I hear someone breathing in there."

Probably she was on the floor, having a coronary. A herd of lunatics just got out of a big yellow school bus and descended on her porch.

"You better open up if you're in there," Grandma yelled. "We got a bounty hunter out here."

The door cracked open, the security chain in place. "Edna? Is that you?" the woman asked.

Grandma Mazur squinted at the eyes behind the door. "Yep, it's me," she said. "Who are you?"

"Esther Hamish. I always sit by you at bingo."

"Esther Hamish!" Grandma said. "I didn't know you were the one who bought this house."

"Yep," Esther said. "I had some money

socked away from Harry's insurance policy, God bless him, may he rest in peace."

Everyone made the sign of the cross. Rest in peace, we all said.

"Well, we come to see about the rental," Grandma told Esther. "This here's my granddaughter. She's looking for a place."

"How nice," Esther said. "Let me get the key. You had me going for a minute there. I've never had a school bus park in front of my house before."

"Yeah," Grandma said. "It's new to us, too, but we're getting used to it. I like that it's a nice cheery yellow. It's a real happy color. Problem is, it blocks the view of the street. Of course I guess it could be worse. We could have our view blocked by one of those vans that carries aliens around. I was listening to news on the radio, and they said a bunch of aliens were found dead from heatstroke in one of them vans yesterday. Imagine that. Here these poor creatures travel through space to get to us, all those light years and galaxies away, and then they die from heat stroke in a van."

"What a shame," Esther said.

"I'm just glad it wasn't in front of my house," Grandma said. "I'd feel terrible if I had to find E.T. dead in a van."

SEVEN

ESTHER HAMISH'S RENTAL was a lot like my parents' house. Living room, dining room, kitchen on the ground floor. Three small bedrooms and bath on the second floor. Narrow backyard. Minuscule front yard. A stand-alone, two-car garage to the rear of the property.

The interior was clean but tired. The bathroom and kitchen were serviceable but dated. Again, a lot like my parents' house. And clearly the house was occupied.

"When will it be available?" Valerie asked.

"Two weeks," Esther said. "I have a young family in here now, and they just bought a house. They'll be moving in two weeks."

"Wait a minute," I said. "The paper said immediate occupancy."

"Well, two weeks is almost immediate," Esther said. "When you get to be my age, two weeks is nothing."

Two weeks. I'll be dead in two weeks! Valerie needs to move out of my apartment now.

Valerie turned to my mother. "What do you think?"

"It's perfect," my mother said.

Esther looked at Sally. "Are you the son-in-law?"

"Nope," Sally said. "I'm the bus driver and the wedding planner."

"The son-in-law is a lawyer," my mother said proudly.

Esther perked up when she heard that.

"You should take it," Grandma said to Valerie.

"Yeah," Sally said. "You should take it."

"Okay," Valerie said. "It's a deal."

So here we go again, there's good news, and there's bad news. The good news is I'm getting my apartment back. The bad news is I'm not getting it back soon enough.

"I need a doughnut," I said, more to myself than anyone else.

"That's a good idea," Grandma said. "I could go for a doughnut."

"Back to the bus," Sally said. "We're all going for doughnuts."

Five minutes later, Sally was parked in front of Tasty Pastry. The doors *whooshed* open and everyone tramped out for celebratory doughnuts. Grandma picked out two, my mother picked out two, Valerie got two, and Sally got two. And I got a dozen. I said they were for the office, but if my day didn't improve there was a good chance I'd eat every last one of them.

Renee Platt was behind the counter. "Wow, it's really brave of you to take on the Slayers," she said to me. "I sure wouldn't want to mess with any of those guys."

"Who are the Slayers?" my mother wanted to know.

"Nobody special," I told my mother. "And I didn't take them on."

"I heard you went into their territory with a tank and ran over a bunch of them," Renee said. "Including the head guy. And I heard you're the only one who can identify the Red Devil. And that you've sworn a blood oath to get him."

"Omigod," I said. "Who did you hear that from?"

"Everybody knows," Renee said. "It's all over town."

My mother crossed herself and ate her two doughnuts on the spot.

"It's the Hungarian side of the family," Grandma said. "We're tough. We come from a long line of army deserters and nasty alcoholics."

"Probably we should be going home now," I said. My mother looked like the two doughnuts didn't do it. My mother had her lips pressed so tight together her face was turning blue. I was a trial to my mother.

We all trooped out to the bus and took our seats. "Let me know if you need help rounding up those Slayers," Grandma said to me. "I don't know what they are, but I bet I could kick some Slayer butt."

"They're a gang," Sally said. "A really bad gang. I have to go through their territory to pick up a couple kids on my bus route, and it's like going through a war zone. They have sentries on the corners and soldiers patrolling the streets. And I don't know what it is, but these guys never smile. They just stand there, staring, like the living dead."

"What do gangs do?" Grandma wanted to know.

"They act tough," Sally said. "And these days they control a lot of the drug traffic. And they kill each other."

"I don't know what this world's coming to," Grandma said. "Used to be the mob did that. What's left for the mob to do? No wonder Lou Raguzzi looks so bad. I saw him the other day at Stiva's and his shoes were all run down at the heel. He probably can't afford to buy shoes."

"Lou's doing fine," my mother said. "He's being audited by the IRS. He got those shoes special so he wouldn't look too successful."

Everyone crossed themselves at the mention of the IRS. Street gangs and the mob paled in comparison to fear of the tax code.

"I'm going to have to take off," Sally said, stopping in front of my parents' house. "I have to get across town to start picking the little dudes up."

"Thanks for the ride," Grandma said, making her way down the bus steps. "Maybe I'll see you tonight. There's a

good viewing at Stiva's. Charley White-
head's laid out, and the Knights of Colum-
bus should be there tonight. They always
put on a good show. They're the best of
the lodges."

I took Valerie's diaper bag, and my
mother took Valerie's purse, and we all
followed Grandma off the bus and up to
the house.

"I have to go, too," I said, depositing the
diaper bag in the hallway.

"It was nice of you to help your sister
find a place," my mother said to me.

I hiked my own bag onto my shoulder.
"Thanks, but it was self-serving."

"It would have been self-serving to order
her out of your apartment. Finding her a
house was a nice thing to do."

I took my bag of doughnuts, called
good-bye to everyone, and let myself out.
I climbed into Ranger's truck, and I sat
there for a moment, trying to calm myself.
I was going to be in big trouble if the rumors got back to the Slayers. The Slayers
wouldn't like being run over and hunted
down by a pasty-faced white woman. It
wasn't the sort of thing that earned gangland prestige points. Not much I can do
about it now, I thought. The best I could

do was to stay away from them and try to keep a low profile. With any luck, the Slayers would be busy selling drugs and shooting each other and not have time for me.

I rolled the engine over, drove the length of the block, turned at the corner, and headed for Joe's house. Security check. I wanted to see for myself that the house was still standing, that no further damage had been done. I'd moved out of the house, but there were still ties. Just as there were still ties to Morelli. Truth was, I'd broken up with him so many times it was beginning to feel like the normal thing to do. For that matter, I wasn't sure if we'd actually broken up. It felt more like a reorganization.

Morelli's street was pretty much deserted, except for a van in front of Morelli's house. The van belonged to Joe's cousin, Mooch. Mooch was covering the graffiti, painting Joe's front door a bright red. The graffiti was still on the sidewalk, but it didn't look as if anything new had been added. I slowed but I didn't stop. Mooch didn't look around from his work, and I didn't call out.

Next stop was Carol Cantell. I wasn't

obligated to check on her *every* day, but I'd become attached to Carol. How could you not like someone who held up a Frito-Lay truck and then ate the evidence?

I parked in front of the Cantell house and walked to the porch. Carol's sister, Cindy, opened the door before I rang the bell.

"We were in the front room, and we saw you pull up in the truck," Cindy said. "Is something wrong?"

I looked around Cindy to Carol. "Social visit. I wanted to make sure everything was okay."

"I'm feeling a lot better," Carol said. "I think I got the chips out of my system."

Cindy leaned closer. "Boy, you smell great," she said to me. "You smell like . . . I don't know. Not exactly perfume."

"It's shower gel," I said. "I borrowed it from a guy I know."

Carol came over and sniffed at me. "Is he married?"

"No."

"Would he like to be?"

The question stuck with me until I was well out of Cantell's neighborhood. I hadn't a clue to the answer. I worked with

Ranger, I drove his truck and I was living in his apartment, and yet I knew almost nothing about him. A few facts. He'd been married when he was very young, and he had a daughter in Florida. He'd dropped out of college to join the army. While in the army, he'd been Special Forces. That was about it. He never shared his thoughts. He rarely showed emotion. A smile once in a while. His apartment yielded little. He had good taste in furniture, leaning toward earth tones, and he had great taste in soap.

It was lunchtime, and I hadn't any idea what to do next, so I parked in the Shop n Bag lot and ate two of the doughnuts. I was scraping a blob of custard off my shirt when my phone rang.

"Where are you?" Morelli wanted to know.

"I'm in the Shop n Bag lot, and I'm eating lunch."

"Have you heard the rumors?"

"There are so many. Which ones are you talking about?"

Morelli gave an exasperated sigh.

"Oh," I said. "Those rumors. Yeah, I heard those rumors."

"What are you going to do about them?"

"I'm sort of hiding."

"You'd better hide really well, because I'll put you under house arrest if I find you."

"On what charges?"

"Reckless endangerment of self and driving me nuts. Where are you hiding? You're not staying with your parents. I checked."

"I'm staying at a friend's place."

"Is it safe?"

"Yep." Except from the friend.

"I'd feel better if you sounded more scared," Morelli said. "These guys are crazy. They're unpredictable and irrational. They operate under a whole different set of rules."

Morelli disconnected and it was my turn to give an exasperated sigh. I was trying hard *not* to be scared.

I decided as long as I was in the lot I might as well do some food shopping, so I locked the truck and ambled into the store. I got a box of Frosted Flakes, a loaf of nice mushy white bread, a jar of peanut butter (the good kind that's been hydrogenated and is full of trans fats and sugar), and a jar of nongourmet olives.

I was pushing my cart down the sanitary products aisle when Mrs. Zuch spotted me.

"Stephanie Plum!" she said. "I can't remember when I last saw you. I see your grandmother all the time, and I hear all about your exploits."

"Whatever Grandma said, it's not true."

"And this business about the Slayers . . ."

"That's especially not true."

"Everyone's talking about it. How you single-handed put them out of business. It's a shame about the killer."

"Killer?"

"You know, the contract that's out on you. I hear they brought someone in from California. I'm surprised you're out and about like this. You don't even look like you're wearing a bulletproof vest, or anything."

Was she serious? "It's all rumor," I said. "None of it's true."

"I understand," Mrs. Zuch said. "And I think it's admirable that you're being so brave and so modest. But if it was me, I'd be wearing the vest."

"I don't think the Slayers spend a lot of time in Shop n Bag."

"You could be right," Mrs. Zuch said. "But just in case, I think I'll move on now."

And Mrs. Zuch put distance between us.

I made an effort not to furtively look over my shoulder while I wheeled my shopping cart to check out.

My phone rang when I got to the truck.

"What's all this noise about a contract killer?" Connie wanted to know. "Have you talked to Joe?"

"I talked to Joe, but he didn't say anything about a killer."

"Vinnie just wrote a bond on a kid from Slayerland, and all the kid could talk about was how you're going down."

I rested my forehead on the steering wheel. This was out of control. "I can't talk now," I told Connie. "I'll call you back."

I dialed Morelli, and I did some deep breathing while I waited.

"Yeah?" Morelli said.

"It's me. You know when you asked me if I heard the rumors? Just exactly what rumors were you referring to?"

"Your vow to rid the world of Slayers rumor. Your vow to identify the Red Devil rumor. Oh yeah, and the contract killer rumor. That's my personal favorite."

"I just heard about the contract killer. Is it true?"

"Don't know. We're checking. Are you still in the Shop n Bag lot?"

A little alarm went off in my brain. He wouldn't actually try to catch me and lock me up in his house, would he?

"I did some grocery shopping, and I'm on my way back to the office," I told him. "Let me know if you hear anything."

I disconnected, plunged the key into the ignition, and took off, driving in the opposite direction of the office. This was dandy. Now I had to hide out from the Slayers *and* from Morelli.

I had time to kill before I met Lula for our movie date and capture, so I headed for the mall. When in doubt . . . shop. I parked at the Macy's entrance and meandered through the shoe department. My credit card was pretty much maxed out, and I didn't see anything worth going to debtors' prison over, so I wandered out of Macy's and hit the Godiva store. I collected all the loose change in the bottom of my bag, and I got two pieces of chocolate. If you buy chocolate with loose change the calories don't count. And anyway, one of the pieces was a raspberry truffle, so it was fruit. And fruit is healthy, right?

My cell phone rang while I was eating the second truffle.

"I thought you were going back to the office," Morelli said.

"Changed my mind at the last minute."

"Where are you?"

"Point Pleasant. I had some time, so I thought I'd take a walk on the boardwalk. It's such a nice day. A little windy here, though."

"Sounds like there are a lot of people there."

"I'm in a pavilion."

"Sounds more like a shopping center."

"And you called, why?" I asked.

"They've released your car. I had it detailed and all the graffiti came off. You can pick it up anytime."

"Thanks. That's great. I'll send my dad over for it."

"You can run, but you can't hide, Cupcake," Morelli said. "I'll find you."

"You are such a cop."

"Tell me about it."

I disconnected and left the mall. It was almost six, so I headed for Lula's house. I ate the rest of the doughnuts while I sat in traffic on Route 1.

Lula was outside, sitting on her stoop, waiting for me. "You're late," she said. "We're gonna miss the beginning of the movie. I hate that."

"Traffic," I told her. "And anyway, I'm only five minutes late. We have lots of time."

"Yeah, but I gotta get popcorn. You can't watch no mutant movie without popcorn. And probably I need soda and some candy to balance out all that salt and grease on the popcorn."

I parked in the multiplex lot and took a last look at the Pancek file. "Harold Pancek," I read to Lula. "Twenty-two years old. Blond hair, blue eyes, Caucasian. Chunky build. Five feet ten inches tall. No identifying characteristics. This is the guy who took a leak on the rosebush. He's got a low ticket bond. We're not going to make a lot of money on him, but we need to bring him in anyway."

"On account of we're professionals," Lula said.

"Yeah. And if we want to keep the job, we haven't got a choice."

I pulled the file photo, and Lula and I studied it.

"He reminds me of someone," Lula said. "I can't put my finger on it."

"SpongeBob SquarePants. Yellow hair. No neck. Body by Lego."

"That's it. Skin like a sponge."

I slipped the photo and the authorization to capture into my shoulder bag. I also had cuffs, a stun gun, and defense spray in the bag. My gun was in Morelli's cookie jar. Ranger's gun was in the truck. God knows what Lula had in her bag. Could be a loaded rocket launcher.

We crossed the lot and entered the theater. We got our tickets, our popcorn, our soda, our M&Ms, Jujubes, Twizzlers, and Junior Mints.

"Look there," Lula said. "SpongeHead is collecting tickets."

The smart thing would be to cuff him now. Any number of things could go wrong if I waited. He could go home sick. He could recognize me and leave. He could decide he hated his job and quit, never to be seen again.

"I've been dying to see this movie," Lula

said, her arm wrapped around a tub of popcorn that was big enough to feed a family of eight.

"We really should cuff him now. If we wait he could get away."

"Are you kidding me? I got my popcorn. I got my soda. I got my Twizzlers. And on top of that, we've never been to a movie together. We never do anything together except work. I think this here's quality bonding time. And what about that hot mutant? Don't you want to see the mutant?"

She had me there. I wanted to see the mutant. I approached Pancek and handed him my ticket. I looked him in the eye and smiled. He smiled back, blank-faced, and tore my ticket in half. He did the same to Lula. No glimmer of recognition for either of us.

"This is gonna be a snap," Lula said, taking a seat. "On our way out we'll clap the cuffs on ol' Harold and trot him off to jail."

AFTER NINETY MINUTES of mutant action, Lula was ready to bag Pancek.

"We could be as good as those mutants,"

Lula said to me. "You know the only difference between us and those mutants?
Costumes. They had cool costumes. I'm
telling you, you can't go wrong with capes
and boots. And you need an insignia.
Maybe we should get an insignia. Something with a lightning bolt."

Pancek was in the aisle directing people
to the exit. Lula walked past Pancek,
turned, and stood at his back. I was a few
steps behind Lula.

I smiled at Pancek. "Harold Pancek?" I
asked. Like I was some long-lost friend.

"Yeah," he said. "Do I know you?"

"Stephanie Plum," I said. "I'm a recov-
ery agent for Vincent Plum Bail Bonds."
And *click*, the cuff was on his wrist.

"Hey," he said. "What the hell do you
think you're doing?"

"You failed to show for a court hearing.
I'm afraid I'm going to have to take you in
to get rescheduled."

"I'm working."

"You're leaving an hour early today," I
told him.

"I gotta tell my boss."

I snapped the second bracelet on him
and gave him a nudge toward the door.
"We'll make sure your boss knows."

"No, wait a minute. On second thought, I don't want anyone to know. This is embarrassing. Jeez, is everyone looking?"

"Not everyone," Lula said. "I think there's a guy over by the popcorn counter who's not looking."

"It's all a big mistake, anyway. I'm not the one who killed her rosebush."

"I suppose it was the phantom leaker," Lula said.

"It was Grizwaldi's dog. He lifts his leg on that bush every day. This is discrimination. I don't see Grizwaldi's dog getting hauled into court. Everybody knows he pisses on everything, but it's okay because he's a dog. It's not fair."

"I see your point," Lula said. "Not that it makes any difference. We're still gonna cart your chunky ass off to jail."

Pancek dug his heels in. "No way. I'm not going to jail."

"You're making a scene," I told him.

"Fine. I'll make a scene. I have a cause."

"The mutants would never have stood for this," Lula said. "Those mutants didn't put up with anything."

I gave Pancek a yank forward and maneuvered him through the lobby, up to the exit door. I was talking to him all the way, trying to get him to cooperate. "It's not like you're going to get locked away," I said. "We have to bring you to the station to reschedule. That's just the way it's done. We'll get you bonded out again as soon as possible."

I held the door open and nudged Pancek out the door, into the lot. Cars were at least ten rows deep, parked under the glare of the overhead security lights. I was parked five rows back.

Lula and I led Pancek through three rows of cars and stopped. An SUV was idling in the aisle between parked cars. A silver compact was nose-to-nose with the SUV. A black guy in a silky white oversized warm-up suit was standing beside the SUV, talking to a white male dressed head to toe in Abercrombie & Fitch. Both men were late teens. From what I could see of the silver car, there was a couple in the backseat and a girl in the passenger-side front seat.

"We don't want to be seeing this," Lula said. "Used to be you had to go looking for the dope, and now the dope comes to you."

I called the Hamilton Police and told

them they had a problem in the multiplex lot. Then I called the theater and told them to send security into the lot.

The guy in the silky suit and the kid kept talking. The silky suit was stoic and the white kid was agitated. The girl in the front passenger seat got out of the car. Impatient.

"This isn't good," Lula said. "She should never have got out of the car. These are gang guys. They got a philosophy about women makes Eminem sound like he's writing nursery rhymes."

Three big guys in homey clothes, all wearing red scarves flying from pants pockets, got out of the SUV and did their *I'm a big bad gang member* shuffle over to the negotiation. One of the big guys jabbed a finger into the Abercrombie & Fitch kid's chest and got into his face. The kid pushed back. The gang guy took out a gun and held it to the kid's head.

"Crap," Lula said on a sigh.

I looked over my shoulder, wondering what was taking security so long. Probably this happened all the time and no one wanted to come into the lot until the police arrived.

The girl's eyes were wide. Deer caught in the headlights. The remaining gang members turned on her, walking her backward, trapping her against Ranger's truck. Another gun was drawn. A knife appeared.

I pressed the panic button on the truck's remote and the truck alarm went off.

Everyone jumped.

The SUV guys piled into their car, backed up, and left the lot, burning rubber.

I did a double hit on the panic button, and the alarm went silent. I turned to Lula and realized Pancek was missing. We'd forgotten to keep watch over Pancek. Worse than losing Pancek, he'd taken off wearing a sixty-dollar pair of cuffs.

Lula was looking around, too. "Don't you hate when they take off like that?" she said. "If there's one thing I can't stand it's a sneaky felon."

"He can't have gone far. You take one side of the lot and I'll take the other, and we'll meet in the theater."

There was the sound of a car engine coming to life in the second row. A car was gunned out of its parking space, and the car roared off toward the exit. I caught a glimpse of yellow hair on the guy behind the wheel.

"Guess we don't have to search the lot no more," Lula said. "Bet it's hard to drive with those cuffs on. Think you should have cuffed him behind his back like the book says."

"He didn't seem dangerous. I was trying to be nice to him."

"See where that gets you. Never be nice to people."

I unlocked the truck and climbed in. "Maybe he's dumb enough to go home," I said to Lula. "We'll check out his house."

We pulled out of the lot, and I saw two Hamilton Township PD cars angled into the curb, lights flashing, half a block down. One was a squad car and the other was unmarked. The SUV was in front of the squad car. The occupants of the SUV were palms down on the SUV hood, getting searched.

I eased past the police cars and recognized Gus Chianni. He was standing back, letting the uniforms do their job. Most of the Hamilton cops were strangers to me. I knew Chianni because he was one of Morelli's longtime drinking buddies.

I stopped and powered my window down. "What's going on?" I asked Chianni.

"Speeding," he said, smiling. "We were answering your call and ran across this SUV doing eighty in a twenty."

"It's the car I called in."

His smile widened. "I figured." He took a step back and looked at Ranger's truck. "You steal this?"

"Borrowed."

"Bet Joe's happy about that."

All the cops knew Ranger's truck.

"Gotta go," I said. If Chianni was here, Morelli wasn't far behind.

The guy in the white silk warm-up suit turned his head sideways and stared at me. His face held no expression, but his eyes were like still pools in the river Styx. Black and bottomless and terrifying. He gave a slight nod, as if to say he knew who I was. His right hand lifted off the SUV hood and he made the sign of a gun, thumb up, index finger extended. He mouthed the word *bang* at me.

Chianni saw it, too. "Be careful," he said to me.

I went out to the highway and drove in the opposite direction to what I would ordinarily take to get to the Burg.

"This is bad," Lula said when we were on the highway. "That guy recognized you. He knew who you were. And it wasn't because he saw you in the lot just now, either. None of them saw us in the lot. That guy was no-shit evil, and he knew who you were."

I pushed it aside and concentrated on driving. I didn't want the fear to grab hold of me. Careful was good. Scared was counterproductive. I went a couple miles out of my way, but I was able to reach Pancek's house without running into Morelli.

Pancek's house was dark, and his car wasn't in sight. I slowly drove around several blocks looking for the car. Big zero. He could have stashed the car in a friend's garage, and he could be hiding in his dark house, but I didn't think that was the case. I suspected he'd gone to someone he trusted and was trying to get out of the cuffs.

I took Lula home, and then I went back to Ranger's apartment on Haywood Street. I parked the truck on a side street and walked the distance to the underground garage. I looked up at the building. Again, floors five and six were lit. I

remoted myself through the security gate
and scurried across the garage to the elevator. Ranger's Turbo and the Porsche
Cayenne were still in place. A black Ford
Explorer was parked on the side wall, plus
a black GMC Sonoma was parked next to
the SUV.

I stepped into the elevator, remoted myself up to the seventh floor, and held my
breath. The elevator doors opened to the
austere foyer, and I jumped out.

I listened at the door to Ranger's apartment, didn't hear anything, held my
breath, and let myself in. Everything
seemed just as I'd left it. Very calm. Tem-
perature a little on the cool side. Dark—
like Ranger. I flipped the lights on as I
walked through the apartment. I said hello
to Rex in the kitchen and set the grocery
bags on the counter. I plugged my cell
phone in to recharge, and I put the food
away.

I wondered about floors five and six.
For two nights now, they'd been lit. A variety of black cars were coming and going
in the garage. So I was guessing floors five
and six were offices. Although I suppose
they could also be apartments. Either way
I needed to be careful where I parked the

truck and careful when I moved about the building.

I made a peanut and olive sandwich and washed it down with one of Ranger's Coronas. I shuffled off to the bedroom, dropped most of my clothes on the floor, went into the bathroom to brush my teeth and smell Ranger's soap, and then I crawled into bed.

It had been a really weird day. Not that I haven't had weird days before. Weird days were getting to feel normal. The disturbing part about *this* weird day was that there'd been steadily escalating indicators of personal danger. I'd done my best to stay sane, to keep my fear in check, but the fear was actually riding very close to the surface. I'd been involved in some scary situations in the past. This was the first time a contract to kill me had been put into motion.

EIGHT

I OPENED MY eyes and had a moment
of panicky confusion. The room was dark
and felt unfamiliar. The sheets were
smooth and smelled like Ranger. And
then it all clicked into focus. Again, I was
the one who smelled like Ranger. I'd
washed my hands and face before bed and
the scent had lingered.

I switched the bedside light on and
checked the time. It was almost eight A.M.
My day hadn't even started, and already I
was late. It was the bed, I decided. It was
the best bed I'd ever slept in. And, while I
worried about Ranger returning, when I
was in the apartment I felt safe from everything else. Ranger's apartment felt serene
and secure.

I rolled out of bed and padded into the

bathroom. It was Friday. Most people are happy on Friday because their workweek ends. I had the sort of job that never ended. Connie worked a half day on Saturday. Vinnie worked when he didn't have anything better to do. We weren't sure when Lula worked. And I worked all the time. Okay, so it wasn't always nine-to-five working. But it was always looking. Opportunities for capture popped up where you least expected—at supermarkets, airports, shopping malls, and movie theaters.

And while on the subject of movie theaters, if I was a better bounty hunter I could probably take weekends off. When you botch a capture, like I did last night, you have to work twice as hard to make repairs. Pancek knew what I looked like now. And he knew I was after him.

I'd had plenty of opportunity to buy shower gel yesterday, but I'd conveniently forgotten. So now I had to once again use Ranger's shower gel. What a hardship, eh? And then I had to dry off with one of his thick, superabsorbent towels. Another hardship I forced myself to endure. All right, I admit it, I was liking Ranger's lifestyle. And even more difficult to admit,

I was liking the stolen intimacy. I was going to have to say a lot of Hail Marys for that one.

And I was going to pay a price when Ranger returned. Even if I was long gone by the time he walked through his front door, even if I washed and ironed his sheets and replaced his shower gel, Ranger would know his home had been violated. The guy was a security expert. Probably there were cameras everywhere. Not in his apartment, I was guessing. But chances were good that there were cameras in the garage, the elevator, and his outer foyer. No one had come up to bust me, so I had to assume that either the cameras weren't monitored or else Ranger had been contacted and was allowing me to stay.

I got dressed in sneakers and jeans and a stretchy white scoop-neck T-shirt. I swiped some mascara on my lashes, and I headed for the kitchen. I dropped a handful of Frosted Flakes into Rex's food dish, and I poured out a bowl for myself. I was late so I didn't take time to make coffee. I needed to stop at the office first thing. I'd get coffee there.

I unplugged my phone, grabbed my short denim jacket and shoulder bag, and

locked up behind myself. I took the elevator to the garage, suffering through the
moment of fear when the elevator doors
parted and I was exposed. Even if I'd been
discovered on camera, I wanted to delay
confrontation as long as possible. No sense
pushing the issue and jeopardizing my
tenancy. I needed a place to stay, and I was
already in trouble with Ranger. Might as
well get the most out of it, right?

I looked out and saw no one. I stepped
out, the doors closed behind me, and I
heard voices in the stairwell.

Ranger's two cars were directly in front
of me. There were three black SUVs to
my right. And there was a blue Subaru
SUV and a silver Audi sedan to my left. I
made an instinctive choice and jumped
behind the Subaru, crouching low, hoping
I was out of sight. I didn't know who had
access to the garage, but I figured Ranger's
men would belong to the black SUVs.

The door to the stairwell opened, and
Tank and two other men came out. All
three got into one of the black SUVs and
left the garage. I waited a couple beats before I scuttled across the floor, remoted
the gate open, and made my escape.

THE BONDS OFFICE was on Hamilton, in the middle of the block. A one-lane alley ran behind the office, servicing a rear entrance and parking for two cars. I parked Ranger's truck on a side street, and I entered the office through the back door . . . just in case Morelli was on the prowl. I was in a mood to avoid the unpleasant.

"Uh oh," Lula said when she saw me. "It's never good when you gotta sneak in through the back."

I went straight for the coffeepot. "I'm being careful."

"I can appreciate that," Lula said. "What's the plan for the day?"

"I need a different car. I can't blend in when I drive Ranger's truck." To be more specific, I can't blend in when I park the truck for the night. Ranger's men were constantly traveling the streets around the Bat Garage. I didn't want to take a chance on one of them spotting the truck. "I was hoping you could follow me to my parents' house. I'm going to leave the truck in their garage. And then we can go car shopping."

"Car shopping! I love car shopping."

I added creamer and sipped some coffee. "You're not going to love this kind of car shopping. I have no money. I'm looking for a wreck." I turned to Connie. "And while we're on the subject of no money, as I'm sure you already know . . . Pancek ran off with my only cuffs."

"Lula told me. Take a pair from the S and M box in the back when you leave."

There used to be a thriving sex shop on Carmen Street. Rumor had it they were the biggest supplier of dildos, whips, and body chains for the tristate area. Nine months ago, the owner decided he was tired of paying his insurance premium to the mob and told his collection agent to take a hike. Shortly after that, the store mysteriously burned to the ground. An entire crate of cuffs came out of the fire almost completely unscathed, and Vinnie bought the crate on the cheap.

"How come you're going to leave the truck at your parents' house?" Lula wanted to know. "Why don't you just give it back?"

"I thought I'd keep it a while longer, just in case. You never know when you might need a truck." And I can't get into Ranger's apartment if I hand the keys back to Tank.

"A couple new skips came in this morning," Connie said. "I'll get the paperwork together later today, and you can pick the files up tomorrow."

"I suppose after you get your new car you're going to want to go looking for Harold Pancek," Lula said.

"I suppose I am."

"And I suppose I should go with you since he's so slippery."

I looked at the stack of files on the filing cabinet. At least a month's worth. "What about the filing?"

"I can do the filing any old time. It's not like filing's a matter of life or death. I got good priorities. I take our friendship seriously. When you're going out on these dangerous manhunts I feel an obligation to ride along and protect your skinny ass. Just 'cause a man looks like SpongeBob doesn't mean he can't turn violent."

"You're pathetic," Connie said to Lula. "You'll do anything to get out of filing."

"Not anything," Lula said.

TEN MINUTES LATER, I had Ranger's truck safely tucked away in my parents' garage.

My dad had retrieved Uncle Sandor's Buick from the police and the Buick and Ranger's truck were now locked up together.

"What a nice surprise," Grandma said when she saw me at the kitchen door.

"I can't stay," I told Grandma and my mother. "I just wanted to tell you I'm leaving Ranger's truck in the garage."

"What about *our* car?" my mother wanted to know. "Where's your father going to park the LeSabre?"

"You never use the garage. The LeSabre is always parked in the driveway. Look outside. Where is the LeSabre? *In the driveway.* I had to drive around it to get to the garage."

My mother was cutting vegetables for soup. She stopped cutting and looked over at me, wide-eyed. "Holy mother. There's something wrong, isn't there? You're in trouble again."

"Did you steal the truck?" Grandma asked hopefully.

"I'm not in trouble, and there's nothing wrong. I told Ranger I'd take care of his truck while he's out of town. I was going to use it, but I've changed my mind. It's too big."

My mother didn't really want to know the truth, I told myself. The truth wasn't good.

"It is big," Grandma said. "And you know what they say about the size of a man's truck."

"I'm off," I said. "Lula's waiting for me."

Grandma trotted after me. She stopped at the front door and waved at Lula. "What are you girls doing?" Grandma asked. "Are you chasing down a killer?"

"Sorry," I said. "No killers today. I'm going car shopping. I need something to tide me over until I get the insurance check from the Escape."

"I'd love to go car shopping," Grandma said. "Wait a minute while I tell your mother and get my purse."

"No," I said. But she was already running around the house, gathering her things.

"Hey," Lula yelled from the curb. "What's the holdup?"

"Grandma's coming with us."

"The Three Musketeers ride again," Lula said.

Grandma bustled out of the house and climbed into the Firebird's backseat. "What have you got?" Grandma asked

Lula. "You got 50 Cent? You got Eminem?"

Lula slid Eminem into the slot, punched up the sound system, and we motored off like distant thunder.

"I've been thinking about your car problem," Lula said, "and I know a guy who's got cars to sell. He don't ask a whole lot either."

"I don't know," I said. "If you buy a used car at a lot you usually get a guarantee."

"How much do you want to spend?" Lula asked.

"A couple hundred."

Lula slanted a look at me. "And you want a guarantee for that kind of money?"

She was right. A guarantee was unrealistic. In fact, it was unrealistic to think I could find a car that actually ran for that kind of money.

Lula hauled out her cell phone, scrolled through the phone book, and dialed a number. "I have a friend who needs a car," she said when the phone connected. "Un hunh," she said. "Un hunh, un hunh, un hunh." She turned to me. "Do you need a registration?"

"Yes!"

"Yeah," Lula said into the phone. "She'd like one of those."

"Isn't this fun," Grandma Mazur said from the backseat. "I can't wait to see your new car."

Lula disconnected, turned out of the Burg, and headed across town. When we got to Stark Street Lula hit the automatic door locks.

"Don't worry," Lula said. "I'm just locking the doors for good measure. We aren't going into the bad part of town. Well, okay, maybe it's a *bad* part of town, but it's not the *worst* part of town. We're not going into gangland. This here is the part of town where the unorganized criminals live."

Grandma had her nose pressed to the glass. "I've never seen anything like this," she said. "Everything's got writing on it. And there's a building that's been all burned out and now it's boarded up. Are we still in Trenton? Does the mayor know about this? How about Joe Juniak? Now that he's a congressman he should be looking into these things."

"I used to work on this street when I was a ho," Lula said.

"No kidding?" Grandma said. "Isn't that something. Are there any working ladies out now? I sure would like to see one."

We kept a lookout for working ladies but none turned up.

"Slow time of the day," Lula said.

Lula made a right onto Fisher, went one block, and parked in front of a narrow two-story house that looked like it was decaying from the bottom up. Clearly it had once been part of a row of attached houses, but the houses on either side had disappeared and only their connecting walls remained. The lots had been mostly cleared of debris, but the landscaping was war zone. An occasional piece of pipe remained, mixed into smatterings of crushed rubble that hadn't made the last truck out. A nine-foot-high razor wire fence had been erected around each of the lots. Refrigerators, washing machines, gas grills, lawn furniture, and a couple ATVs, all with varying degrees of rust, were displayed in the one lot. The second lot was filled with cars.

"These lots are owned by a guy named Hog," Lula said. "Besides the lots he's got a garage on the next block. He buys junker cars at auction, fixes them up enough to get them running, and then sells them to dummies like us. Sometimes he gets cars from other sources, but we don't want to talk about that."

"Those would be the cars without registration?" I asked.

"Hog can get a registration for any car you want," Lula said. "It's just you gotta pay extra for it."

Grandma was out of the Firebird. "Those lawn chairs with the yellow cushions look pretty nice," she said. "I might have to take a look at them."

I jumped out after her and grabbed her by the purse strap. "Don't leave my side. Don't wander off. Don't talk to anyone."

A large guy with skin the color of hot chocolate and a body like a cement truck strolled over to us. "Lula tells me somebody wants to buy a car," he said. "You be happy to know you came to the right place because we got some fine cars here."

"We don't want too fine a car," Lula said. "We're sort of shopping for a bargain."

"How much of a bargain?"

"Two hundred dollars and that includes plates and registration."

"That don't even cover my overhead. I got expenses. I got middlemen."

"Your middlemen are all in jail," Lula said. "The only expenses you got is filling your car with gas so you can drive over to the workhouse to pick up your sorry-ass relatives."

"Ouch," Hog said. "That's nasty. You're getting me all excited."

Lula gave him a smack on the side of the head.

"I love when you do that," Hog said.

"Do you have a car, or what?" Lula said. "Because we can go down the street to Greasy Louey."

"'Course I got a car," Hog said. "Don't I always have a car? Have I ever failed you?" He looked at Grandma and me. "Which of you lovely ladies is buying this car?"

"Me," I said.

"What color you want?"

"A two-hundred-dollar color."

He turned and considered the motley collection of cars huddled together behind the razor wire. "Two hundred dollars don't get you much of a car. Maybe you be better to rent a car from Hog." He walked over to a silver Sentra. "I just got this car. It needs some body work, but it's structurally sound."

Needs some body work was a gross understatement. The hood was crumpled and attached to the car with duct tape. And the left rear quarter panel was missing.

"The thing is," I said to Hog, "I need a car that blends in. People would notice this car. They'd remember that they saw a car with only three fenders."

"Not in this neighborhood," Hog said. "We got lots of cars look like this."

"Look at her," Lula said. "She look like she gonna spend a lot of time in this neighborhood?"

"How about this car?" Grandma called out from across the lot. "I like this car."

She was standing in front of a purple Lincoln Town Car that was about a block long. It had terminal rust creeping up from the undercarriage, but the hood was attached in the normal fashion, and it had all its fenders.

"You could put a whole pack of killers in this car," Grandma said.

"I didn't hear that," Hog said. "Don't matter to me who you hang with."

"We don't hang with them. We arrest them," Grandma said. "My granddaughter's a bounty hunter. This here's Stephanie Plum," she said proudly. "She's famous."

"Oh crap," Hog said, eyes bugged out. "Are you shitting me? Get out of here. You think I want to die?" He craned his neck, looking beyond us, up and down the street. "Not only would the brothers like to get hold of her, I hear they brought someone special in from the coast." He scrambled behind a car, putting some distance between the two of us. "Go away. Shoo."

"*Shoo?*" Lula said. "Did I hear you say *shoo*?"

"Some Slayer ride by here I be a dead man," Hog said. "Get her off my lot."

"We came here to buy a car, and that's what we're gonna do," Lula said.

"Fine. Take a car," Hog said. "Take anything. Just go away."

"We want this pretty purple car," Grandma said.

Hog gave Grandma another of the bug-eyed looks. "Lady, that's an expensive car. That's a Lincoln Town Car. That's no two-hundred-dollar car!"

"We wouldn't want to cheat you," Lula said. "So we'll just wander around awhile and see if we like something less expensive."

"No. Don't do that," Hog said. "Take the friggin' Lincoln. I got the keys in the house. I'll just be a minute."

"Don't forget the plates and the registration," Lula said.

Five minutes later, I had a temporary plate taped to my rearview window, Grandma was strapped into the passenger seat, and Lula was a car length ahead of us, en route back to the office.

"I feel like a movie star in this car," Grandma said. "It's like a big limousine. Not everybody can afford a car like this, you know. It must have belonged to somebody special."

A gangster or a pimp, I thought.

"And it rides real smooth," Grandma said.

I had to admit the ride was smooth. The car was about the same size as Sally's bus and took two lanes to make a corner, but the ride was smooth.

Lula and I parked in front of the bonds office, and we all got out to reorganize.

"Now what?" Lula said. "Are we going after Harold Pancek?"

"Yeah," Grandma said. "Are we going after Harold Pancek?"

"Lula and I are going after Harold Pancek," I said. "I should take you home first."

"No way! What if you need an old lady to quiet him down?"

My mother would cut me off from pineapple upside-down cake for the rest of my life if she knew I took Grandma on a bust. Then again, I'd just driven Grandma down Stark Street, so I was most likely screwed already.

"Okay," I said. "You can go with us, but you have to stay in the car."

I felt obligated to say this but it was an empty demand because Grandma never stayed in the car. Grandma was always the first out of the car. I was taking her along because I really didn't think we were going to find Pancek at home. Pancek had been here for a couple years but hadn't seemed to put down roots. According to Connie's background search, Pancek's relatives and longtime friends were in Newark. I was guessing that after last night Pancek skipped back to Newark.

A gray late-model sedan drove by, hooked a U-turn in the middle of traffic, and parked behind the purple Lincoln. Morelli.

"Uh oh," Lula said to me. "You got that look."

"What look is that?"

"That *oh shit* look. That's not a look from a woman who got some last night."

"It's complicated."

"I've been hearing that a lot lately," Lula said.

Morelli got out of the car and walked over, looking like a cop who'd just gotten rear-ended. The anger was tightly controlled, and the gait was deceptively relaxed.

"Isn't this a nice coincidence," Grandma said to Morelli. "I didn't expect to see you until tomorrow night."

Neither rain, nor sleet, nor snow, nor shoe sale at Macy's could get me out of Saturday dinner with my parents. Like a spawning salmon, I was expected to return to my birthplace. Unlike a salmon, I didn't die, although sometimes I wished I could, and the migration took place weekly.

"I need to talk to Stephanie," Morelli said with his best effort at a pleasant smile, his hand at my neck, his fingers curled into the back of my shirt to discourage escape.

"Gee, we were right in the middle of something," I said. "Can it wait?"

"Afraid not," Morelli said. "We need to talk *now*."

I followed him to his car, and we stood with our backs to Lula and Grandma to keep them from eavesdropping.

"Gotcha," Morelli said.

"Now what?"

"Now I take you back to my house and lock you in the bathroom. If you're real nice to me, I'll bring the television in for you."

"You're not serious."

"About the television? Afraid not, I've only got one, and I'm not lugging it up the stairs."

I gave him one of those looks that said *get real*.

"There's a contract on you," Morelli said, "and I ride by and see you standing here like a duck in a shooting gallery. A dead girlfriend doesn't do me much good."

Well, at least he thought I was still his girlfriend. "I was hoping the contract was just rumor."

"My sources tell me there's a guy in town from L.A. He goes by the street name Junkman, and it's widely believed he was brought in by the Slayers to take you out. From all reports, this is a very bad guy. Lots of talk about him. Virtually no useable information. At this point, we don't even have a description."

"How do you know he's real?"

"The sources are good. And the brothers on the street are scared. Just so you don't feel too special, it appears you aren't the only one on his list. It's said to include a cop and two rival gang members."

"Who's the cop?"

"Someone in gang intelligence. We don't have a name."

"I think it's sweet of you to want to lock me in your bathroom, but it doesn't fit into my plans. And last time I was in your house we had a major disagreement over all this."

Morelli ran a fingertip around the scoop neckline of my T-shirt. "First of all, it wasn't much of a disagreement. A disagreement in my family involves restraining orders and bloodshed. Second, I like this little white T-shirt." He hooked a finger into the neckline and looked inside.

"Excuse me?" I said.

"Just checking." More of the smile.

"You wouldn't really lock me in your bathroom, would you?"

"Yep."

"That might be considered kidnapping."

"Your word against mine."

"And it's disgustingly arrogant and macho."

"Yeah," Morelli said. "That's the best part."

I looked back at Grandma and Lula. "How do you expect to accomplish this?"

"I thought I'd drag you into my car and carry you kicking and screaming into my house."

"In front of Grandma and Lula?"

"No," Morelli said. "I can't do it in front of your grandmother." The smile faded. "Can we get serious? This isn't just rumor. These guys are out to get you."

"What am I supposed to do? I live here. I can't go into hiding for the rest of my life."

Morelli's pager buzzed, and he looked at the readout. "I hate this thing," he said. "You're going to be careful?"

"Yes."

"You're going to get off the street?"

"Yes."

He gave me a fast kiss on the forehead and took off.

Grandma and Lula watched Morelli drive away.

"I don't usually like cops," Lula said, "but he's hot."

"He's a looker all right," Grandma said. "And he's got a way about him. There's nothing like a man with a gun."

"He don't get his way from a gun," Lula said. "His way is natural born."

I did some mental knuckle cracking and sidled up to the big purple Lincoln, hoping it would shield me from potential sniper fire. Morelli had done a good job of rattling my nerves. Stating the obvious to Morelli, that I lived in Trenton and couldn't hide for the rest of my life, wasn't a declaration made from bravery. It was a declaration tinged with desperation and maybe even a little hysteria. I was backed into a corner, the victim of circumstances. And I was at a loss how to fix it.

The best I could come up with on short notice was a temporary survival plan. Hide out in Ranger's apartment at night. Search for Pancek by day. The Pancek search was a good thing because I suspected after our initial trip to Canter Street, the search would shift to Newark, far away from the Slayers.

"Everybody in the car," I said. "We're going on a Harold hunt."

I DOCKED THE Lincoln in front of Pancek's row house, and we all got out and stood on the stoop while I rang the bell. There was no answer, of course. I rang again. I dialed his number on my cell phone. We could hear the phone ring on the other side of the door. The machine picked up. I left a message.

"Hi, this is Stephanie Plum," I said. "I need to talk to you." I left my cell number and disconnected.

I tried Pancek's next-door neighbor.

"He left early this morning," she said. "Must have been around seven. I went out to get the paper, and he was loading up his car. Usually you take grocery bags into the house, but he was taking them out."

"Did he say anything?"

"No. But that wasn't unusual. He's sort of an odd guy. Not real friendly. Lived in there all alone. I never saw anyone else go in. Guess he didn't have a lot of friends."

I left my card with her, and I asked her to call if Pancek returned.

"Now what?" Grandma wanted to know. "I'm ready to catch this guy. Where do we go next?"

"Newark. His family is in Newark."

"I don't know if I can go with you," Grandma said. "I'm supposed to go to the mall with Midgie Herrel at one o'clock."

I TOOK ROUTE 1 to Route 18 and got on the Jersey Turnpike. Grandma was home, waiting for Midgie. Sally, Valerie, and my mom were busy planning the wedding. Lula was sailing along with me in the purple Lincoln, riding shotgun, nosing through a big bag of food we bought before leaving Trenton.

"What do you want first?" she asked. "You want a sandwich or a Tastykake?"

"The sandwich." We had about forty Tastykakes. We couldn't chose which kind we wanted, so we got a bunch of everything. I have a cousin who works at the

Tastykake factory in Philadelphia, and she said they make 439,000 Butterscotch Krimpets a day. I intended to eat three of them when I was done with the sub. And maybe I'd follow them up with a coconut layer cake. It's important to keep your strength up on a manhunt.

By the time we got to Newark, Lula and I had almost emptied the food bag. My jeans were feeling unusually tight and my stomach felt seasick. I suspected the queasy stomach was more fear of death than overeating. Still, it would have been good if I'd stopped after the third Tastykake.

Pancek's mother had posted the bond. I had her address plus the address of Pancek's former apartment. I knew Pancek drove a dark blue Honda Civic, and I had his plate number. It would be nice to find the Civic parked in front of one of the addresses.

Lula was reading a map, directing me through Newark. "Turn left at the next corner," she said. "His momma's house is on the first block, two houses in on the right side."

NINE

LULA AND I were in a neighborhood that looked a lot like parts of the Burg. The homes were modest redbrick row houses, their front stoops set into sidewalk. Cars were parked on both sides, narrowing the street to barely two lanes. It was early afternoon and not much was happening. We drove past Pancek's mother's house, looking for the Civic. We did a four-block grid but came up empty.

By late afternoon we'd talked to Pancek's mother, two former neighbors, his former girlfriend, and his best buddy from high school. No one was giving Pancek up, and we hadn't run across his car.

"We're all out of Tastykakes," Lula said. "It's either time to go home or time to go shopping."

"Time to go home," I said.

Pancek's best buddy was married, and I couldn't see the wife putting up with Pancek. The girlfriend thought Pancek should rot in hell. That was a direct quote. His neighbors barely knew him. That left his mother. I had a feeling Mrs. Pancek knew more than she was telling us, but from today's performance it was obvious she wasn't ready to rat on her son.

We'd run down all our leads, and there wasn't anything left to do short of staking out the mother's house. I was all in favor of a job well done, but Pancek wasn't worth a stakeout. A stakeout was a major bummer.

Morelli called on my cell phone. He didn't waste time with hello or how are you. Morelli got right to the heart of it. "Where are you?"

"I'm in Newark, looking for a skip."

"I don't suppose you'd consider staying there. Maybe getting a room."

"What's up?"

"We have a dead guy here. Gunned down on the street, and then had his nuts surgically removed."

"Gang member?"

"Big time. Cut. Had a J freshly carved into his forehead."

"Would that be J for Junkman?"

"That would be my guess," Morelli said. "Are you scared yet?"

"I'm always scared."

"Good. I'm drinking Pepto-Bismol by the case. I hate this. Every time my pager goes off I get an eye twitch, terrified that someone found your body."

"At least we don't have to worry about me getting my nuts surgically removed."

There was a moment of silence. "That's sick," Morelli finally said.

"I was shooting for levity."

"You failed." And he disconnected.

I told Lula about the killing, and we went in search of the turnpike.

"These gang guys are crazy," Lula said. "It's like they're alien invaders, or something. Like they don't know how to live on planet Earth. Hell, they're not even hot aliens. Not that it would matter, but if they were hot looking they'd at least be interesting, you see what I'm saying?"

I wasn't seeing what she was saying. I was taking slow, even breaths, and I was working at controlling my heart rate.

I dropped Lula off at the office, and I drove to Ranger's building. I could see someone in the lobby, talking to the guard at the desk. A car pulled out of the garage, and the gate slid back into place. Too much activity, I thought. Too early for me to sneak inside.

I parked halfway down the block, and I watched the people coming and going. I called Connie, gave her the Haywood Street address, and asked her to check on the building.

"That's Ranger's building," Connie said.

"You know about it?"

"The RangeMan offices are there. Ranger moved his business into that building about a year ago."

"I didn't know."

"Well, it's not like it's the Bat Cave," Connie said. "It's an office building."

So what was with the top-floor apartment? It was filled with Ranger's clothes. Clearly he lived there at least part-time. I was disappointed, and I was relieved. I was disappointed because I hadn't discovered some big secret place. And I was relieved because maybe I hadn't invaded Ranger's private space. The relief was unwarranted, of course. His clothes were there. His shower gel, his deodorant, his razor was there. It might not be the Bat Cave, but it was Ranger's private space.

"Anything else?" Connie wanted to know.

"Nope," I said. "That was it. See you tomorrow."

By seven o'clock the building looked just about empty. The fifth and sixth floors were lit, but the lobby door appeared locked, and garage traffic seemed to have stopped. I locked the Lincoln, walked the short distance to the garage, and let myself into Ranger's apartment.

I dropped my keys into the dish on the sideboard and went to the kitchen to say hello to Rex. I had a beer and a peanut butter sandwich, and I moved to the den to take another crack at the television. After ten minutes of pushing buttons on the remote I had the picture up but no sound. I went to school with a guy who owned an appliance store. I called him at the store, and he gave me a remote lesson. Hooray, now I could watch and *hear* television. Home sweet home.

I'D SET THE alarm on the bedside clock, so I could get out earlier in the morning. It was Saturday, but I suspected the security industry didn't slow for weekends, and I didn't want to take a chance on getting kicked out of the one place I felt safe.

I borrowed a black hooded sweatshirt from Ranger's closet. The sweatshirt was miles big, but it was the best I could do by way of disguise. I pulled the hood up, rode the elevator down, and I reached the Lincoln without a problem. Connie wouldn't be in the office for a couple hours, so I crossed the river into Pennsylvania and headed for Yardley. Yardley was just a short distance from Trenton, but it was light years from Slayerland. Junkman would not be patrolling Yardley looking for Stephanie Plum.

I parked in a public lot, locked my doors, and powered my seat back. It was 7:30 A.M., and Yardley was sleeping in.

I called Morelli at nine o'clock. "What are you doing?" I asked.

"Bob and I are at the car wash. Then we're going to Petco to get some dog food. It's a pretty exciting morning."

"I can hear that. Anything new going on?"

"Nothing you want to know about. I hope you're some place far away."

"Far enough. I'll be on my cell phone if you have breaking news. And don't forget, my mother's expecting us to show up for dinner tonight."

"You're going to have to pay up, Cupcake. I don't do dinner without reimbursement."

"I'll run a tab for you." And I disconnected.

Truth is, I missed Morelli. He was sexy and smart and his house felt homey. His house didn't have the aphrodisiac shower gel, but it had Bob. I really missed Bob. Go figure that one. Okay, so I had to carry his poop in a plastic bag back to the house. It didn't seem like such a big deal anymore.

I left the lot and cruised through town. I turned onto Hamilton, drove past the office, and parked on a side street. Then I entered the office through the back door.

Connie looked up from her computer when I walked in. "Using the back door again?"

"I'm trying to decrease my visibility."

"Good call."

Vinnie rarely came in on a Saturday, and Lula was always late. I poured myself a cup of coffee, and took a seat across from Connie. "Any new shootings, firebombings, rumors of my imminent death?"

"Nothing new." Connie slid the mouse across the mouse pad and clicked. "I've got three new skips. I'm printing out the search results for you now. The original paperwork is somewhere in the mess of unfiled documents stacked on the cabinets."

Oh boy. Lula hadn't filed anything in so long there were more files on top of the cabinets than there were in the drawers.

"We have to go through those stacks," Connie said, coming out of her chair. "And we might as well file them while we search. We're looking for Anton Ward, Shoshanna Brown, and Jamil Rodriguez."

An hour later, we had the documentation for all three skips, and we'd filed more than half of the outstanding cases.

The front door crashed open, and Lula marched in. "What's going on here?" she asked. "I miss anything?"

Connie and I gave Lula a cold ten-second stare.

"Yeah?" Lula asked.

"We just spent an hour doing your filing so we could find the paperwork on three new skips," Connie said.

"You didn't have to do that," Lula said. "I got a system."

"You weren't here," Connie said. "Where the hell were you? You were supposed to be here at nine."

"I'm never here at nine on Saturdays. I'm always late on Saturdays. Everybody knows that." Lula poured herself a cup of coffee. "Did you hear the news? I was listening to the radio on the way in and they said the Red Devil robbed the deli-mart on Commerce Street this morning. And he shot the clerk ten times in the head. That's a lot of times to get shot in the head."

The Red Devil again. Getting more bold. More ruthless. It seemed like years had passed since my Escape got fried and Eddie got shot. I dropped into my seat at the desk and added Connie's search information to the three files.

Shoshanna Brown was wanted for possession. She was a repeater. I'd picked Shoshanna up for priors, and I knew she wouldn't be hard to find. Probably she didn't have a ride to court.

Jamil Rodriguez was caught shoplifting a variety of electronics from Circuit City. When they searched him they found a loaded Glock, a box cutter, a sandwich bag filled with Ecstasy, and a human thumb in a sealed vial of formaldehyde. He claimed to have no knowledge of the thumb.

Anton Ward had a high bond. He'd gotten into a fight with his girlfriend and had stabbed her repeatedly with a steak knife. The girlfriend had lived, but she wasn't happy with Anton. Anton had made bail but had failed to show for court. He was nineteen with no priors. Or at least no priors as an adult. Vinnie had a notation on Ward's bond document that there were gang tattoos on Ward's arm. One of the tattoos was a paw print accompanied by the letters CSS. Ward was a Comstock Street Slayer.

I paged through the file, looking for the photo. The first photo was a profile. The second was full on. I saw the second photo and froze. Anton Ward was the Red Devil.

"You don't look too good," Lula said. "Are you okay? You look whiter than usual."

"This is the devil guy."

Connie grabbed the file. "Are you sure?"

"It's been four days, but I'm pretty sure that's him."

"I didn't give him to you when I ran the neighborhood check because I couldn't find him," Connie said. "I didn't have time to go through the stacks of unfiled folders."

"Oops," Lula said.

Connie looked through the folder and read from the computer search. "Anton Ward. Dropped out of high school when he was sixteen. No work history. Lives with his brother." She flipped to the bond document. "His bond was secured by someone named Francine Taylor. She put her house up as collateral. Vinnie has a note that the daughter, Lauralene, is very pregnant, very young, and expecting to marry Anton Ward." Connie handed the file back to me. "I hate to give this to you. Ordinarily this would go to Ranger."

"No problem," I said. "I'm turning it over to the police." Trenton PD didn't have the manpower to pursue every skip. This was fine by me because it meant my job was secure. Anton Ward would be different. He was involved in a cop shooting and a possible murder. Trenton PD would find the manpower to go after Anton Ward.

I called Morelli and told him about Ward.

"I don't want you anywhere near this guy," Morelli said.

I felt the muscles knot around my spine. Morelli's a cop. He's Italian, I told myself. He can't help himself. Cut him some slack.

"Could you rephrase that?" I asked Morelli. "I think what you meant was *be careful.*"

"I said exactly what I meant. I don't want you anywhere near Anton Ward."

So here's the unfortunate truth. I called Morelli because I didn't want to go anywhere near Anton Ward. Problem is, when Morelli issues it as a demand my ears go flat against my head, my eyes narrow, and I take a stance with my head down, ready to lock horns. I don't know why I do this. I think it might have something to do with curly hair and being born in Jersey. And needless to say, this isn't the first time it's happened.

"And I suppose it's okay for you to go after him?" I said to Morelli.

"I'm a cop. We go after criminals. That's why you called me, right?"

"And I'm a fugitive apprehension agent."

"Don't take this the wrong way,"

Morelli said, "but you're not a great apprehension agent."

"I get the job done."

"You're a magnet for disaster."

"Okay, hotshot," I said. "I'll give you
twenty-four hours to get him . . . and
then he's mine."

I put my phone back into my bag and
looked over at Lula.

"Guess you told him," Lula said. "If it
was me I would have given him forever.
To begin with, those people all live over
in Slayerland. And if you want to think
about something else, Anton hasn't got a
lot to lose being that he just made Swiss
cheese outta someone's head."

"I got carried away."

"No shit. And how are you expecting to
find someone Morelli can't find? Morelli's
good."

Morelli'd issued his ultimatum before I'd
finished giving him all the information.
"Morelli doesn't know about Lauralene
Taylor. And, as we all know, the girlfriend
is always the ticket to the skip."

"I'm hoping he don't need Lauralene on
account of I don't want to have to follow
your ass into Slayerland," Lula said.

I tucked the three new files into my bag.

"Lauralene doesn't live in Slayerland. She lives on Hancock Street."

"Hey, that's my neighborhood," Lula said.

Lula leaned over me and sniffed. "Boy, that Ranger truck smell stays with you. You've been outa that truck for a whole day, and you still smell like Ranger." She took a step back. "There's something different about you. I can't put my finger on it."

"She's fat," Connie said.

Lula's face creased into a broad smile. "That's it. Look at those chubby cheeks and that bootie. And you got love handles that go all the way around. You go girl, you're on your way to being a big woman like Lula."

I looked down at myself. They were right! I had a roll of fat hanging over the waistband of my jeans. Where'd that come from? I was almost certain it wasn't there last night.

I ran into the bathroom and examined my face in the mirror. Definite chubbiness. Apple cheeks. Two chins. Shit. It was the stress. Stress released a hormone that made you fat, right? I was pretty sure I read that somewhere. I checked out my jeans again. I'd had a stomachache all morning. Now I knew why. I popped the top snap and felt some relief as more fat oozed out.

I went back to Lula and Connie. "It's the stress," I said. "It's releasing hormones that are making me fat."

"Good thing I brought doughnuts with me," Lula said. "Have one of the chocolate-covered cream-filled and you'll feel better. Don't want to let that stress grab hold of you."

CONNIE LET ME out the back door and locked up after me. We'd filed the remaining folders and eaten all the doughnuts. Connie was going to a baby shower at the firehouse this afternoon. Lula had a hair appointment. I was going to spend the day being careful.

I slipped out of the alley, wearing the hooded sweatshirt with the hood up, and I did a fast scan of the side street. No gang guys in baggy pants and do-rags waiting to gun me down. Good deal.

I cruised into the Burg, and I parked one street over from my parents' house. I walked head down around the block, cut through the Krezwickis' yard, and hopped the fence into my parents' backyard.

My mother shrieked when she saw me at the back door. "Holy mother," she said, hand over her heart. "I didn't recognize you at first. What are you doing with the hood up on that sweatshirt? You look like a maniac."

"I was chilly."

She put her hand to my forehead. "Are you coming down with something? There's a lot of flu going around."

"I'm fine." I removed the sweatshirt and hung it over the back of a kitchen chair. "Where is everybody?"

"Your father's running errands. And Valerie took the girls shopping. Why?"

"Just making conversation."

"I thought maybe you were going to make a big announcement."

"What would I announce?"

"It's getting obvious," my mother said.

"Okay, so I've moved out of Morelli's house. It's not like it's the end of the world. We haven't even totally broken up this time. We're still talking to each other."

"You moved out? But aren't you pregnant?"

I was stunned. Pregnant? Me? I looked down at my belly. Yikes. I *did* look pregnant. I was on the pill, but I guess there could have been a slip-up. I did a fast calculation and stifled a sigh of relief. I wasn't pregnant.

"I'm *not* pregnant," I said.

"It's the doughnuts," Grandma said. "I know a doughnut butt when I see one."

I looked around for a knife. I was going to kill myself. "I've been under a lot of stress," I said.

"You could get that fat sucked out," Grandma said. "I saw a show on it last night. They showed a doctor sucking a whole load of fat out of some woman right on television. I almost threw up watching it."

The front door crashed open, and Mary Alice galloped in. Valerie followed with the baby. Angie followed Valerie.

Angie and Mary Alice immediately went to the television. Valerie brought the baby into the kitchen with her.

"Look who's here," Grandma said to Valerie. "Stephanie came early, and she's not even going to leave right away."

Valerie set the diaper bag on the floor

and looked at me wide-eyed. "Oh my gosh," she said. "You're pregnant!"

"That's what we thought, too," Grandma said. "Turns out she's just fat."

"It's stress," I said. "I need to relax. Maybe I'm drinking too much coffee."

"I'm telling you, it's the doughnuts," Grandma said. "The Plum side of the family finally caught up with you. You don't watch out you're going to look like your Aunt Stella."

Stella had to have someone else tie her shoes.

"Your pants aren't buttoned," Mary Alice said to me as she galloped through. "Did you know that?"

Okay. Fine. I'll never eat again. Not ever. I'll drink water. But wait a minute, suppose the Junkman finds me and I get shot. I could end up on life support, and I could need the extra fat. Maybe the extra fat is a good thing. An act of God!

"What have we got for dessert?" I asked my mother.

"Chocolate cake and vanilla ice cream."

If God had wanted me to lose weight he

would have made sure there was creamed spinach for dessert.

ALBERT KLOUGHN ARRIVED at six o'clock sharp.

"I'm not late, am I?" he asked. "I was working, and I lost track of time. I'm sorry if I'm late."

"You're not late," my mother said. "You're just in time."

We all knew who was late. Joe. The pot roast and green beans and mashed potatoes were set on the table, and Joe's chair was empty. My father sliced up the roast and took the first piece. Grandma plopped a glob of potatoes onto her plate and passed right. My mother looked at her watch. No Morelli. Mary Alice made horse sounds with her tongue and galloped her fingers around her water glass.

"Gravy," my father said.

Everyone jumped to attention and passed him the gravy.

I had a plate heaped with meat and potatoes smothered in gravy. I had a buttered roll, four green beans, and a beer. I'd taken the food, but I hadn't yet dug in. I was

having an inner dialogue with my stupid
self. Eat it, the stupid self was saying. You
need it to keep up your strength. And
suppose you get run over by a truck tomorrow and die? What then? You'll have
dieted for nothing. Eat and enjoy!

My mother was watching. "You're not
that fat," she said. "I always thought you
were too thin."

Kloughn picked his head up and looked
around. "Who's fat? Am I fat? I know I'm
a little roly-poly. I've always been like
that."

"You're perfect, Snuggy Uggums,"
Valerie said.

Grandma knocked back her glass of
wine and poured another.

A car door slammed shut at the curb,
and everyone sat straight and still in their
seat. A moment later, the front door
opened, and Morelli walked in.

"Sorry I'm late," he said to my mother.
"I was stuck at work." He moved next to
me, dropped a friendly kiss on the top of
my head, and took his seat.

There was a collective sigh of relief. My
family feared Morelli was my last shot at
marriage. Especially now that I was fat.

"What's new?" I asked Morelli.

"Nothing's new."

I made a show of looking at my watch.

"Don't push it," Morelli said softly, smiling for the family. "Are you still driving the truck? I didn't see it out front."

"It's in the garage."

"Are you really going after Ward?"

"It's my job."

Our eyes locked for a moment, and I felt the handcuff clamp around my left wrist.

"You've got to be kidding," I said, holding my wrist up for inspection, the remaining bracelet dangling loose.

"Private joke," Morelli said to the rest of the table. Then he clicked the other half of the cuffs onto his right wrist.

"Kinky," Grandma said.

"I can't eat like this," I told Morelli.

"You eat with your right hand, and I cuffed the left."

"I can't cut my meat. And besides, I have to go to the bathroom."

Morelli gave his head a single shake. "That is so lame," he said.

"I do," I said. "It's the beer."

"Okay," Morelli said. "I'll go with you."

Everyone sucked in some air. A piece of pot roast fell out of my father's mouth, and my mother's fork slipped from her fingers and clattered onto her plate. We weren't the sort of family who went to the bathroom together. We barely admitted to *using* the bathroom.

Morelli looked around the table and gave a small defeated sigh. He reached into his shirt pocket, extracted the key to the cuffs, and released me.

I popped out of my seat and ran upstairs to the bathroom. I locked the door, opened the window, and climbed out onto the roof over the back stoop. I'd used this escape route since junior high. I was good at it. I dangled myself off the roof, and I dropped to the ground.

Morelli grabbed me, spun me around, and trapped me against the back of the house. He leaned into me and grinned. "I knew you'd go out the window."

In a perverse way, I liked that Morelli had me figured out. It was reassuring to know he paid attention. "Very clever of you."

"Yep."

"Now what?"

"We go back to the table. And when dinner is over, we go home . . . together."

"And what happens in the morning?"

"We sleep late, read the Sunday paper, and take Bob for a walk in the park."

"And Monday?"

"I go to work, and you stay home and hide."

I did a major head slap. "Unh," I said.

His eyes narrowed. "What?"

"To begin with, I'm afraid to hide in your house. I'm afraid to hide in my apartment or in my parents' house. I don't want to endanger anyone, and I don't want to make it easy for the bad guys to find me. And if that isn't enough, I *hate* when you order me around. I'm in law enforcement, too. I'm key to this mess. We should be working together."

"Are you crazy? What did you have in mind? I should use you for bait?"

"Maybe not bait."

Morelli grabbed the front of my shirt, pulled me to him, and kissed me.

It was a great kiss, but I didn't know what the heck it meant. It seemed to me a breaking-up kiss would have had less tongue.

"So," I said, "do you want to explain that?"

"There's no possible explanation. I am

so messed up. You frustrate the shit out of me."

I knew the feeling. I was the mess-up queen. There was a contract on my head, and I was weirdly involved with two men. I didn't know which was more frightening.

"I'm going to take the coward's way out and leave," Morelli said. "That whole thing with the handcuffs got a little freaky. I should go back to work anyway. We have a twenty-four-hour watch on Ward's brother's house, so stay far away. I swear if I see you anywhere near there I'm going to have you arrested."

I did another eye roll and returned to the house. I was doing so many eye rolls these days I was getting head pains.

SUNDAY MORNING I took a good look at myself in the mirror in Ranger's bathroom. Not a pretty sight, I decided. The fat had to go. I showered and got dressed, borrowing a black T-shirt from Ranger. The T-shirt was nice and roomy and hid the fat roll.

It had been easy to find the T-shirt. It was perfectly folded and stacked on a shelf, along with twenty other perfectly folded black T-shirts. It had been easy to find the hooded sweatshirt I'd previously borrowed. The hooded sweatshirt had been perfectly folded and stacked on a shelf, along with six other perfectly folded black hooded sweatshirts. Doubly impressive because it's damn hard to perfectly fold a hooded sweatshirt. I counted thirteen black cargo pants, thirteen black jeans, thirteen perfectly ironed long-sleeved black shirts that matched the cargo pants. Black cashmere blazer, black leather jacket, black jeans jacket, three black suits, six black silk shirts, three lightweight black cashmere sweaters.

I started opening drawers. Black dress socks, black and dark gray sweat socks. Assorted black athletic clothes. There was a small safe and a locked drawer. I was guessing the locked drawer held guns.

None of this especially interested me. The ugly truth is, I'd finally lost the fight for dignity, and I was searching for Ranger's underwear. Not that I was going to do anything kinky with it. I just wanted to see what he wore. Hell, I thought I'd shown a lot of restraint to have gone this long without snooping.

I'd now searched the entire dressing room, and unless Ranger kept his underwear in his safe, it appeared to me that he went commando.

I did one of those stupid fanning motions with my hands that women used to do in movies back in the forties to signify heat. I had no idea why I did it. It did nothing to cool me off. I was thinking about Ranger in his black cargo pants, and my face felt sunburned. I had other body parts that were pretty warm, too.

I had one drawer left. I slowly opened the drawer and peeked inside. A single pair of black silk boxers. Just one pair. What the heck did that mean?

I was feeling a little perverted, so I carefully closed the drawer, went into the kitchen, opened the refrigerator door, and let the cold air wash over me.

I looked down and couldn't see my toes past my belly. Mental groan. "No more junky breakfast cereal," I told Rex. "No more doughnuts, chips, pizza, ice cream, or beer."

Rex was in his soup can so it was hard to tell what he thought of the plan.

I got the coffee going, fixed myself a small bowl of Ranger's cereal, and added skim milk. I like this cereal, I told myself. This is delicious. And it would be even more delicious with some sugar and chocolate. I finished the cereal and poured out a mug of coffee. I took the coffee into the den, and I turned the television on.

By noon I was bored with television, and the apartment was starting to feel claustrophobic. I hadn't heard a word from Morelli, and I took that as a bad sign both romantically and professionally. I dialed his cell and held my breath while it rang.

"What?" Morelli said.

"It's Stephanie. I'm just checking in."

Silence.

"Since I haven't heard from you I'm assuming you don't have Ward."

"We've been watching the brother's house, but so far Anton's a no-show."

"You're watching the wrong house. You need to get to him through the girlfriend."

"I don't have any leverage with the girlfriend."

"I do. The girlfriend's mother used her house as collateral on the bond. I can threaten the mother with foreclosure."

More silence. "You could have told me this yesterday," he finally said.

"I was sulking."

"Good thing you're cute when you sulk. What's the plan?"

"I'll visit the mother and apply some pressure. I'll pass whatever information I get on to you, and you can do the takedown."

TEN

ANTON WARD'S GIRLFRIEND, Lauralene Taylor, lived at home with her
mother on Hancock Street. I wanted to
question the Taylors, and I thought it was
best to do it alone. Less threatening that
way, and I didn't think I'd need help. This
was basically a fishing trip in a neighborhood that was hard times but not in the
red zone on the danger meter.

Houses were small, in varying degrees
of disrepair, and largely multiple family.
The population was ethnically mixed. The
economy was a hair above desperate.
Mostly the inhabitants were working
poor.

I drove past Francine Taylor's house,
didn't see any activity, and decided it was
safe to approach. I parked the Lincoln a

couple houses away, locked up, and walked back.

The Taylor house was better than most in the neighborhood. The exterior was a faded lime green, halfway between bare wood and fresh paint. Shades looked inexpensive, but had been neatly raised to the same level on all windows. The small porch was covered with green indoor-outdoor carpet. Porch furnishings consisted of a rusted metal folding chair and a large glass ashtray filled with butts.

I hesitated a moment, listening before knocking. I didn't hear any yelling behind the closed door, no gunshots, no big dog snarling. Just the muffled hum of a television. So far, so good. I rapped once and waited. I rapped a second time.

A very pregnant kid opened the door. She was a couple inches shorter than me, dressed in pink sweats not designed for maternity. Her face was round and smooth with baby fat. Her hair had been straightened and bleached honey blond. Her skin was dark, but her eyes had an Asian tilt. Much too pretty for Anton Ward, and much too young to be pregnant.

"Yeah?" she said.

"Lauralene Taylor?"

"You're either a cop or social services," she said. "And we don't want none."

She tried to close the door, but my foot was in the way.

"I represent Anton's bond agent. Is Anton here?"

"If Anton was here, you'd be dead."

Lauralene sounded like she thought that would be a good thing, giving me pause to rethink my opinion of her. "Anton needs to reschedule his court date," I said.

"Yeah, like that's gonna happen."

"Your mother used this house as collateral. If Anton doesn't show up for court your mother will lose her house."

"Anton will take care of us."

Mrs. Taylor came to the door, and I introduced myself.

"I have nothing to say to you," Francine Taylor said. "You're talking about the father of my unborn grandchild. You need to take this up with him."

"You signed the bond document," I said. "You used your house as collateral. If Anton doesn't show up for court you'll lose this house."

"He won't let that happen," Francine said. "He has connections."

"He has no connections," I said. "If he stays in the area we'll catch him, and he'll go to jail. His only other option is to run. And if he runs, he's not going to take a pregnant woman with him. And he's not going to care if you keep this house. You'll be on the street with nothing."

It was the truth. And I could see that Francine knew it. She wasn't as dumb as her kid.

"I knew I shouldn't have put the house up for him," Francine said. "It was just I wanted him to turn out good for Lauralene."

"This dump isn't worth nothing anyway," Lauralene said.

"I work hard to make my payments on this house," Francine said. "It's a roof over your head. And it's gonna be the only roof over your baby's head. And I'm not losing it for no worthless Anton Ward."

"It don't matter what anyone thinks," Lauralene said. "I'm not giving up Anton, and there's nothing you can do about it. He's gonna marry me. And he's gonna take me out of this hole. We got plans."

I gave Francine my card and asked her to call if she had information on Ward. I wished Lauralene luck with the baby, and she told me to kiss her ass. I try not to be judgmental, but it was a little frightening that Lauralene Taylor and Anton Ward were reproducing.

I returned to the Lincoln and sat there awhile, watching the Taylor house. I'd had a bowl of rabbit food for breakfast and nothing for lunch. I was starving and there was no food in the Lincoln. No Krispy Kremes, no Big Mac, no supersize fries.

I had two new skips, but I wasn't motivated to find them. And Harold Pancek was out there, but truth is, I didn't care much about him either. I cared about Anton Ward. I wanted to see Ward locked up. I would have preferred not to be the one doing the capture, but at the moment I felt relatively safe. So I decided to sit tight.

I was still watching the Taylor house at four o'clock. I was bored out of my mind and hungry enough to eat the upholstery. I called Lula, told her I was on Hancock, and asked her to bring me something nonfattening to eat.

Five minutes later, the Firebird pulled to the curb behind me, and Lula got out. "What's happening?" she asked, handing over a brown paper lunch bag. "Did I miss anything?"

"I'm hanging out to see if Lauralene has a date tonight."

I looked in the bag. It contained a bottle of water and a hard-boiled egg.

"You gotta stay away from the carbs," Lula said. "That's how I lost all my weight. I went on that protein diet. Then I sort of fell off the wagon and gained all the weight back, but it was still my favorite diet, except for the time I ate two pounds of bacon and threw up."

I ate the egg and drank the water. I thought about eating the bag, but I was worried it was carbohydrate.

"I guess I should stay with you in case something dangerous happens, and you need someone to squish somebody," Lula said.

I looked over at her. "Nothing better to do?"

"Not a damn thing. I'm between men right now. And there's nothing on television worth watching." She pulled a deck of cards out of her purse. "I figured we could play rummy."

At six o'clock Lula said she had to have a bathroom break. She took off in the Firebird, and she returned a half hour later with powdered sugar on her shirt.

"That's really rotten," I said. "You've got a lot of nerve sneaking out to get food and not bringing any back for me."

"You're on a diet."

"It's not the starvation diet!"

"Well, I was going to stop home to use the bathroom, and then I thought why not use the bathroom at Dunkin' Donuts? And then I couldn't very well use their bathroom without buying some dough- nuts. That'd be rude, right?"

I gave her an Italian hand signal that didn't mean left turn.

"Boy, you get cranky when you don't get a doughnut," Lula said.

A little over an hour later, streetlights were on, and Hancock Street was settled in for the night. Lula and I couldn't play cards in the dark, so we were passing the time with twenty questions.

"I'm thinking of something that's ani- mal," Lula said. "And my ass is asleep. What makes you so sure Lauralene's gonna have a date tonight?"

"She's got news for Anton, and I'm bet- ting she's going to use it to make him come see her."

Just then, the Taylors' front door opened and Lauralene stepped out.

"You're pretty smart," Lula said. "You're always thinking. You know all about manipulative female shit."

Lauralene looked right and left, and Lula and I froze. We were just a couple houses down. Easily in sight. Fortunately, we weren't under a streetlight, and Lauralene didn't appear to have picked us out. She was wearing the same pink sweat suit. She wasn't carrying a purse. She set off down the street, walking away from us.

"She's going to meet him," Lula said. "And she don't want her mama to know."

Lauralene turned the corner, and I started the car engine. I left my headlights off, and I carefully followed after Lauralene. She walked two blocks and got into the backseat of a parked car. The car was in shadow, hard to tell the make, impossible to see the occupants at this distance. It looked to be a compact, possibly dark green.

I stopped several houses back and idled at the curb. There were no cars parked between Lauralene and me.

"We're sort of exposed, sitting here like this," Lula said. "She could turn around and see us."

I agreed, but I didn't want to drive past

Lauralene and risk having her recognize me. Better to take our chances being parked in the dark.

After a short time, the car in front of us started to rock.

"Look at this," Lula said. "She's seven months pregnant, and they're doing the nasty in the backseat of a friggin' compact. They didn't even bother to go out of the neighborhood."

"They must have been in a hurry," I said.

"Well, excuse me, but I think that's tacky. He could at least of had the courtesy to steal something with a bigger backseat. This here's a pregnant woman he's slippin' it to. I mean how much effort does it take to find a Cadillac? All those old people over in Hamilton Township got Caddies. Those cars are just sitting around waiting to get stolen."

"He's doing more than slippin'," I said. "I've never seen a car rock like that."

"He's gonna ruin the shocks if he keeps this up."

Some loud groaning sounds carried back to us, and Lula and I rolled our windows down so we could hear better.

"Either he's real good or else she's going

into labor," Lula said. She leaned forward
and squinted. "Am I looking at a moon?
What the hell is he doing? How'd he get
his ass plastered against the rear window
like that?"

The sight was both horrifying and
mesmerizing.

"Maybe we should go get him before he
finishes up," Lula said. "It'll be easier to
get the cuffs on him when he's got a boner
and can't move real fast."

Lula was probably right, but I couldn't
see myself slapping cuffs on Anton Ward
while his flag was flying. Last month
Morelli and I rented a porno flick, and
there was some boinking in it. And okay,
so it was fun in a car crash kind of way.
But that was film, and this is Anton Ward
in the flesh, rocking the car with pregnant
Lauralene Taylor. Yikes. I was as close as I
wanted to get.

"Uh oh," Lula said. "The car's stopped
rocking."

We stuck our heads out and listened.
Quiet.

"He don't impress me as being the type
to stick around," Lula said.

We jumped out of the Lincoln and scurried up to Ward's car. I had cuffs shoved

into the waistband of my jeans, and I was holding Ranger's Maglite in one hand and pepper spray in the other. Lula was fumbling in her purse, looking for her gun as she ran.

I took a deep breath, prayed to God that Anton and Lauralene had their clothes on, and flashed the Maglite into the car interior.

"What the fuck?" Anton Ward said, bare ass gleaming under the Maglite.

"Oops," I said. "Sorry, I thought you were done."

"Guess they must have been changing positions," Lula said, looking into the car.

"You fat cow," Ward yelled at Lauralene. "You set me up." And he punched her in the face.

I dropped the Maglite and the spray, and reached into the car to secure Ward, but he was a man in motion, and I only succeeded in grabbing his pants. He wriggled out of the pants, hurled himself out of the opposite side of the car, and took off running.

I ran after him, down the street to the corner. He turned the corner and kept going. He was younger and probably in better shape than me, but he was running buck naked with the exception of socks. I figured eventually the socks were going to slow him down, not to mention the outdoor plumbing swinging in the breeze.

I could hear Lula pounding the pavement half a block back. Nice to know someone was slower than me.

Ward cut through a narrow alley between houses, jumped a fence, and fell when he caught his foot on the top of the fence. He scrambled to his feet, but he'd lost ground to me. I went over the fence and tackled him.

He wasn't a real big guy, but he was a nasty fighter. We rolled around on the ground, swearing and clawing. Turns out it's not that easy to grab hold of a naked guy. Not that I was feeling fussy about where to grab, mostly I just couldn't get a grip on anything. He caught me with a knee to the stomach, and I rolled off him in a rush of pain.

"Stand clear," Lula yelled. "I've got him!" And Lula fell on top of Anton Ward, doing a perfect repeat of Roger Banker.

There was a woof of air that got squished out of Anton Ward's body when Lula made contact, and then Ward didn't move. He was on his back, spread-eagled, eyes open and fixed.

Lula toed him. "You aren't dead, are you?"

Ward blinked.

"He isn't dead," Lula said. "Too bad, hunh?"

I cuffed him, and Lula and I hauled him to his feet.

"Guess we don't have to search him for weapons," Lula said. "That's a big advantage to chasing down a naked guy."

"Come on," I said to Ward. "We're going back to the car."

"I'm not going nowhere," he said.

"Don't mess with me," I told him. "I've only had an egg to eat today, and I'm feeling really vicious."

"Not only that, but I wouldn't mind having a reason to sit on you again," Lula said. "I'm working at perfecting my technique. That was my new special move. I'm even going to give it a name. You know how the Rock has all them wrestling moves like the *People's Elbow* and the *Rock Bottom*? I'm gonna call mine the *Lula Bootie Bomb*."

Ward did some mumbling and started walking. "You're as good as dead," he said to me.

"We're so scared, we're shaking," Lula said. "Look at me. I'm shaking. We're getting threatened by some ugly-ass naked guy. You think we're scared of you? You can't even keep your baggy-ass clothes on."

"You mess with me, and you mess with the Nation," Ward said. "Only reason bounty hunter bitch hasn't tasted the brothers so far is she's being saved for Junkman." Ward smiled at me. "You're gonna like Junkman. They tell me he's got a way with bitches."

We turned the corner, and I could see the Lincoln at the curb, but no Ward car.

"Fuck," Ward said. "That cow took off with my car."

No big disaster, except his clothes were in the car. Lula and I both looked at Ward.

"He isn't going in my Firebird like this," Lula said. "I'm not sitting his nasty bare ass on my Firebird seat."

I didn't want his bare ass on my upholstery, either. I wasn't in love with the Lincoln, but it was all I had right now.

"I'll call Morelli," I said. "They can come pick him up."

"You have Ward in cuffs?" Morelli said, after a deadly pause.

"Yeah, and I thought you could come get him."

"You were supposed to call me for the takedown."

"I forgot. It happened kind of fast. You know, took me by surprise."

Ten minutes later, two squad cars pulled up. Robin Russell got out of the first car and walked over to me.

"Oh man," she said, "he's naked. I'm not getting paid enough for this job."

"Wasn't our fault he's naked," Lula said. "We caught him in the act. He was in the backseat of a Hyundai, humping like a big dog."

Carl Costanza followed Russell. He checked Ward out and grinned at me. "You want to tell me the details?"

"No," I said. "You're going to have to make them up as you go."

"Joe's gonna love this," Costanza said. "Where is he?"

"He's waiting at the station. He was afraid he'd be up for homicide if he didn't calm down before he saw you."

Robin slung a friendly arm around Costanza's shoulders. "I have a real big favor to ask . . ."

"No way."

Robin Russell narrowed her eyes. "You don't even know what I was going to say."

"You were going to try to sweet-talk me into putting this guy's bare ass in my squad car."

"I was not," Russell said. "Well, all right, I was." She locked eyes with Costanza. "What would it take?"

Costanza smiled at her.

"You're a disgrace to the uniform," Russell said to Costanza.

"I try."

Russell wrapped her hand around Ward's arm and tugged him forward. "I'm going to sit you on my Trenton *Times*," she said to Ward. "And I don't want to see your butt move off that newspaper."

"That was fun," Lula said. "That was worth waiting for."

It was satisfying to have captured Ward, but I don't know if I'd classify the experience as fun. I dropped Lula at her Firebird, thanked her for her help, and then I went on to the police station. I would have preferred to crawl back to Ranger's apartment and let my mind go numb in front of his big-screen TV, but I had to make sure I was credited for the capture. And I had to pick up my body receipt.

The police station isn't in the high-rent part of town, and the public lot is across the street and unguarded. It was too late, too dark, and I was too worried to take a chance on the public lot, so I parked illegally in the lot reserved for cop cars. I had myself buzzed in through the back door, and I went directly to the desk. Ward was there, chained to a wooden bench, still naked. Someone had draped a towel over his lap.

"Hey, bitch," Ward said to me. "Want to take a peek under the towel? Take one last look at the big boy?"

Then he made slurpy kissy sounds at me.

I'd already seen more of the "big boy" than I wanted, and it wasn't that big or that fascinating. And the kissy sounds were really getting on my nerves. I kept my head down at the desk, waiting for my paperwork. I didn't want to see Morelli. I didn't know if he was in the building. If I got out before he found me, that would be cool. I figured time and space were my friends at this point.

There was a new cop behind the desk, going slow, making sure he was getting it right. I had a hard time not ripping the body receipt out of his hands.

"In a hurry?" he asked.

"Things to do."

I took the receipt from him, turned on my heel, and marched out of the building. I avoided eye contact with Ward, just in case the towel had slipped or, even worse, was moving. The back door closed behind me, and I shrieked when Morelli grabbed me and pulled me to one side.

"Jeez," I said, hand over my heart. "You scared the crap out of me. Don't sneak up on me like that." Although, truth is, I'm not sure I shrieked because I *didn't* know who it was or because I *did* know who it was.

"Are you okay?"

"Yeah, I think I'm okay. I'm just having some heart palpitations. I have them a lot these days."

"Now that you've had a chance to see Ward up close, are you sure he's the Red Devil?"

"Yes."

"And he was in the car when Gazarra got shot?"

"Yes."

A patrol car pulled up to the back door for delivery. Morelli and I stood aside while two cops hauled Lauralene out of the backseat.

"What did she do?" I asked.

"Ran a red light in a stolen car, driving without a license."

Lauralene's eyes were red from crying.

"She's had a bad night," I said to Morelli. "And she's pregnant. Maybe you can talk to her. She looks like she could use a friend."

I called Francine and told her Ward had been captured. Then I told her Lauralene was at the cop shop.

"Now what?" Morelli said.

"I'm going home. Stick a fork in me, I'm done."

"And home is where?"

"It's a secret."

"I could find you if I put some energy to it," he said.

"I'd tell you if I thought I could trust you."

Morelli sent me a tight smile. He couldn't be trusted. We both knew it. He'd drag me out of my hiding place against my wishes if he thought it was the right thing to do.

"Do you need an escort out of here? Are you in public parking?"

"No, I'm illegally parked in the chief's spot."

Morelli looked over at the reserved space. "The Lincoln? What happened to the truck?"

"Too high profile."

MY CELL PHONE rang at six forty-five Monday morning.

"Junkman tagged the second gang member on his list," Morelli said. "You don't want to know the details, but it took us less time to locate all the body parts this time since we knew where to look."

Not good information on an empty stomach.

I rolled out of bed and went to the kitchen to say good morning to Rex. I made coffee and drank it with my meager bowl of healthy, tasteless cereal. After two cups of coffee I still wasn't motivated to start my day, so I went back to bed.

The phone rang again at eight o'clock. It was Connie.

"You remembered about Carol Cantell, right?"

"Sure. What was I supposed to remember?"

"She's got court today."

Shit. I'd completely forgotten. "What's her court time?"

"She's supposed to be there at nine, but her case probably won't be heard until after lunch."

"Call her sister and have her go over to Carol's house. I'll pick Lula up at the office in a half hour."

No time for a shower. I borrowed a hat and another shirt from Ranger and pulled on my one remaining pair of clean jeans. I was in the elevator when I realized I'd buttoned the top snap on the jeans. Hooray. The diet was working. Good thing, too, because I was hating every minute of it and would love an excuse to quit.

I remoted the gate open and ran to the car. I was parking closer now that I was driving the Lincoln. Not as afraid of discovery by Ranger's men. I was on the cell phone at the first red light, calling Cantell.

"What?" she yelled into the phone. "What?"

"It's Stephanie Plum," I said, in my most reassuring, soothing voice. "How are things going?"

"I'm fat . . . that's how it's frigging going. I have nothing to wear. I look like a blimp."

"You remembered your court date?"

"I'm not going. I can't get into any of my clothes, and everyone's going to laugh at me. I ate a truckful of chips, for crying out loud."

"Lula and I are coming over to help. Just hang in there."

"Hurry up. I'm losing it. I need salt. I need grease. I need something crunchy in my mouth. I'm running a fever here."

CINDY WAS SITTING on Carol's front porch when we drove up.

"She won't let me in," Cindy said. "I know she's in there. I can hear her pacing."

I rapped on the front door. "Carol, open the door. It's Stephanie."

"Have you got food?"

I crinkled a bag of Cheez Doodles so she could hear it through the door. "Lula and I stopped on the way over and bought Doodles to get you through the court session."

Carol cracked the door. "Let me see."

I shoved the Cheez Doodles at her. She

grabbed the bag from me, ripped it open, and shoved a handful of doodles into her mouth.

"Oh yeah," she said, sounding a lot like Lowanda doing phone sex. "I feel better already."

"I thought you were over the doodle craving," Lula said.

"I'm not good with stress," Carol said. "It's a glandular thing."

"It's a mental thing," Lula said. "You're a nut."

We all followed Carol upstairs to her bedroom.

"I did my hair, and I put on my makeup, and then I went to get dressed, and I just sort of had a brain fart," Carol said.

We stood at the doorway and surveyed the disaster area. It looked like her closet exploded, and then her room was ransacked by monkeys.

"Guess you couldn't decide what to wear," Lula said, stepping over the clothes carnage that littered the floor.

"Nothing fits!" Carol wailed.

"Would have been good if you'd discovered that yesterday," Lula said. "You ever think of preparing ahead?"

I was picking through the crumpled

piles of clothes on the floor, looking for slacks with elastic waistbands, bulky tops, scarves that matched. "Help me out here," I said. "Let's start with the slacks. Black would be good. Everything goes with black."

"Yeah, and it don't show the cellulite lumps," Lula said. "Black is real slimming."

Ten minutes later we had Carol squashed into black slacks. The button was open at the waist but you couldn't see it under the hip-length dark blue cotton shirt.

"Good thing you got this nice big roomy shirt," Lula said to Carol.

Carol looked down at it. "It's a nightgown."

"Do you have any roomy shirts that aren't nightgowns?" I asked her.

"They all have doodle stains on them," she said. "It's hard to get those orange smudges out of stuff."

"You know what I think?" I said. "I think this outfit looks good. No one will know you're wearing a nightgown. It looks just like a shirt. And the color is good for you."

"Yeah," Lula and Cindy said. "The color is good."

"Okay," I said, "we're ready to go."

"I've got her purse and jacket," Cindy said.

"I've got a towel so she don't get doodle crumbs on herself on the way to the courthouse," Lula said.

"I can't do it!" Carol sobbed.

"Yes, you can," we all said. "You can do it."

"Hit me," Carol said. "I need a hit."

I gave her a new bag of Cheez Doodles. She tore the bag open and scarfed a handful of doodles.

"You gotta pace yourself," Lula said to Carol. "You got a long day ahead of you, and you don't want to run out of doodles."

Carol clutched the bag to her chest and we nudged her forward, down the stairs, out to the car.

I GOT CAROL Cantell settled in at the courthouse and then I left. Lula and Cindy were with Cantell. Cindy had four unopened bags of doodles. Lula had cuffs and a stun gun. They promised to call me if a problem developed.

I would have stayed with Cantell to see how things turned out but I was feeling grungy. I needed a shower. And I needed to put distance between me and the Cheez Doodles. Ten more minutes with Cantell and I would have wrestled her for the remaining bags.

I drove past Ranger's building, but there was too much activity to chance a run for the elevator. So, what are the alternative shower and lunch possibilities? Morelli's house was one alternative. I had a key to the house, and I still had some clothes there. Convenient but not smart, I thought. Not a good time to return. Too many unresolved issues. And Junkman could be watching the house.

Better to go to my parents' house. It was easier to sneak in through the back, and I could feel relatively confident that I wasn't seen.

ELEVEN

IT WAS CLOSE to noon when I cruised into the Burg. Sally's bus was parked in front of my parents' house, and my father's car was missing from the driveway. Probably there was a big wedding discussion going on, and my father was hiding out at the Elks Lodge.

On first pass I didn't see any Slayers with boom boxes or automatic weapons. Of course, if someone was skinny enough he could be crouched behind Mrs. Ciak's hydrangea bush. I thought better safe than sorry, and I did my Saturday night routine, driving halfway around the block to park. I had the sweatshirt on again with the hood up. I locked the Lincoln, and once again, I cut through the Krezwickis' yard.

I didn't want my mother to do another freak-out, so I took the sweatshirt off before I opened the back door.

Sally, Valerie with the baby, my mother, and Grandma Mazur were at the kitchen table.

"You're hiding from someone, aren't you?" my mother said to me. "That's why you keep sneaking in the back."

"She's hiding from them gang members who want to kill her," Grandma said. "Does anyone want that last piece of cake?"

"That's ridiculous," my mother said. "We don't have gangs in Trenton."

"Wake up and smell the coffee," Grandma said. "We got Bloods and Craps and Latin Queens. And that's just to name a few."

"I was in a rush this morning, and I didn't have time to take a shower," I said to my mother. "Is it okay if I shower here?"

"Of course it's okay," my mother said. "Did you really break up with Joseph again?"

"I moved out of his house. I'm not sure how broken up we are."

My mother went still, radar humming.

"If you're not living with Joseph, where are you living?"

This got everyone's attention.

"I'm staying in a friend's apartment," I said.

"What friend?"

"I can't say. It's . . . a secret."

"Omigod," my mother said. "You're having an affair with a married man."

"I'm not!"

"Isn't that something," Grandma said.

Sally snapped the band on his wrist.

"What was that for?" Grandma asked.

"I thought a really bad word," Sally said.

Yeesh. "I'm not going to discuss this," I told everyone. "This is stupid." And I flounced off to take a shower.

An hour later, I was showered and shampooed, and I was peering into my mother's refrigerator. I didn't have nearly so much blubber hanging over the waistband of my jeans today. Amazing how the fat disappears when you stop eating. The downside was that I felt mean as a snake.

"What are you looking for?" my mother wanted to know. "You've been standing there with the door open for ten minutes."

"I'm looking for something that won't make me fat."

"You're not fat," my mother said. "You shouldn't worry."

"She's got to be careful of the Plum side of the family," Grandma said. "This is when it starts. Remember how Violet was always so thin? Then she hit her thirties and ballooned up. Now she has to buy two seats when she gets on an airplane."

"I don't know what to eat!" I said, arms flapping. "I've never had to worry about weight before. What the hell am I supposed to friggin' eat?"

"Depends what kind of diet you're doing," Grandma said. "Are you doing Weight Watchers, Atkins, South Beach, The Zone, The Slime Diet, The Sex Diet? I like the Slime Diet, myself. That's where you're only allowed to eat things that got slime . . . like oysters and slugs and raw bull's balls. I was going to try the Sex Diet, but I couldn't figure out some of the rules. Every time you get hungry you're supposed to have sex. Only thing is, they didn't say what kind of sex you're supposed to have. Like, whether you should have it alone or with someone else. And what about that oral sex stuff? I never did

a lot of that personally. Your grand-
father wasn't much for experimenting,"
Grandma said to me.

My mother went to the cupboard,
poured herself a tumbler of whiskey, and
chugged it.

"So what kind of diet are you on?"
Grandma asked me.

"I'm on the Tastykake diet," I said, helping myself to a Butterscotch Krimpet.

"Good for you," Grandma said. "That's
a good choice."

"I'm going back to work," I told everyone, putting my hood up, ducking out the
back door.

Mrs. Krezwicki was at her kitchen window when I scuttled through her yard.
She leveled a gun at me, sighting with one
eye. I pushed the hood back and waved,
and she lowered the gun and reached for
the wall phone. Calling my mother, no
doubt.

I got into the Lincoln and drove to the
office.

"I heard from Lula at the courthouse,"
Connie said. "Cantrell's doing okay."

"How about Ranger? Have you heard
from Ranger?"

"Not a word."

Rats. He wasn't supposed to be back for at least another week, but I didn't want to take any chances on being caught in his bed. Or even worse, in his shower!

Connie's eyes fixed on my hat. "That looks like Ranger's hat."

"He gave it to me." It was a perfectly good fib. If he gave me his truck, why not his hat?

Connie looked like she bought it.

"I wish Ranger would get his butt back here," Connie said. "I'm not happy about you going after Rodriguez. What kind of a person would carry a thumb around with him?"

"A crazy person?"

"It's creepy. If you want, I can call Tank to go with you."

"No!" Last time I went out with Tank he broke his leg. Then his substitute got a concussion. I was hell on Ranger's Merry Men. Bad enough I was squatting in his apartment, I didn't want to compound the damage by wiping out his workforce. And if I was being totally honest, I'd have to admit that time spent with Tank was un-comfortable. Tank was Ranger's right-hand man. He was the guy who watched Ranger's back. He was entirely trustworthy, but he rarely spoke, and he never shared his thoughts. I'd reached a sort of telepathic state with Ranger. I hadn't a clue what was in Tank's mind. Maybe nothing at all.

"I'm a lot more worried about Junkman than I am about Rodriguez," I said to Connie.

"Have you seen Junkman?"

"No."

"Do you know what he looks like?"

"No."

"Do you know why you're on his list?"

"Does there have to be a reason?"

"There's usually a reason," Connie said.

"I can identify Ward as the Red Devil, and I bounced Eugene Brown off my Buick."

"That could be it," Connie said. "Or it could be something else."

"Like what?"

Connie shrugged. "I don't know gangs, but I know something about the mob. Usually when someone's targeted for take-out, it's about power . . . keeping it or getting it."

"How does that relate to me?"

"If it's an entire gang that's out to get you, you move far away. If it's only one member, you can eliminate the problem by eliminating the member."

"Are you suggesting I kill Junkman?"

"I'm suggesting you try to find out why Junkman has you on his list."

"I'd have to penetrate the Slayers."

"You'd have to catch one and make him talk to you," Connie said.

Catch a Slayer. It sounded like a kid's game.

"You could hide out until Ranger gets back," Connie said.

What she meant was, I could hide out until Ranger gets back and eliminates Junkman for me. Ranger was good at solving problems like that. And it was tempting to let him solve mine, but that's not the sort of thing you do to someone you like. That's not even the sort of thing you do to someone you hate. Not when the problem is solved by murder.

I'd already been there, and it didn't feel great. I was pretty sure Ranger had once killed a man to protect me. The man had been insane and determined to end my life. His death had been ruled a suicide, but in my heart, I knew Ranger had stepped in and done the job. And I knew

there'd been an unspoken agreement between Ranger and Morelli. Don't ask,
don't tell.

Morelli was a cop, sworn to uphold the
law. Ranger had his own set of laws. There
were things that fell in the gray zone between Morelli and Ranger. Things Ranger
was willing to do if he felt it necessary.
Things Morelli could never justify.

"I'll think about it," I told Connie. "Let
me know if you hear from Ranger."

I'd parked in the small lot behind the
bonds office. I left through the back
door, got into the Lincoln, and I called
Morelli.

"What's happening with Anton?" I
asked. "Did he make bail?"

"It's set high. I don't think anybody's going to step forward for him."

"Have you talked to him? Did he tell
you anything interesting? Like about
Junkman?"

"He's not talking," Morelli said.

"Can't you make him?"

"I could, but I misplaced my rubber
hose."

"You said Junkman was a hired gun,
right? That he was from L.A."

"We're not sure if that information is right anymore. The source hasn't turned out as reliable as we'd hoped. We know there's a guy out there who uses the tag Junkman. And we know he's working his way through a list. That's really all we're sure of."

"And I'm on the list."

"That's what we were told."

And that's what Anton confirmed. "It would be helpful to know why I'm on the list."

"Whatever the reason, it would help your cause if you'd quit your job and look like a nonthreatening house-wife. Or maybe go away for a couple months. These guys have a short atten-tion span."

"Would you miss me if I went away?"

There was a long silence.

"Well?" I asked.

"I'm thinking."

I called Lula next.

"Carol's up in about ten minutes," Lula said. "How are we supposed to get home?"

"I'm on my way. Parking's a pain. Call me when you're on the sidewalk in front of the building, and I'll swing by and pick you up."

I REACHED THE courthouse and drove around the block. My phone rang on the second pass.

"We're out," Lula yelled. "We got Carol with us, too. And we all need a bar!"

"How did she do?"

"Probation and counseling. It was her first offense, and she'd already paid for all the Fritos she ate. We had a lady judge who weighed about two hundred pounds and was real sympathetic."

I turned the corner and saw them at the curb. Lula and Cindy were smiling. Carol looked shell-shocked. She was ghostly white, clutching a bag of Cheez Doodles to her chest, and she was visibly shaking.

They all piled into the backseat, with Carol sitting between Cindy and Lula.

"Carol doesn't know the court session is over," Lula said, grinning. "Carol's in a state. We gotta get Carol a big-ass margarita."

I drove over to the Burg, and I parked in front of Marsillio's. It was a nice safe place to get a drink. If anybody messed with you at Marsillio's, Bobby V. would kick their butt. Or even worse, he'd make sure they didn't get a table.

We guided Carol into Marsillio's, sat her at a table, and used the napkin to brush some of the doodle dust off her.

"Am I going to jail?" Carol asked.

"No," Cindy said. "You're not going to jail."

"I was afraid I was going to jail. Who would take care of my kids?"

"I'd take care of your kids," Cindy said. "But you don't have to worry about it, because you're not going to jail."

Alan, the owner, rushed over with a margarita for Carol.

"Am I going to jail?" she asked.

THREE MARGARITAS LATER, we poured Carol into the Lincoln, and I dumped her at Cindy's house.

"Boy," Lula said. "She was really hammered."

With any luck she'd throw up a bag or two of Doodles. Don't get me wrong, I love Doodles, but they aren't exactly diet food when you snarf them by the truckload.

It was late afternoon, so I took Lula to the office. I parked in the rear lot, and we went in through the back door.

Connie was on her feet when she saw us. "I've got a bunch of files," she said. "Everyone take a couple and put them away. I don't want another file mess."

I took my stack of files and arranged them alphabetically. "Joe tells me no one bonded out Anton Ward this time."

"He's being held on a big bucks bond, and no one has the collateral to cover it. His brother called, but Vinnie wouldn't take the bond. The only way Ward's going to get out is with a signature bond, and no one's going to write a signature on Anton Ward."

"What's the charge?"

"Armed robbery and accessory."

"Ain't no justice in this world," Lula said. "That scrawny piece of garbage will plea-bargain and get off with a couple years."

Connie filed the last of her folders. "I don't think he'll plea-bargain. I don't think he'll talk at all. If he gives up any Slayers, he's as good as dead."

There was a burst of rapid-fire gunshots from the back of the building, and we all instinctively went to the floor. The shooting stopped, but we stayed down.

"Tell me I'm hallucinating," Lula said. "I don't want to believe this."

After a couple minutes we got to our feet and tiptoed to the back door. We put our ears to the door and listened.

Perfectly quiet.

Connie cracked the door and peeked out. "Okay," she said. "It makes sense now."

Lula and I peeked out, too.

The Lincoln was totally spray painted with gang graffiti and riddled with bullet holes. The tires were shot out, and the windows were shattered.

"Hunh," Lula said. "Guess you're going to need alternative transportation."

What I needed was a new life. I felt myself gnawing on my lip again and immediately forced myself to stop.

"You're kind of white," Connie said to me. "Are you okay?"

"They found me. I was driving a new car, and I parked in the back, and they figured it out."

"Probably watching the office," Lula said.

"I'm trying real hard not to freak," I told them.

"Play the role," Lula said. "That's what we do. We pick a role and we play it. What role you want to play?"

"I want to be smart, and I want to be brave."

"Go for it," Lula said.

Connie closed and locked the door. She went to the ammo storage area, rummaged through boxes, and came up with a Kevlar vest.

"Try this on for size," she said to me.

I slipped it on, flattened the Velcro closures, and covered the vest with the hooded sweatshirt.

Lula and Connie stood back and looked at me. I was wearing Ranger's black hat, black T-shirt, black sweatshirt.

"It's the damnedest thing," Lula said. "Now you just don't smell like Ranger, you're even starting to look like him."

"Yeah," Connie said. "How come you still smell like Ranger?"

"It's this new shower gel I bought. It smells like Ranger." Can I fib, or what?

"I'm gonna go buy a gallon," Lula said. "What's it called?"

"Bulgari."

I WAS BACK to using Ranger's truck. I was parked two blocks from his building, waiting for the sun to set and the building to clear out. Another couple minutes and I thought it would be safe for me to make a move. I'd been waiting for over two hours. That was okay. It had given me time to think.

Connie was right. I needed to find out why I was on the list. Eventually, Street Crimes or the Criminal Intelligence unit would get the information, but I was having a hard time finding the patience for "eventually."

I'd had a stupid, crazy idea while I was at the bonds office. It was so stupid and crazy I couldn't bring myself to say it out loud. Trouble was, the idea wouldn't go away. And I was beginning to think it wasn't so stupid and crazy.

What I needed was a snitch. I needed to find a Slayer who could be bribed into talking. I didn't have a lot of money to use as a bribe, so I figured I'd have to resort to violence. And then I needed to find this Slayer outside of Slayerland. No way was I getting caught within Slayer boundaries.

So how am I going to catch a lone Slayer out of his 'hood? Turns out there's one sitting in jail. Anton Ward. All I have to do is bond him out, and he's mine. Okay, so I don't have all the details worked out, but it has potential, right?

The sun was down, and the streets were empty. Time to take a look at the building, I decided. I locked the truck, I pulled the hood over Ranger's ball cap, and I walked the two blocks to the gate. Floors five and six were lit. And there was a single window showing light on the fourth floor. Only the night guard was left in the lobby. Now or never, I thought. I remoted myself through the gate, crossed the garage, and took the elevator without a hitch. I let myself into the apartment and relaxed.

The apartment was nice and empty. Just as I'd left it. I dropped the keys to the truck in the dish on the sideboard. I shrugged out of the sweatshirt and vest and went to the kitchen.

Rex was running on his wheel. I tapped on the side of the cage and said hello. Rex

paused for a moment, whiskers twitching.
He blinked once and went back to
running.

I opened the refrigerator and looked inside. Then I looked down at my waistline.
Still some fat oozing over the top of my
jeans, but there was less fat than yesterday.
I was moving in the right direction. I
closed the refrigerator door and hustled
out of the kitchen before the beer got
to me.

I watched television for a while, and
then I took a shower. I told myself I was
taking a shower to relax, but the truth
was, I wanted to smell the soap. Sometimes I was able to forget I was living in
Ranger's space. Tonight wasn't one of
those times. Tonight I was very aware that
I was using his towels and sleeping in his
bed. It was a kind of Russian roulette, I
thought. Each night I walked into the
apartment and spun the barrel. One of
these nights Ranger would be here waiting for me, and I was going to take it between the eyes.

I toweled off and went to bed in panties
and T-shirt. The sheets were cool and the
room was dark. The panties and T-shirt
felt skimpy in Ranger's bed. I would be

much more comfortable if I was fully
dressed. Socks, jeans, two or three shirts
buttoned to the neck, tucked into the
jeans. Maybe a jacket and hat.

It was the shower, I decided. The hot
water and the delicious soap. And the
towel. It had me all overheated. I could
fix that . . . but I'd go blind. At least that
was the threat when I was growing up in
the Burg—you abuse yourself and you'll
go blind. It hadn't totally stopped me—
but it had me worried. I really didn't
want to go blind. Besides, what if I was
in the middle of something and Ranger
walked in? Actually, that sounded pretty
good.

No! It didn't sound good. What was I
thinking? I was sort of attached to Joe.
Maybe. So where the heck was he when I
needed him? He was at home. Probably. I
could go over there, I thought. I could
walk in and tell him I'd just taken a shower
with this great soap that always makes me
feel sexy. And then I'd explain to him how
I got carried away with the towel . . .

Good grief. I switched the light on. I
needed something to read, but there were
no books, no magazines, no catalogues. I
wrapped myself in Ranger's robe, curled

up on the couch, and turned the television on.

I WOKE UP to the *Today* show. I was still in Ranger's robe. I was on the couch. And I was feeling cranky. It didn't help that Al Roker was on the television screen, talking to some woman from Iowa, and Al was looking happy as could be. Al always looked happy. What's with that?

I said good-bye to Al and beamed the television off. I dragged myself into the bathroom but decided to forego the shower. I brushed my teeth and got dressed in the clothes on the floor.

I was desperate for coffee, but it was almost eight o'clock, and I needed to get out of the building. I clapped Ranger's hat on my head, stuffed myself into the vest and sweatshirt, and took the elevator to the garage. The elevator doors opened just as a car approached the gate. I flattened myself against the side and returned to the seventh floor. I waited in the seventh-floor foyer for ten minutes, and I tried it again. This time the garage was empty.

I left the garage, and I walked to the truck. The sky was overcast and a misting rain had started to fall. The buildings on either side of Comstock were redbrick and cement. No trees, no shrubs, no lawns to soften the landscape. It felt nicely urban when the sun was shining. Today it felt grim.

I drove to the office and parked the truck in full view on the street. Connie was already at work. Lula hadn't yet arrived. I saw no sign of Vinnie.

I went straight to the coffeepot and poured out a cup for myself. "I haven't seen a lot of Vinnie lately," I said to Connie. "What's the deal?"

"He's got hemorrhoids. He comes in for an hour to bitch and complain, and then he goes home to sit on his rubber doughnut."

Connie and I both smiled at this. Vinnie deserved hemorrhoids. Vinnie *was* a hemorrhoid.

I sipped my coffee. "So you're the one writing bonds now?"

"I'm doing the low money bonds. Vinnie gets off his doughnut to do guys like Anton Ward."

"I need a favor."

"Uh oh," Connie said. "I got a bad feeling about this."

"I want you to help me bond out Anton Ward. I need to talk to him."

"No way. Un uh. Nope. No can do. Forget it."

"This was your idea! You were the one who said I had to find out why I was on Junkman's list."

"And you think Ward is going to tell you out of gratitude?"

"No. I was planning on beating it out of him."

Connie considered that. "Beating might work," she said. "Who's going to slap him around?"

"Me and Lula. You could do it, too, if you want."

"So let me get this straight," Connie said. "We bond him out. Then we escort him from the jail to the trunk of Lula's Firebird and take him somewhere for further discussion."

"Yeah. And then when we're done we can revoke his bond."

"I like it," Connie said. "Did you think of this all by yourself?"

"Yep."

"Think of what all by herself?" Lula said, swinging through the front door.

"Man, it's crappy out there. It's gonna rain cats and dogs all day."

"Stephanie's got a plan to bond out Anton Ward and beat some information out of him," Connie said.

Lula's mood changed to smiley face. "No shit? Are you messin' with me? That's inspired. You aren't gonna leave me out, are you? I'm good at smackin' people around. And I'd just love to smack Anton Ward around."

"You're in," I said to Lula. "We just have to figure some things out first. Like, where are we going to take him for his beating?"

"It has to be someplace isolated, so no one hears him screaming," Lula said.

"And it has to be cheap," I said. "I haven't got any money."

"I have just the place," Connie said. "Vinnie has a house in Point Pleasant. It's right on the beach, and no one's going to be around now. The season's over."

"That's a great plan," Lula said. "The arcade will still be open, and in between beatin' on Anton Ward I can play the claw machine."

"Do you think we'll have to beat him a

lot?" I asked Connie. A bunch of her relatives were mob, and I figured she knew about these things.

"I hope so," Lula said. "I hope he don't talk for days. I love Point Pleasant. And I haven't beat on anyone in a while. I'm looking forward to this beating."

"I've never actually beat anyone," I said.

"Don't you worry about it," Lula said. "You just stand back and leave it to me."

"We have to do this right," Connie said. "We don't want anyone to know we have Ward. We're going to have to make it look like he just disappeared."

"I've already thought it through," I said. "You can call Ward's brother back and tell him we'll bond Ward out if he agrees to wear a personal tracking unit. We just got one in from iSECUREtrac, right?"

"We haven't used it yet," Connie said. "Haven't even taken it out of the box."

"If Ward agrees to the PTU we say we have to have him released into our custody so we can install the unit. Then we tell everybody we have to install the transmitter here, at the office. We tell them after the unit is in place Anton is free to go.

"We cuff Anton on his release and bring him back to the office, but instead of strap-

ping the transmitter on him, we dump him
in Lula's trunk. All she has to do is back up
to the rear door, and Anton's off to Point
Pleasant. Then we pretend Anton escaped.
We can say he used the lavatory at the
office, and he went out through the
window."

"Brilliant," Lula said. "You're a criminal
genius."

"I like it," Connie said. "Let's do it."

We all did a high five.

"It'll take me some time to set this up,"
Connie said. "I'll arrange it for the end of
the business day. Then it won't be suspicious if we close the office down and disappear. In the meantime, you two should
take a drive to Point Pleasant and make
sure it's okay to use the house." She took a
key from a mess of keys she kept in her
top drawer. "This is the key to the house.
He doesn't have a security system. It's just
a little bungalow on the beach." She wrote
the address on a sticky note and gave it
to me.

LULA AND I didn't do a lot of talking on
the way to Point Pleasant. Hard to say
why Lula fell into silence. Mine was

brought on by a mixture of disbelief and terror. I couldn't believe we were going to do this. It was insane. And it was all my idea.

I was driving Ranger's truck, and Lula was reading the map. We'd reached the ocean, and we were looking for Vinnie's street. The rain was steady and the little shore houses that seemed cute and colorful in July sunshine looked sad in the dismal gray gloom.

"You turn left onto the next street," Lula said. "And you go all the way to the end. It's the last house on the right. Connie says it's painted salmon and turquoise. I'm hoping she's wrong about the paint."

"This is like a ghost town," I said. "Not a single house has a light on."

"Better for us," Lula said. "But it feels spooky, don't it? It's like we're in some horror movie. *Nightmare in Point Pleasant.*"

I got to the last house on the right and darned if it wasn't painted salmon with turquoise trim. It was a small two-story bungalow that faced the ocean. No garage, but there was a driveway separating Vinnie's house and an almost identical bungalow next to him. At this time of year a car parked in the driveway would be reasonably well hidden.

I pulled the truck into the driveway, and I cut the lights. Lula and I squinted through the rain to the bungalow's back door. Above the door was a hand-painted sign that said SEA BREEZE.

"Bet Vinnie had to think a long time to come up with that name," Lula said.

I put my hood up, and Lula and I sprinted through the rain and huddled together on the small back stoop while I fumbled with the key. I finally got the door open, we both jumped inside, and I slammed the door shut behind us.

Lula shook her corn-rowed head, sending water flying. "Could we possibly have picked a crappier day to do this?"

"Maybe we should wait a couple days until the weather is better." The heartfelt, cold-feet statement of the year.

"I don't want to be no alarmist or nothing, but you wait a couple days and you might not be around to beat on this guy."

TWELVE

THE BACK DOOR to Vinnie's beach bungalow opened to the kitchen. The floor was yellow-and-white linoleum that looked relatively new. The counters were red Formica. The cabinets were painted white. The appliances were also white. GE. Midgrade. A small white wood table, covered with a blue-and-white checked plastic tablecloth, sat to one side. There were four chairs at the table.

Beyond the kitchen was a combination living room and dining room. The carpet was gold and showing wear. The dining room table was white and gold, French provincial. Probably confiscated from a bad bond. The living room furniture was overstuffed brown velour. Tasteful in an upper-end whorehouse sort of way. End

TEN BIG ONES 311

tables were dark fruitwood, Mediter-
ranean style. Hand-stitched pillows with
messages were everywhere. KISS ME I'M
ITALIAN. HOME IS WHERE THE HEART IS.
SUMMER STARTS HERE.

There was a downstairs bathroom and a
small downstairs bedroom. Both rooms
looked out at the driveway.

"Here's where we'll beat Anton," Lula
said, standing in the bathroom. "Just in
case there's blood, it'll be easy to clean up
with all this tile."

Blood? My stomach went sick and little
black dots floated in front of my eyes.

Lula kept going. "And there's only that
one little frosted window over the tub. So
nobody can see us. Yep, this is gonna be
good. Nice and private. No neighbors
around. That's important on account of
he's probably gonna be screaming in pain,
and we don't want no one to hear."

I sat down on the toilet and put my head
between my legs.

"You okay?" Lula asked.

"I've been dieting. I think I must be
weak from hunger."

"I remember when I was dieting, and I
felt like that," Lula said. "And then I discovered that protein diet, and I was eating

all those pork roasts. I felt real good on the protein diet. Except sometimes I'd overdo it. Like when I found that sale on boiled lobsters. And I was eating all those lobsters and melted butter. I'm telling you that butter went through me like goose grease."

I didn't want to hear about goose grease right now. I stayed on the toilet, taking deep breaths, and Lula went exploring upstairs.

"There's two bedrooms and a bathroom up there. Nothing special. Looks like it's for kids and guests," Lula said, returning to the bathroom. "Maybe we should get you food."

I didn't need food. I needed someone to intervene and stop me from kidnapping a guy and beating him bloody. I left the bathroom and walked through the living room to the front door. I opened the door and stepped out onto the covered front porch. There was a minuscule front yard, just big enough for an aluminum and nylon webbed chaise and a small table.

A boardwalk ran the length of the beach for as far as the eye could see. Beyond the boardwalk, the wet sand was the color and texture of fresh concrete. The ocean was loud and scary. Big gray rollers crashed onto the beach, conjuring visions of tsunamis barreling in, gobbling up Point Pleasant.

The wind had picked up, driving the rain across the porch in sheets. I retreated back into the house and locked the door. We pulled every shade and closed every curtain and then we left.

I called Connie when we hit White Horse. "What's up?" I asked.

"It's all set," Connie said. "Ward and his brother bought the whole enchilada. Ward's being held at the prison on Cass Street. I have to get there before four o'clock to bond him out."

I PICKED CONNIE up at three thirty and dropped her at the prison. We decided Ward might not be happy to see Lula and me, so we waited in the truck. In a half hour, Connie emerged with Ward cuffed behind his back. Ranger's truck was a four-door supercrew cab with a full back-seat and steel rings conveniently bolted into the floor, just right for securing leg shackles. Connie got in back with Ward, and I swung the truck out into traffic.

Ward didn't say anything. And I didn't say anything. And Lula didn't say anything. All of us being careful not to rock the boat. Ward thinking he was going home. And Lula and Connie and me thinking we were going to beat the crap out of him.

I parked curbside when I reached the office. We took our time off-loading Ward, making a show of it as best we could in the rain. We wanted people to witness the fact that we'd brought him this far. The whole time I was having heart palpitations, and I couldn't get the phrase "harebrained scheme" out of my head.

We finally brought him inside and sat him in the chair in front of Connie's desk. The plan was to give him a shot at talking to us. If he refused to cooperate we'd hit him with the stun gun, blindfold him, and trundle him out to the Firebird.

"I want to know about Junkman," I said.

He was slouched in the chair. Hard to do when your hands are cuffed behind your back, but he managed. He cut his eyes to me under half-lowered lids. Sullen. Insolent. He didn't say anything.

"Do you know Junkman?" I asked.

Nothing.

"You better answer her," Lula said.

"Otherwise we might get upset, and then I'd have to sit on you again."

Ward spit on the floor.

"That's disgusting," Lula said. "We don't put up with that. You don't watch your step, I'll give you enough volts to make you pee your pants." And she showed him her stun gun.

"What the hell is this?" Ward said, sitting up straighter. "I thought I was supposed to get hooked up to a monitor. What's with this stun gun bullshit?"

"We thought you might want to talk to us first," Lula said.

"I got rights, and I'm being violated," Ward said. "You got no business keeping me cuffed. Either put the fucking monitor on me or turn me loose."

Lula got into his face and wagged her finger at him. "Don't you use that language in front of ladies. We don't tolerate that."

"I don't see no ladies," Ward said. "I see a big fat black . . ." And he used the *c* word. The mother of all swear words. Even better than the *f* word.

Lula lunged at him with the stun gun, and Ward jumped out of his chair.

Connie was on her feet, too, trying to

contain the disaster. "Don't let him get to the door!" she yelled.

I sprang into action, blocking his way. He turned and ran for the back door. Connie and Lula both had stun guns in hand.

"I got him. I got him," Lula shouted.

Ward lowered his head, and gave Lula a head butt to the stomach that knocked her on her ass. Connie rounded on him in a crouch, and they sized each other up. Ward sidestepped and bolted around her. He wasn't smart, but he was nimble.

I took a flying leap and tackled him from behind. We both went down, I rolled off, and Connie swooped in and tagged him with the stun gun.

"Unh," Ward said. And he went inert.

We all popped our heads up to see if anyone was looking in the front window.

"We're in the clear," Connie said. "Quick, help me drag him behind the file cabinets before someone sees him."

Ten minutes later we were set to go. Ward was cuffed and shackled. We wrapped him in a blanket and carted him out the back door to Lula's car. We dumped him in the trunk, and we all made the sign of the cross. Then Connie slammed the trunk lid shut.

"Holy Mary Mother of God," Connie said. She was breathing heavy, and her forehead was beaded with perspiration.

"He isn't going to die in there, is he?" I asked Connie. "He can breathe, right?"

"He'll be fine. I asked my cousin Anthony. Anthony knows these things."

Lula and I didn't doubt for a moment that Anthony knew all about stuffing bodies in trunks. Anthony was an expediter for a construction company. If you treated Anthony right, your construction project moved along without a hitch. If you decided you didn't need Anthony's services, you were likely to have a fire.

Connie locked the office, and we all piled into the Firebird. Twenty minutes into the trip Anton Ward came to life and started yelling and kicking inside the trunk.

It wasn't that loud from where I was sitting, but it was unnerving. What must he be feeling? Anger, panic, fear. What was I feeling? Compassion? No. In spite of Connie's expert assurances, I was worried Ward would die, and we'd have to bury him in the dark of night in the Pine Barrens. I was going straight to hell for this, I thought. It was all adding up. I was for sure beyond Hail Marys.

"This guy's creeping me out," Lula said. She punched a number on her CD player and drowned Ward out with rap.

Ten minutes later I could feel my cell phone vibrating. It was hooked to my Kevlar vest, and I couldn't hear the ring over the rap, but I could feel the vibration.

I flipped the phone open and yelled, "What?"

It was Morelli. "Tell me you didn't bond out Ward."

"There's a lot of static here," I said. "I can't hardly hear you."

"Maybe it would help if you turned the radio down. Where the hell are you, anyway?"

I made crackling, static sounds, disconnected, and shut my phone off.

HARD TO TELL when the yelling and kicking stopped, but there were no sounds coming from the trunk when Lula parked in Vinnie's driveway and cut the engine.

It was still raining, and the street was dark. No lights shining from any of the houses. The ocean roiled in the distance, the waves thundering down onto the sand and then swooshing up the beach.

It was pitch black when we huddled around the rear end of the Firebird. I had a flashlight. Connie had the stun gun. Lula was hands free to open the trunk.

"Here goes," Lula said. "Here's the plan. Soon as I get the lid up we want Stephanie to shine the light in his eyes in case the blanket's come undone, and then Connie can zap him."

Lula opened the trunk. I switched the light on and aimed it at Ward. Connie leaned forward to zap Ward, and he kicked out at Connie. He caught Connie square in the chest and knocked her back four feet onto her keister. The stun gun flew out of Connie's hand and disappeared into the darkness.

"Shit," Connie said, scrambling to get to her feet.

I ditched the flashlight, and Lula and I wrestled Ward out of the trunk. He was bucking and swearing, still wrapped in the blanket. We lost our grip and dropped him twice before we got him into the house.

As soon as we were in the kitchen, we dropped him again. Connie closed and locked the kitchen door, and we stood there breathing hard, dripping wet, gaping at the pissed-off guy writhing around on the linoleum. He stopped wriggling when the blanket fell away.

He had big baggy homey pants that had slipped off his boney ass and were around his knees. He was wearing cotton boxers with red and white stripes. His oversize four-hundred-dollar basketball shoes were unlaced in hood fashion. He looked pretty bad, but it was an improvement over the last time I saw him.

"This is kidnapping," he said. "You can't do this, bitch."

"Of course we can," Lula told him. "We're bounty hunters. We kidnap people all the time."

"Well, maybe not *all* the time," I said.

Connie looked pained. Kidnapping wasn't actually allowed. We could detain and transport people if we had the right documentation.

"If you stop flopping around we'll stand you up and sit you on a chair," I told him.

"We'll even pull your pants up, so we don't have to look at Mr. Droopy hanging out," Lula said. "I've seen enough of Mr. Droopy to last a long time. It's not that great."

We dragged him to his feet, pulled his

pants up, and plopped him onto one of the wooden kitchen chairs, securing him with a length of rope that we wrapped and knotted around his chest and the chair back.

"You're at our mercy now," Lula said. "You're going to tell us what we want to know."

"Yeah, right. I'm real scared."

"You should be scared. If you don't start talking about Junkman, I'm gonna hit you one."

Ward gave a bark of laughter.

"Okay, that's it. I guess we have to persuade you," Lula said. "Go ahead, Stephanie, make him talk."

"What?"

"Go ahead and hurt him. Slap him around."

"You're going to have to excuse us for a moment," I said to Ward. "I need to talk to my associates in private."

I pulled Lula and Connie into the living room. "I can't slap him around," I said.

"Why not?" Lula wanted to know.

"I've never slapped anyone around before."

"So?"

"So, I can't just walk up to him and hit

him. It's different when someone attacks you, and you get lost in the heat of the moment."

"No, it's not," Lula said. "You just be thinking he hit you first. You just walk up to him, and you imagine him punching you in the face. And then you punch him back. Once you get started, I bet you'll like it."

"Why don't you hit him?"

"I could if I wanted," Lula said.

"Well, then?"

"I just don't think it's my place. I mean, you're the one needs to know about Junkman. And you're the bounty hunter. I'm just a bounty hunter assistant. I figured you'd want to do it."

"You figured wrong."

"Boy, I never had you figured for chicken," Lula said.

Unh. I walked back to Ward and stood in front of him. "Last chance," I said.

He waggled his tongue at me and spit on my shoe.

I made a fist, and I told myself I was going to hit him. But I didn't hit him. My fist stopped just short of his face, and my knuckles sort of bumped against his forehead.

"That's pathetic," Lula said.

I dragged Lula and Connie back into the living room.

"I can't hit him," I said. "Someone else is going to have to hit him."

Lula and I looked at Connie.

"*Fine,*" she said. "Get out of my way."

Connie marched up to Ward, squared her shoulders, and gave him a light slap.

"Jeez," Lula said. "Is that bitch slap the best you can do?"

"I'm an office manager," Connie said. "What do you want from me?"

"Well, I guess it's up to me," Lula said. "But I'm pretty rough when I get going. He'll be all bruised and bloody and cut up and stuff. We might get into trouble for that."

"She has a point," I said to Connie. "It'd be best if he didn't look too beat up."

"How about if we all kick him in the nuts," Lula said.

We repaired to the living room.

"I can't kick him in the nuts," Connie said.

"Me either," I said. "He's just sitting there. I can't kick a guy in the nuts when he's just sitting there. Maybe we should turn him loose. Then we could chase him around the house and get into the moment."

"No way," Connie said. "He already knocked me on my ass once tonight. I'm not giving him another shot at it."

"We could burn him with lighted cigarettes," Lula said.

We looked at each other. None of us smoked. We didn't have any cigarettes.

"How about if I get a stick," Lula said. "Like a broomstick. And then we could hit him like he was a piñata."

Connie and I did a grimace.

"You could really hurt someone like that," Connie said.

"So what we want to do is inflict maximum pain without hurting him?" Lula asked. "Hey, how about sticking him with a needle? I hate when I get stuck with a needle. And it only makes a tiny hole in you."

"That has potential," Connie said. "And we can stick him in places that won't show."

"Like his dick," Lula said. "We could use his dick for a pincushion."

"I'm not touching his dick," I said.

"Me either," Connie said. "Not even

with rubber gloves. How about his feet? You could stick the needle between his toes and then nobody would see it."

"I bet you got that idea from Anthony," Lula said.

"Dinner table conversation," Connie said.

We fanned out and looked for a needle. I took the downstairs bedroom and found a sewing kit in the closet. I selected the biggest needle in the kit, and I brought it into the kitchen.

"Who's going to do this?" I asked.

"I'll take his shoe off," Connie said.

"And I'll take his sock off," I said.

That left Lula with the sticking.

"I bet you think I can't do it," Lula said.

Connie and I made some encouraging sounds.

"Hunh," Lula said. And she took the needle.

Connie took Ward's shoe off. I removed his sock. Then Connie and I stepped back to give Lula room to operate.

Ward was looking nervous, and he was shuffling his shackled feet around.

"This here's a moving target," Lula said. "I can't do my best work like this."

Connie got another length of rope and tied Ward's ankles to the chair legs.

"This little piggy went to market," Lula said, touching the little toe with the tip of the needle. "And this little piggy stayed home . . ."

"Just stick him," Connie said.

Lula grabbed Ward's big toe, closed her eyes, and rammed the needle into Ward dead center between two toes. Ward let out an unearthly scream that raised every hair on my body.

Lula's eyes flew open. Her eyes rolled back into her head, and Lula crashed over in a dead faint. Connie ran into the bathroom and threw up. And I staggered outside and stood in the rain, on the front porch, until the clanging stopped in my head.

By the time I got back to the kitchen, Lula was sitting up. The back of her shirt was soaked in sweat and sweat beaded on her upper lip.

"Must have been something I ate," she said.

The toilet flushed and Connie joined us. Her hair was a wreck, and she'd washed off most of her makeup. It was a sight that was more frightening than Lula with the needle.

Ward's eyes were dilated black. If looks could kill we'd all be dead.

"So, are you ready to talk?" Lula asked Ward.

Ward shifted the death look to Lula.

"Hunh," Lula said.

We all went into the living room.

"Now what?" I asked Connie and Lula.

"He's pretty tough," Lula said.

"He's not tough at all," I said. "He's a jerk. We're a bunch of wimps."

"How about if we lock him up here and don't give him any food," Lula said. "I bet he'll talk when he gets hungry."

"That could take days."

Connie looked at her watch. "It's getting late. I should be heading for home."

"Me, too," Lula said. "I gotta get home to feed the cat."

I looked over at Lula. "I didn't know you adopted a cat."

"It's more like I'm thinking about it," Lula said. "I'm thinking of stopping at the pet store on the way home and getting a cat, and then I'm going to have to feed him."

"So what are we going to do with this idiot?" Connie asked.

We swung our attention back to Ward.

"I guess we leave him here for now," I said. "Maybe we can think of something overnight."

We cut the ropes away, stood Ward up, shoved him into the bathroom, and cuffed him to the main pipe of the pedestal sink. He had one hand free, and he was within reach of the toilet. We removed everything from the medicine chest. We left the ankle bracelets in place and attached an extra length of chain to the shackle and wrapped the extra chain around the base of the toilet. Then we closed the door on him.

"This feels a little like kidnapping," I said.

"No way," Lula said. "We're just detaining him. We're allowed to do that."

"I'm thinking about changing careers," Connie said. "Something more sane . . . like being the detonator on the bomb squad."

We turned the lights out and locked up. We piled into Lula's car and left Point Pleasant.

"I never even got to play the claw machine," Lula said.

RANGER'S TRUCK WAS still parked in front of the bond office. It wasn't covered with graffiti or riddled with bullet holes. I thought that was a good sign. I got out of the Firebird and unlocked the truck with the remote. Then I stood back, held my breath, and started the truck with the remote. I blew out a sigh of relief when the truck didn't explode.

"You're in business," Lula said. "See you tomorrow. Be careful."

I got into the truck and locked the doors. I sat there for a moment in the dark, enjoying the silence, not sure what to think of the day. I was tired. I was depressed. I was appalled.

I jumped when someone rapped on the driver-side window. I sucked in some air when I saw the guy. He was big. Over six feet. Hard to tell his build in the dark. But I was guessing he was heavily muscled. He was wearing an oversize black hooded sweatshirt, and his face was lost in shadow inside the hood. His skin in the dark looked as black as the sweatshirt. His eyes were hidden behind dark glasses. He could be one of Ranger's men. Or he could be a messenger from the dead. Either way, he was freaking scary. I released the emergency brake and put the truck in gear in case I needed to lay rubber.

I cracked the window an inch. "What?" I asked.

"Nice truck."

"Un hunh."

"Yours?"

"For now."

"You know who I am?"

"No."

"You wanna know?"

"No."

Pretty amazing that my voice was staying steady, because my heart was racing, and I had a cramp in my large intestine.

"I'll tell you anyway," he said. "I'm your worst nightmare. I'm Junkman. And I'm not just gonna kill you . . . I'm gonna eat you alive. You can take that as a literal promise."

His voice was deep, the inflection serious. No smile in his voice, but I knew he was getting off on the moment. I'd run into his type before. He fed off fear, and he was hoping to see fear in my face. I was looking into his mirrored lenses, my face reflecting back at me. I decided my face wasn't showing much. That was good. I was learning from the men in my life.

"Why do you want to kill me?" I asked.

"For fun. And you can think about it for a while because I gotta cut the balls off a cop before I let myself enjoy *you*."

There was more to it than fun, I thought. He wasn't a kid. He probably got the muscle and the attitude in prison. He was brought in by the Slayers, and I thought Connie was right, Junkman wanted something from these killings besides satisfying his blood lust. Not to trivialize the blood lust. I was guessing Junkman liked to kill. Probably emasculated his victims for a show of power over the enemy, and I was betting he also liked the blood on his hands.

He gave me some kind of gang sign language and stepped back from the truck. "Make the most of your last hours on earth, bitch," he said.

A black Hummer came out of nowhere and pulled up beside me. Junkman got in, and the Hummer disappeared down the street. No chance to get the plate.

I sat perfectly still and rigid until I could no longer see the Hummer taillights. The instant the lights vanished from my field of vision, all my bravado vanished as well. Tears poured out of my eyes, and it was painful to swallow. I didn't want to die. I had more doughnuts to eat. I had nieces to spoil. If I died, poor Rex would be orphaned. And Morelli. Don't even go there, I thought. I didn't know what to think about Morelli, but I wished I'd told him I loved him. I'd never said it out loud. I'm not sure why not. Just never felt right, I guess. And I always thought I'd have lots of time. Morelli had been a part of my life since I was a kid. It was hard to imagine a life without him, but sometimes it was equally hard to imagine his role in my future. I couldn't get past two months of cohabitation with him without going nutty. Probably not a good sign.

I had a dilemma now. My eyes were leaking, and my nose was running. I was trying real hard not to progress to open-mouthed sobbing. *Stop it!* I told myself. Get a grip. Easier said than done. I was feeling vulnerable and incompetent. The vulnerable and incompetent Stephanie wanted to run to Morelli. The stubborn

Stephanie hated to give in. And the halfway intelligent Stephanie knew it would be a bad thing to leave Ranger's truck sitting in front of Morelli's house. Junkman would recognize it if he rode by, and Morelli's house would be a target for God knows what.

I took the path of mindless action. I stepped on the gas, and I let the truck take me someplace. Of course, it took me to Ranger's building. I parked in my usual spot, two blocks from the garage entrance. I reached under the seat and helped myself to Ranger's gun. It was a semiautomatic. I was pretty sure it was loaded. To say I wasn't a gun person was a gross under-statement. I wasn't sure I knew how to fire the gun, but I figured I might be able to scare someone with it.

I retreated into my hooded sweatshirt, locked the truck, and walked head down in the rain to the garage. Minutes later I was in Ranger's apartment with the door bolted behind me. I left the gun and the truck keys on the sideboard. I ditched the sweatshirt, hat, and Kevlar vest. I removed my wet shoes and socks. My jeans were soaked from the knee down, but I'd lived with them like that for the entire day, and

I could endure a few minutes more. I'd stopped whimpering, and I was starving.

I stuck my head into Ranger's refrigerator and pulled out one of his low-fat plain yogurts. No way was I going to die with a roll of fat hanging over my waistband.

I scraped the last smidgen of yogurt from the cup and looked at Rex. "Yum," I said. "I'm stuffed."

Rex was running on his wheel and didn't bother to respond. Rex was a little slow. He didn't always see the humor in sarcasm.

"Probably I should call Morelli," I said to Rex. "What do you think?"

Rex was noncommittal on the subject, so I dialed Morelli.

"Hey," Morelli said.

I gave him my smiley voice. "It's me. Sorry we had a bad connection this afternoon."

"You've got to practice your crackle. You've got too much phlegm in it."

"I thought it was pretty good."

"Second rate," Morelli said. "What's up? Are you going to tell me about Ward? It seems he's disappeared."

"He escaped from us."

"Apparently he escaped from everybody. His brother hasn't seen him either."

"Hmmm. That's interesting."

"You didn't kidnap him, did you?"

"Kidnap is an ugly word."

"You didn't answer my question," Morelli said.

"You don't really want me to, do you?"

"Jesus."

"I have something else to tell you before this conversation goes down the drain. I met Junkman today. About an hour ago. I was in Ranger's truck, parked in front of the office, and Junkman rapped on my window and introduced himself."

There was a long empty space where nothing was said, and I could feel the electric mix of emotion traveling the phone line. Astonishment that this had happened. Fear for my safety. Anger that I'd allowed contact. Frustration that he couldn't fix the problem. When he finally spoke it was in his flat cop voice.

"Tell me about it," Morelli said.

"He was big. Around six foot two. And he was chunky. It looked like muscle, but it was hard to tell for sure. I didn't get to see his face. He was wearing dark glasses. And he had a big oversize sweatshirt hood over his head."

"Caucasian,   Hispanic,   African-American?"

"African-American. Maybe some Hispanic. He had a slight accent. He said he was going to kill me, but he had to kill a cop first. He said he was doing it for fun, but I think that's just part of it. When he left he gave me a hand signal. Probably some gang thing. Definitely not Italian."

"It's almost ten o'clock. What were you doing in front of the bonds office at nine o'clock?"

"Lula and Connie and I were out looking for Ward."

"Where were you looking?"

"Around."

There was another big silence and I sensed things were going to deteriorate now, so I moved to wrap it up. "Gotta go," I said to him. "Turning in early tonight. I just wanted to check with you. And I wanted to tell you I . . . uh, like you." *Shit.* I chickened out! What was it with me that I couldn't say the big *L* word? I am such a dope.

Morelli sighed into the phone. "You are such a dope."

I returned the sigh and disconnected.

"That went well," I said to Rex. *Yeesh.*

THIRTEEN

IT WAS TEN o'clock at night, and I was
bone tired. I'd been cold and wet all day. I
had just had an embarrassing phone conversation with Morelli. And one cup of
nonfat, unfruited, unsweetened, unchoco-
lated yogurt wasn't doing it for me.

"Sometimes sacrifices need to be made,"
I told Rex. "Sometimes you have to sacrifice weight loss for the pleasure of eating a
peanut butter sandwich on worthless
white bread."

I felt a lot better after I ate the peanut
butter sandwich on the worthless white
bread, so I passed on the milk with the 2
percent butterfat and drank a glass of
Ranger's watery, tasteless skim. Am I righ-
teous, or what?

I said good night to Rex, and I switched

the light off in the kitchen. I was too tired and cold for television. And I was too grungy just to crawl under the covers. So I dragged myself to the shower.

I stood in the shower until I was pruney and toasty warm. I pulled on red bikini undies and dropped one of Ranger's black T-shirts over my head. I dried my hair, and I climbed into bed.

Heaven. Too bad the bed, the shirt, the whole comfy apartment wasn't actually mine. Too bad it belonged to a guy who could be a little scary. This brought me around to thinking about the lock on the front door. Did I throw the bolt when I came in?

I got out of bed, padded to the front door, and checked the locks. All locked. Not that it mattered with Ranger. He had a way with locks. Didn't matter if it was a deadbolt, a slide bolt, a chain. Nothing stopped Ranger. Fortunately, Ranger wasn't due home. And the average garden-variety thief, rapist, murderer, gang guy didn't have Ranger skills.

I slumped back to bed and closed my eyes. I was safe for at least a couple more days.

I STRUGGLED OUT of sleep thinking something was wrong. I was caught at the edge of a dream, and something was pulling me awake. It was the light, I thought. Dim but annoying. I'd fallen asleep and left a light burning somewhere in the apartment. Probably did it when I checked the locks. Probably I should get up and turn the light off.

I was on my stomach with my face smushed into the pillow. I squinted at the bedside clock. Two o'clock. I didn't want to get out of bed. To quote Grandma Mazur, I was snug as a bug in a rug. I closed my eyes. The hell with the light.

I was trying hard to ignore the light when I heard the faint rustle of clothing from the far side of the room. If I was a man this would have been the point where my gonads ran for cover and hid inside my body. Since I didn't have any gonads, I kept my eyes closed and hoped death came quickly.

After about twenty seconds of this I got impatient with waiting for death. I opened my eyes and rolled onto my back.

Ranger was leaning one shoulder against the doorjamb, his arms loosely crossed over his chest. He was dressed in his usual working outfit of black T-shirt and black cargo pants.

"I'm trying to decide if I should throw you out the window, or if I should get in next to you," Ranger said, not looking especially surprised or angry.

"Are there any other options?" I asked him.

"What are you doing here?"

"I needed a safe place to stay."

His mouth curved at the corners. Not quite a smile but definite amusement. "And you think this is safe?"

"It was until you came home."

The brown eyes were unwavering, fixed on me. "What scares you more . . . getting thrown out the window or sleeping with me?"

I sat up in bed, pulling the covers up with me. "Don't flatter yourself. You're not that scary." *Liar, liar, pants on fire!*

The almost smile stayed in place. "I saw the gun and the flak vest when I came in."

I told him about the death threat from Junkman.

"You should have asked Tank for help," Ranger said.

"I don't always feel comfortable with Tank."

"And you feel comfortable with me?"

I hesitated with my answer.

"Babe," Ranger said. "You're in my bed."

"Yes. Well, I guess that would indicate a certain comfort level."

His attention dropped to my chest. "Are you wearing my shirt?"

"I have to do laundry."

Ranger unlaced his boots.

"What are you doing?"

He looked over at me. "I'm going to bed. I've been up since four this morning, and I just drove nine hours to get home. Half of it in pouring rain. I'm beat. I'm going to take a shower. And I'm going to bed."

"Um . . ."

"Don't look so panicked. You can sleep on the couch, or you can leave, or you can stay in the bed. I'm not going to attack you in your sleep. At least it's not my plan right now. We can figure this out in the morning."

And he disappeared into the bathroom.

Heaven help me, I didn't want to give up the bed. It was warm and comfy. The sheets were silky smooth. The pillows were soft. And the bed was big. I could stay on my side, and he could stay on his side, and we'd be fine, right? Clearly, he didn't think my staying was a sexual invitation. We were adults. We could do this.

I turned on my side, face to the wall, back to the bathroom, lulled into sleep by the distant sound of the shower and the rain on the window.

I CAME AWAKE slowly, thinking I was back at Morelli's house. I could feel the warmth from the man next to me, and I edged closer. I reached out, and the instant my fingertip touched skin I realized my mistake.

"Oops," I said.

"Babe," Ranger said, wrapping his arms around me, gathering me close to him.

I meant to push away, but I was distracted by the scent of the sexy shower gel mingled with warm Ranger. "You smell great," I told him, my lips brushing against his neck as I spoke, my mind suddenly not totally connected to my mouth. "I thought of you every time I took a shower. I *love* this stuff you use."

"My housekeeper buys it for me," Ranger said. "Maybe I should give her a raise."

And he kissed me.

"Oh *shit*," I said.

"Now what?"

"I'm sorry. I'm having a major guilt attack over Morelli."

"While we're on the subject, why aren't you in *his* bed?"

"Same old, same old."

"You had a fight, and you moved out."

"More like a disagreement."

"I'm seeing an unhealthy pattern of behavior here, Babe."

Tell me about it. "I didn't want to move back home because Junkman was looking for me, and I didn't want to endanger my family." Plus they'd drive me crazy. "I was going to sleep in the truck, but it led me here. The GPS was on. I just followed it backwards."

"And broke into my apartment?"

"I had a key. You don't seem especially upset or surprised that I borrowed your apartment."

"With the exception of the seventh floor, the entire building inside and out is monitored. Tank called me when you pulled up to the gate. I assumed you had a good reason for needing the apartment, so I told him to let you stay."

"That was nice of you."

"Yeah, I'm a nice guy. And I'm late for work." He rolled out of bed, stood at bedside, pressed speaker phone, and hit a button.

A woman's voice came on. "Good morning," she said. "Welcome home."

"Breakfast for two this morning," Ranger said. And he disconnected.

I looked over at him. He was wearing the black silk boxers. They sat disturbingly low on his hip, and his hair was mussed from sleep. How I'd managed to stop kissing him and give in to the guilt was a mystery. Even now, I was having a hard time not jumping across the bed and grabbing him.

"What was that?" I asked, thankful my voice didn't sound as breathless as I felt.

"Ella and Louis Guzman manage this building for me. I work here, and sometimes I sleep here. That's about it. Ella makes it easy for me. She does the cooking, the cleaning, the laundry, the shopping."

"And she brings you breakfast?"

"She'll be at the door in ten minutes. I've never had a woman here before, so she's going to be curious. Just smile and endure it. She's a very nice lady."

I WAS DRESSED and had my teeth brushed when Ella rang the bell. I opened the door to her, and she bustled in carrying a large silver tray.

"Hello. Good morning!" she said, all smiles as she swept past me.

She was small and robust with short black hair and bright bird eyes. Early fifties, I thought. She was wearing bright red lipstick. No other makeup. She was dressed in black jeans and a black V-neck knit shirt. She set the tray on the dining room table and laid out two place settings.

"This is Ranger's usual breakfast," Ella said to me. "If you would like something different I'd be happy to make it for you. Maybe some eggs?"

"Thank you. This will be fine. It looks lovely."

Ella excused herself and retreated, closing the door behind herself. She'd brought hot coffee in a silver pot with matching cream and sugar, a platter of sliced fruit and berries, a small silver dish of lox, and two small pots of cream cheese. A white linen napkin covered a basket of sliced, toasted bagels.

Ranger was in the bedroom, lacing his boots. He was dressed in his usual uniform, hair still damp from the shower.

"What is *that*?" I said, arm straight, finger pointing to the dining room.

He rose out of the chair and walked to the doorway. "Breakfast?"

"You eat like this everyday?"

"Every day that I'm here."

"What about the tree bark and wild roots?"

He poured the coffee and took some fruit. "Only when I'm in a third world jungle. And I'm almost never in one of those."

"I've been eating that cardboard cereal in your cupboard."

Ranger cut his eyes to me. "Babe, I looked in my cupboard. You've got Frosted Flakes in there."

"So," I said, "is this the Bat Cave?"

"This is an apartment I keep in my office

building. I have similar buildings and apartments in Boston, Atlanta, and Miami. It turns out security is big business these days. I supply a variety of services to a wide range of clients. Trenton was my first base of operation, and it's the place I spend most of my time. My family is still in Jersey."

"Why all the secrecy?"

"We're not secretive about the office buildings, but we try to keep a low profile."

"We?"

"I have partners."

"Let me guess—the Justice League. The Flash, Wonder Woman, and Superman."

Ranger looked like he was thinking about smiling.

"Okay, forget the partners," I said. "I want to get back to the Bat Cave. Is there a Bat Cave?"

Ranger took a bagel and speared some lox onto it. "You're going to have to work harder for that one. It's not in the phone book, and GPS isn't going to take you there."

A challenge.

Ranger glanced at his watch. "I have five minutes. Tell me about Junkman."

"Not much to tell. He wants to kill me. I told you everything I know last night."

"What are you doing about it?"

"Connie and Lula and I kidnapped a Slayer. The plan was to get him to talk to us about Junkman, but we haven't had any luck."

Ranger finished his bagel and pushed back from the table to finish his coffee. "Kidnapping a Slayer is good. Why wouldn't he talk?"

"He didn't want to."

Ranger paused with the coffee cup halfway to his mouth. "You're supposed to persuade him."

"We were going to slap him around, but when we got him tied to the chair it turned out none of us could hit him."

Ranger burst out laughing and coffee sloshed out of his cup onto the table. He put the coffee down and reached for his napkin, trying not to laugh, not having a lot of luck at it.

"Jeez," I said. "I think that's the first time I've ever seen you laugh like that."

"There's not a lot to laugh about when you're knee deep in garbage. And that's where we usually operate." He swiped his napkin across the table, blotting up the coffee spill.

"If you have all this, why do you still do fugitive apprehension?"

"I'm good at it. And someone has to do the job."

I followed him into his dressing room and watched him open the locked drawer and remove a gun. I was working hard at keeping my eyes focused above his waist, but I was thinking *no underwear!*

"Do you still have your Slayer hidden away?" he asked.

"Yes."

"Is he secure?"

"Yes," I said.

"My day is filled, but we can talk to him tonight. In the meantime, don't have any contact with this guy. Don't feed him. Let him worry." He clipped the gun to his belt. "I need the truck. Use one of the Porsches. The keys are in the plate on the sideboard. The communication room and gym are on the fifth floor. Feel free to use the gym. Ella and Louis live on the sixth floor. You can intercom number six if you need anything. She'll be in today to make the bed and clean and pick up laundry. She'll do your laundry if you leave it out for her." He glanced at his watch again. "I have a meeting scheduled. I'm assuming you want to live here a while longer?"

"Yes." I didn't have a lot of good choices.

His mouth curved into the almost smile. "You're going to be indebted to me, Babe. You want to start working on that guilt problem."

Oh boy.

He grabbed me and kissed me, and I felt my toes curl. And I wondered how long it would take me to get him undressed. And just exactly how many minutes did he have before the meeting. I didn't think I needed a lot of time. After all, he wasn't wearing any undies. That would help, right?

"I have to go," he said. "I'm late."

Thank God, he was late. There were no minutes. No time to cheat on Joe. No time to send myself straight to hell. I smoothed the wrinkles from his shirt where my fingers had gripped the material. "Do you know where the truck is?"

"It's in the garage. I had Tank bring it in last night. All the cars and trucks are equipped with GPS tracking. We always know where they are."

Great. Really glad I went to the trouble to park two blocks away.

I showered and dressed and left the apartment, being careful not to run into any of the men. I suspected they were also careful not to run into me. The arrangement felt awkward.

I chose the Turbo, parking at the curb when I got to the office, so I could keep an eye on the car. It was one thing to lose a bargain-basement Lincoln; I didn't want to get a bunch of unnecessary holes in Ranger's megabucks Porsche.

"Holy crap," Lula said, staring out the window at the Porsche. "Is that Ranger's Turbo?"

"Yes. He's back, and he needed the truck, so he gave me the 911. He's going to talk to our friend tonight. He said we shouldn't have any contact with him. And he didn't want us to feed him."

"Fine by me," Connie said. "I'm not anxious to repeat yesterday's performance."

"Yeah," Lula said. "That was embarrassing."

"Anything new on the books?" I asked.

"No, but you have three outstandings," Connie said. "Shoshanna Brown, Harold Pancek, and the thumb guy, Jamil Rodriguez. Maybe you want to leave Rodriguez for Ranger."

"We'll see how it goes," I said. "I'm going to pick up Shoshanna Brown this morning."

Lula looked at me hopefully. "Need any help?"

"Not with Brown. I've picked her up before. She's usually cooperative." And to make things even easier, I'd chosen the flashy Turbo. Shoshanna would be at home smoking weed in her rattrap apartment, watching the Travel Channel on her stolen television, and she'd happily trade her freedom for a ride in the Porsche.

Shoshanna lived in the projects on the other side of town. I took Hamilton to Olden and wound my way around, avoiding known Slayer territory. I parked in front of Shoshanna's building and called her. Ordinarily, I'd march up to Shoshanna's front door and encourage her to come with me in person. If I did that today, alone and in the Porsche, the car would be gone the instant I turned my back.

"Yeah, what?" Shoshanna said, answering the phone.

"It's Stephanie Plum. I want you to look out your front window."

"This better be good. I'm watching a show on the best bathrooms in Vegas."

"I came to take you for a ride in Ranger's Turbo."

"Are you shitting me? The Porsche? You came to pick me up in the Porsche? Hold on. I'll be right out. I just gotta put on some lipstick for my new photo. I've been waiting for you anyway. I'm hoping I get sent to the workhouse on account of I got a tooth that's killing me, and they got a good dentist there. I won't have to pay for it or nothing."

Two minutes later, Shoshanna burst out of her apartment and angled herself into the Porsche. "Now this is class," she said. "I hope some of my neighbors are watching. I don't suppose you could drive me past my friend Latisha Anne's apartment so she could see?"

I drove Shoshanna past Latisha Anne's apartment, Shirelle Marie's apartment, and Lucy Sue's apartment. And then I drove her to jail.

Shoshanna was cuffed to the bench

when I left with my paperwork.
"Thanks," she said. "See you next time."

"You might want to think about staying out of trouble."

"It's no *problemo*," she said. "I only get caught when I need dental."

Morelli was waiting for me outside. "Nice car," he said.

"I borrowed it from Ranger to get Shoshanna. She jumped right in."

"Clever."

I was choking on guilt. My throat was dry and my chest was hot. I could feel sweat beginning to prickle at the roots of my hair. I happen to be excellent at rationalizing away acts of dumbness, but this one had me for a loss. I'd slept with Ranger! Not sexually, of course. But I'd been in his bed. And then there was the evil shower gel. And the kisses. And heaven help me, there'd been desire. A lot of desire.

"It was all because of the shower gel," I said.

Morelli's eyes narrowed. "Shower gel?"

I made a major effort not to sigh. "Long story. You probably don't want to hear it. Out of morbid curiosity, what sort of a relationship do we have?"

"It looks to me like we're in the *off* stage of *on again, off again.* Or maybe we're still *on again* . . . but in a remote sort of way."

"Suppose I wanted to change it to full-time *on again*?"

"For starters, you'd have to get a new job. Or even better, no job at all."

"No job?"

"You could be a housewife," Morelli said.

Our eyes locked in stunned disbelief that he'd suggested such a thing.

"Okay, maybe not a housewife," Morelli said.

I sensed a slur on my ability to house-wife. "I could be a housewife if I wanted. I'd be a good one, too."

"Sure you would," Morelli said. "Eventually. Maybe."

"It's just that I was surprised because marriage is usually a prerequisite to being a housewife."

"Yeah," Morelli said. "Isn't that a frightening thought?"

LULA AND CONNIE had their noses pressed against the front window when I got out of Ranger's Cayenne.

"Where's the Turbo? What happened to the Turbo?" Lula wanted to know. "You didn't destroy the Turbo, did you?"

I gave Connie the body receipt. "The Turbo is fine. I swapped it out after I dropped Shoshanna at the police station. It was good for luring Shoshanna out of her house, but it didn't suit my purposes for this afternoon. I thought we'd go looking for Pancek again, and we need a backseat in case we get lucky."

I was standing with my back to the door, and I saw Connie's eyes go wide.

"Be still my heart," Lula said, looking past me, through the window to the side-walk.

I figured they were looking at either Johnny Depp or Ranger. My money was on Ranger.

The door opened, and I glanced over my shoulder, just in case, not wanting to miss Johnny Depp. But then not entirely disappointed when it turned out to be Ranger.

He crossed the room and stood close behind me, his hand at my back, heating the skin beneath his touch.

"Tank said you wanted me to stop by," he said to Connie.

Connie took the Jamil Rodriguez file from her desktop. "I originally gave this to Stephanie, but she's got a lot on her plate right now."

Ranger took the file and flipped through it. "I know this guy. The thumb belongs to Hector Santinni. Santinni stiffed Rodriguez on a drug sale, so Rodriguez chopped Santanni's thumb off and put it in a jar of formaldehyde. Rodriguez carries the thumb everywhere. Thinks the thumb gives him an edge."

"So much for the edge," Connie said. "The police have the thumb."

"A lot more where that came from," Ranger said. His hand moved to the base of my neck. "Your call, Babe," he said to me. "Do you want him?"

"Is he a gang guy?"

"No. He's an independent nut case."

"I'll keep him."

"He's probably looking for a new thumb," Ranger said. "So be careful. Most afternoons you can find him at the bar on the corner of Third and Laramie."

His fingertips trailed the length of my spine, triggering feelings I was determined to ignore. And he was gone.

"Damn," Lula said, doing thumbs up,

eyes fixed on the thumbs. "I don't know if I want to go after a guy who's going big game hunting for a thumb. I'm real attached to mine."

I made chicken sounds and did wing flaps.

"Hunh," Lula said. "Smart-ass. What makes you so brave all of a sudden?"

For starters, every move I made in the Cayenne was tracked at RangeMan Central. And if that wasn't enough, I suspected I was being followed. Ranger and Morelli always ran neck and neck in the *vote of no confidence* race. The only difference being in the level of sneakiness. Ranger always won out on sneaky. When there's a code-red danger alert, Morelli rants and raves and tries to lock me away. Ranger just assigns a goon to watch over me. Sometimes the goons are visible. Sometimes the goons are invisible. Whatever the state of visibility, they stick to me like glue, preferring death to the hideous task of informing Ranger they've lost me.

I turned and looked out the window in time to see Ranger pull away in the big bad truck. A shiny black SUV with tinted windows was left idling at curbside behind the Cayenne. "That's what makes me so brave," I said.

"Hunh," Lula said, following my eyes to the SUV. "I knew that."

Lula and I left the bonds office and climbed into the Cayenne. "I thought we'd drive past Pancek's house first," I said. "See if he's returned."

"Are you gonna try to lose the SUV?"

"I can't lose the SUV as long as I'm in this car. It's hooked into a GPS tracking system."

"I bet there's a way to disable it," Lula said. "This is one of Ranger's personal cars, and I bet there's times Ranger doesn't want anyone to know where he's going."

I'd had the same thought, but for now I didn't want to disable the system. And I didn't want to lose my bodyguard. I had the flak vest and sweatshirt in the backseat and Ranger's loaded gun in my purse. I thought I was relatively safe until Junkman made his third hit, but I wasn't taking unnecessary chances.

I glanced back at the SUV. "To tell you the truth, I'm happy to have the added protection."

"I hear you," Lula said.

I drove a block down Hamilton, left-turned into the Burg, and followed the maze of streets that led to Canter. I didn't see the blue Honda Civic parked anywhere near Pancek's apartment. I parked two houses down, put my Kevlar vest on under the sweatshirt, got out of the car, and walked to Pancek's door. I rang the bell. No answer. I rang two more times and returned to the car.

"No luck," I told Lula.

"Are we going back to Newark?"

"Not today. Ranger told me where I can find Rodriguez. I thought I'd go after him while I have an escort."

"On the one hand, that sounds good," Lula said. "Like, we got some help if we need it. On the other hand, if we screw up we got a witness laughing his ass off."

Lula had a point. "Maybe we won't screw up."

"I just hope it's not Tank back there. I wouldn't mind taking Tank home with me someday, and it would put a crimp in my plans to embarrass myself with a lame bust."

The SUV was half a block back. Too far for us to see its occupants. We were debating the embarrassment potential when my phone rang.

"Where are you?" Sally wanted to know. "We've been waiting for twenty minutes."

"Waiting?"

"You were supposed to meet us to get your dress fitted for the wedding."

Crap. "I forgot."

"How could you forget? Your sister's getting married. It's not like this happens every day. How do you expect me to plan this wedding if you forget things?"

"I'll be right there."

"We're at the Bride Shoppe next to Tasty Pastry."

"What'd you forget?" Lula wanted to know.

"I was supposed to go for a fitting for my bridesmaid dress. They're all waiting for me. This will only take a minute. I'll run in and run out, and we can go look for Rodriguez."

"I love wedding dresses," Lula said. "I might buy one even if I never get married. I like the bridesmaid dresses, too. And you know what else I like . . . wedding cake."

FOURTEEN

I PUT THE Cayenne in gear and raced off, doubling back to Hamilton. I took the turn to the parking lot on two wheels and diagonal parked the SUV next to my mother's Buick LeSabre.

Lula and I jumped out of the car and sprinted for the Bride Shoppe. Ranger's men in the SUV barreled in after us. The guy in the passenger seat had one foot on the ground when I turned and pointed at him.

"Stay!" I said. And then Lula and I hustled through the front door.

The Bride Shoppe is run and owned by Maria Raguzzi, a dumpling of a woman in her late fifties. Maria's got short black hair and long black sideburns and fine black hair on her knuckles. She always wears a fat round pincushion on a Velcro wrist bracelet, and for as long as I've known her, she's had a yellow tape measure draped around her neck. She's been married and divorced three times, so she knows a lot about weddings.

Loretta Stonehouser, Rita Metzger, Margaret Durski, Valerie, Grandma Mazur, my mother, and the "wedding planner" were all crammed into the little showroom. Maria Raguzzi and Sally were bustling around, distributing dresses.

Margaret Durski was the first to see me. "Stephanie!" she shrieked. "Omigod, it's been so long. I haven't seen you since Valerie's first wedding. Omigod, I see you in the paper all the time. You're always burning something down to the ground."

Rita Metzger was right behind her. "Stephan*eeeee!*" she said. "Is this so awesome? Here we are all together. Is this cool, or what? And have you seen the dresses? The dresses are to die for. Pumpkin. I love pumpkin."

My mother stared at me. "Are you still gaining weight? You look so big."

I unzipped the sweatshirt. "It's the vest. It's bulky. I was in a hurry and forgot to take it off."

Everyone gaped.

"What is that thing you're wearing?" Rita wanted to know. "It like squashes your boobs. It's very unflattering."

"It's a bulletproof vest," Grandma said. "She's gotta wear one of them on account of she's an important bounty hunter, and there's always people trying to kill her."

"There's not always people trying to kill her," Lula said. "Just sometimes . . . and this is one of them times," she added.

"*Omigod!*" Margaret said.

My mother squelched a groan and made the sign of the cross.

"The fudging vest wasn't in the fudging plan," Sally said. "What the fudge am I supposed to do with this? It's gonna fudging ruin the fudging line of the fudging gown."

"It's a flak vest, not a chastity belt," I told him. "It comes off."

"Cool," he said.

"You should chill," Lula told him. "You're gonna get a embolism you keep that up."

"This is a fudging responsibility," Sally said. "I take my wedding planning seriously." He took a gown off the rack and handed it over to me. "This is yours," he said.

Now it was my turn to gape. "What happened to pumpkin?"

"The other girls are wearing pumpkin. The maid of honor has to have a different color. This is eggplant."

Lula gave a burst of laughter and clapped her hand over her mouth.

Eggplant. Great. As if pumpkin wasn't bad enough. I ripped my vest off and unlaced my shoes. "Where do I go to try this on?"

"There's a dressing room through the pink doorway," Sally said, leading the way, carrying Valerie's gown, staggering under the weight of it.

Five minutes later we were all zipped up. Three pumpkins and an eggplant. And Valerie, who was wearing enough glaring white to make everyone snow-blind. Her breasts bulged out of the bodice neckline, and the back zipper valiantly struggled to hold the dress together. The skirt was bell shaped, meant to disguise leftover baby fat. In actuality, the skirt emphasized her hips and ass.

Valerie tottered over to the three-way

mirror, took a look at herself, and shrieked. "I'm fat!" she yelled. "My God, look at me. I'm a whale. A big white whale. Why didn't someone tell me? I can't go down the aisle like this. The aisle isn't even *wide* enough."

"It's not so bad," my mother said, trying to smooth away the fat bulge at the waistline. "All brides are beautiful. You just need to see yourself with the veil."

Maria came running with the veil, draping the gauze fabric over Val's eyes. "See how much better it looks through the veil?" Maria said.

"Yeah, and if you want to really feel better, you should get a load of Stephanie in the eggplant," Lula said.

"It didn't seem that vegetable when we were looking at swatches," Sally said, eyeing my gown.

"She needs a different makeup palette," Loretta said. "Some eggplant on her eyes to balance the dress. And then some glitter under the brow to open the eye. And more blush."

"A *lot* more blush," Lula said.

"What am I doing getting married anyway?" Valerie said. "Do I really want to get married?"

"Of course you want to get married," my mother said, the panic clear in her voice, her life flashing in front of her eyes.

"Yes," Valerie said. "But do I want to get married to Albert?"

"He's the father of your child. He's a lawyer, sort of. He's almost as tall as you." My mother drew a blank after that and looked to Grandma for help.

"He's cuddle umpkins," Grandma said. "And oogieboogie bear and all them things. What about that?"

"I love this," Lula said, big grin on her face. "I thought I was gonna lose a thumb this afternoon, but here I am in the middle of cuddle umpkins' pumpkin patch." Lula turned to Sally. "What are you going to do? Does the wedding planner get to be an attendant, or something? Or do you just gotta be the wedding planner?"

"I'm singing," Sally said. "I have a lovely russet satin gown. I thought it would continue the fall theme."

"Maybe we should get the Trenton *Times* to cover this," Lula said to me. "Or MTV."

Maria had been jumping from one gown to the next, pinning and tucking. "All done," she said.

Sally took me aside. "You remember about the wedding shower, right? Friday night at the VFW hall."

"Sure. What time?"

"Seven. And it's a surprise, so be careful what you say to Valerie."

"My lips are sealed."

"Let me see you make the zipper," Grandma said. "I always like when a person makes the zipper and throws the key away."

I zipped my lips, and I threw the key away.

LULA SWIVELED IN her seat. "Ranger's guys are still back there."

It was the second time I drove past the bar at the corner of Third and Laramie. Most of the street was residential, if you can call warehousing human misery in squalid brick cubes residential. There were no public parking lots, and curbside parking was nonexistent. Half the cars parked at the curb looked like they hadn't been moved in years.

I double-parked directly in front of the bar, and Lula and I got out. I didn't bother to lock the Cayenne. Ranger's men weren't going to let anything happen to his car. I had cuffs tucked into the back of my jeans. I was wearing the Kevlar vest under the sweatshirt. I had pepper spray in my pocket. Lula was half a step behind me, and I didn't ask what she was carrying. Best not to know.

Heads turned when we entered the bar. This wasn't a place where women went voluntarily. We took a moment to allow our eyes to adjust to the dark interior. Four men at the bar, one bartender, a lone man sitting at a scarred round wood table. Jamil Rodriguez. He was easy to recognize from his photo. A medium-sized black man in a rhinestone do-rag. Cheesy mustache and goatee. A nasty scar etched into his cheek, looking like an acid burn.

He slouched back in his chair. "Ladies?"

"You Jamil?" Lula asked.

He nodded his head yes. "You got business with me?"

Lula looked at me and smiled. "This fool thinks we're gonna buy some."

I pulled a chair up next to Rodriguez. "Here's the thing, Jamil," I said. "You forgot to show up for court." And I slapped a cuff on him.

"You sit around and wait and good things come to you," Rodriguez said. "I been looking for a new thumb." And he pulled a big Buck knife out of his pocket.

The four guys at the bar were paying attention, waiting to see the show. They were young, and they looked hungry for action. I suspected they'd jump in when it was the right time.

Lula pulled a gun out of her tiger print stretch pants and leveled it at Rodriguez. And from the doorway there was the unmistakable ratchet of a sawed-off shotgun. I didn't recognize the guy in black, filling the doorway, but I knew he'd come from the SUV. Not hard to spot one of Ranger's men. Big muscles, no neck, big gun, not much small talk.

"You want to drop the knife," I said to Rodriguez.

Rodriguez narrowed his eyes. "Make me."

Ranger's man blasted a three-foot hole in the ceiling over Rodriguez and plaster flew everywhere.

"Hey," Lula said to Ranger's man. "You want to watch it? I just had my hair done. I don't need no plaster in it. Next time just shoot a hole in this punk-ass loser, will you?"

Ranger's man smiled at her.

Minutes later, we had Rodriguez in the backseat of the Cayenne, cuffed and shackled, and we were on our way to the police station.

"Did you see that hunk of burning love smile at me?" Lula said. "Was he hot, or what? Did you see the size of his gun? I'm telling you, I'm getting a flash. I could have a piece of that."

"How about a piece of this?" Rodriguez said.

"You watch your mouth," Lula said. "You're close to being roadkill. We could throw you out and run over you, and nobody'd know the difference."

I took Third to State and headed south on State. I went one block, stopped for a light, and when the light changed, Harold Pancek passed me going in the opposite direction in his blue Honda Civic.

"Holy cow," Lula said. "Did you see him? That was Harold Pancek. I'd know him anywhere with his yellow square head."

I was already in motion, making an illegal U-turn. I did some aggressive driving and got myself directly behind Pancek. Ranger's guys had been caught by surprise and were struggling to catch up, two cars back. We stopped for another light, and Lula jumped out of the Porsche and ran for Pancek. She had her hand on the passenger-side door when he looked around and saw her. The light changed, and Pancek took off. Lula climbed back into the Porsche, and I closed the gap. I was riding close on his bumper, hoping he'd get demoralized and stop. He was checking his rear mirrors, weaving around traffic, taking side streets in an attempt to lose me.

"He don't know where he's going," Lula said. "He's just trying to get away from you. I bet he's never been in this neighborhood before."

That was my guess, too. We were in a poor section of Trenton, heading toward an even worse section of Trenton. Pancek drove like a bat out of hell down four blocks on Sixth Street.

I hit the brakes when Pancek crossed Lime. Comstock was one block away. Comstock was Slayerland. I wasn't following Pancek into Slayerland.

"Do we have a cell phone number for Pancek?" I asked Lula. "Can we warn him he's in Slayerland?"

"We never got a cell for him," Lula said. "And anyway, it's too late. He's turned up Comstock."

I slowly cruised a couple blocks on Lime, hoping Pancek would pop out of Slayerland. No luck. So I turned around and pointed the Porsche in the direction of North Clinton.

When we got to the station, I left Lula with the Cayenne, and I marched Rodriguez in through the front door. I know it was moronic, but I wanted the guys to see I could capture a man with all his clothes on.

It was close to five and Morelli was gone for the day. Thank God for small favors. I didn't know what to do about Morelli. Thanks to Ranger's stupid shower gel, face-to-face meetings with Morelli were now beyond uncomfortable. Okay, let's be honest. It was more than the shower gel. It was Ranger. The man was deadly sexy.

And he was walking around without underwear. I couldn't stop thinking about it. I gave myself a mental face slap. Get a grip, I told myself. You don't really know for sure.

Just because you didn't *find* any underwear, doesn't mean he doesn't own any. Maybe they were all in the laundry. All right, so this was a little improbable. I was going to go with it anyway, because the thought of standing next to Ranger when he was commando had me in a state.

CONNIE HAD CLOSED up shop by the time I got back to the bonds office, so I dropped Lula at her car, and I returned to the RangeMan building. The black SUV followed me into the garage and parked in one of the side slots. Two of the four slots reserved for Ranger were occupied. The Mercedes and Turbo were in place. The truck was missing. I parked the Cayenne next to the Turbo, walked over to the SUV, and knocked on the passenger-side window.

"Thanks for the help," I said.

The guy in the passenger seat nodded acknowledgment. Neither said anything. I gave them something between a smile and a grimace, and I scurried off to the elevator.

I let myself into the apartment and dropped the keys in the dish on the sideboard. The sideboard also held a bowl of fresh fruit and a silver tray filled with un-opened mail.

I was in the process of selecting a piece of fruit when I heard the lock tumble on the front door. I slipped the bolt back and opened the door to Ranger.

He tossed his keys into the dish and ri-fled through the mail, not opening any. "How was your day?" he asked.

"Good. You were right about Ro-driguez. He was open for business at the bar on Third and Laramie." I didn't have to say more. I was sure Ranger had al-ready gotten a full report.

"Who's getting married?"

"Valerie."

There was a knock at the door, and Ella came in with a food tray.

"Would you like me to set the table?' she asked.

"Not necessary," Ranger said. "You can just leave the tray in the kitchen."

Ella swept past us, deposited the food, and returned to the front foyer.

"Is there anything else?" she asked.

"No," Ranger said. "We're good for the night. Thank you."

I couldn't believe the big bad Special

Forces survival nut lived like this. Clothes washed and ironed, bed made, gourmet food delivered daily.

Ranger locked the door after Ella and followed me into the kitchen. "This is ruining my image, isn't it?" Ranger said.

"All this time, I thought you were so tough. I imagined you sleeping on a dirt floor somewhere."

He uncovered one of the dishes. "There were years like that."

Ella'd brought us roasted vegetables, wild rice, and chicken in a lemon sauce. We filled plates and ate at the counter, sitting on bar stools.

I finished my chicken and looked over at the silver tray. "No dessert?"

Ranger pushed back from the counter. "Sorry, I don't eat dessert. Where are you keeping your Slayer?"

"Vinnie's house in Point Pleasant."

"Who knows about this?"

"Connie, Lula, and me."

He reached across, unzipped my sweatshirt, and released the Velcro tabs on the vest. "This isn't going to help you, Babe," he said. "Junkman shot his last two victims in the head."

I removed the sweatshirt and the vest

and put the sweatshirt back on. It had stopped raining, but it had gotten cooler.

Ranger dialed Ella and told her we were leaving. He got a utility belt and sweatshirt from the dressing room. The black nylon web belt carried a gun, a stun gun, pepper spray, cuffs, and a Maglite, plus ammo. We left the apartment, locked up, and took the elevator. There were two men waiting in the garage. I knew them both. Tank and Hal. They took a black Ford Explorer, and Ranger and I took the Porsche Turbo. Ranger was wearing the sweatshirt. The belt was in the back.

We rolled out of the garage and cut over to Broad. It was a dark, moonless night. The cloud cover was low, threatening more rain. The SUV's headlights stayed constant behind us. Ranger was silent, driving relaxed, his sweatshirt sleeves pushed halfway up his forearms, his watch catching the occasional light from overhead streetlights.

I wasn't nearly so relaxed. I was worried that Anton Ward might have escaped. And I was worried that he might still be there. "You aren't going to hurt him, are you?" I asked Ranger.

Ranger flicked a glance at me via the rearview mirror. "Babe," he said.

"I know he probably killed a couple people," I said. "But I'm sort of responsible for his safety."

"You want to explain that?"

I told Ranger how we bonded Ward out and then kidnapped him.

"Nice," Ranger said.

VINNIE'S STREET WAS totally black, not a single light burning. Ranger tucked the Porsche into the driveway, and Tank pulled the SUV in behind him.

"I can leave you in the car with Hal," Ranger said, getting the belt from the back. "Would you feel more comfortable with that?"

"No. I'm coming in."

The house was quiet, but I could feel Ward's sullen presence. He was in the bathroom, just as we left him, shackled to the toilet and sink pipe. He didn't look happy to see Ranger.

"Do you know who I am?" Ranger asked him quietly.

Ward nodded his head, checking out the belt with the gun and the Maglite. "Yeah, I know who you are."

"I'm going to ask you some questions,"

Ranger said. "And you need to give me the right answers."

Ward's eyes darted from me to Ranger and beyond Ranger to Tank.

"If you don't give me the right answers, I'm going to leave you alone in the house with Tank and Hal," Ranger said. "Do you understand?"

"Yeah, I understand."

"Tell me about Junkman."

"Nothing to tell. He's from out of town. L.A. Nobody even knows his name. Just Junkman."

"Where does he live?"

"Moves around, livin' with the bitches. Always got a new bitch. We're not exactly best friends, you know? Like I don't know his bitches."

"What's the deal with the killing? What's the list about?"

"Hey, man, I can't talk to you about these things. I'm a brother."

Ranger whacked Ward in the knee with the Maglite, and Ward went down like a sack of sand.

"Anybody finds out I talked to you, I'm a dead man," Ward said, holding his knee.

"You don't talk to me and you're going to wish you were dead," Ranger said.

"It's about being Five Star General. Junkman was a lieutenant in the organization out in L.A. He got sent here to take over on account of Trenton's had some leadership problems. Power vacuum after our OG Moody Black got taken out. Only thing, Junkman gotta impress the members first. He gotta eat some serious food, you know. Like he has to make some kills that count. He already took out a Second Crown of the Kings and an enforcer. What he's got left is a cop and sweetie pie, here."

"Why Stephanie?"

"She's a bounty hunter. She collected a bunch of the brothers. And it's not good to get collected by snatch. It's not got a high prestige factor. So for Junkman's last proof of worthiness the council decided he had to give the members some bounty hunter. The plan is he catches the snatch and passes it around to the members before he does her. She's part of the coronation."

My vision got cobwebby, and there was a loud clanging in my head. I staggered out of the bathroom and collapsed on the couch in the living room. My mother and Morelli were right. I needed a new job.

I heard the door to the bathroom close, and Ranger came over and squatted beside me.

"Are you okay?" he asked.

"I'm fine. It was getting boring, so I thought I'd take a nap."

This got me the almost smile. "We're done with Anton Ward. Do you have plans for him?"

"I was going to revoke his bond and put him back in jail."

"And the reason for this?"

"He agreed to wear a PTU and then refused when we got him released, escaping out the bonds office bathroom window before we could install the unit."

"I'll have Tank take care of it. We'll hold him over until tomorrow morning, so we can get the paperwork straight. Did you bring him in blindfolded?"

"He was wrapped in a blanket. It was dark and I doubt he saw much."

IT TOOK FORTY minutes to get back to Trenton and neither of us spoke. Normal for Ranger. Not normal for me. I had a lot of thoughts in my head, but almost none of them were thoughts I wanted to say out loud. Ranger parked the car, and we got out together. When we got in the elevator, he touched the number four button.

"What's on the fourth floor?" I asked.

"Studio apartments that are available to RangeMan employees. I moved one of the men out so you could have your own place until it's safe for you to leave." The doors opened to the fourth floor and Ranger wrapped my hand around a key. "Don't expect me to always be this civilized."

"I'm undone. I don't know what to say."

Ranger took the key back, crossed the hall, and opened the door to 4B. He flipped the light on, gave me the key, and shoved me inside.

"Lock the door before I change my mind," he said. "Hit seven if you need me."

I closed and locked the door and looked around. Kitchenette against one wall. Queen-size bed in an alcove. Writing desk and chair. Comfy-looking leather couch. Coffee table and television. All done in earth tones. Clean and tasteful. The bed was made with fresh sheets. The bathroom had clean towels and a basket of toiletries.

My clothes were freshly washed and folded in a wicker basket at the edge of the sleeping alcove.

I took a shower and got dressed in a clean T-shirt and boxer shorts. The boxers weren't black and silky and sexy like Ranger's. They were soft cotton. Pink with little yellow daisies. Seemed just right for spending an evening alone, pretending life was safe and happy.

It was a couple minutes after ten, so I called Morelli at home. No answer. Painful contraction around my heart, resulting from irrational stab of jealous insecurity. If I was having a hard time keeping my hands off Ranger, Morelli could be having a similar problem. Women followed him down the street and committed crimes, hoping to meet him. Morelli wouldn't have a problem finding a sympathetic body to sleep beside.

Morelli with another woman wasn't an appealing thought, so I sunk into the couch and did some channel surfing, looking for a diversion. I settled on a West Coast ball game. I watched for ten minutes but couldn't get involved. I channel-surfed some more. I looked up at the ceiling. Ranger was three floors above me. It was more comfortable to think about Ranger than to think about Morelli. Thinking about Ranger got me over-heated and frustrated. Thinking about Morelli got me sad.

I shut the television off, crawled into bed, and ordered myself to go to sleep. A half hour later I was still awake. The little room felt sterile. It was safe, but it gave no comfort. The pillow didn't smell like Ranger. And Anton Ward's words kept cycling through my brain. A tear slid out of my eye. Jeez. What was the deal with the tears! It wasn't even that time of the month. Maybe it was my diet. Not enough Tastykakes. Too many vegetables.

I got out of bed, grabbed all my keys, and took the elevator to the seventh floor. I marched across the foyer and rang Ranger's bell. I was ready to ring it a sec-ond time when he opened the door. He was still dressed in the black T-shirt and cargo pants. I was thankful for this. I thought I could manage to keep from rip-ping the cargo pants off him. I wasn't sure about the black silk boxers.

"It's lonely on the fourth floor," I said. "And your sheets are nicer than mine."

"Ordinarily I'd take that as a sexual invitation, but after this morning I'm going to guess you just want my sheets."

"Actually, I was hoping I could sleep on your couch."

Ranger pulled me into his apartment and locked the door. "You can sleep anywhere you want, but I'm not going to be responsible for my actions if you fondle me again when I'm sleeping."

"I didn't fondle you!"

WE WERE AT the breakfast table, and Ranger was watching me eat a croissant.

"Tell me the truth," Ranger said. "Were you really freaked out last night? Or did you just want my sheets and my shower gel and my food?"

I smiled at him while I chewed. "Does it matter?"

Ranger thought about it for a long moment. "Only minimally."

I'd slept on his couch, wrapped in a down comforter, my head on one of his pillows with the wonderful smooth pillowcase. It wasn't as comfy as his bed, but it had been guilt-free.

"I got some bad news while you were in the shower this morning," Ranger said. "Junkman tagged his cop."

My heart stuttered. "Anyone I know?"

"No. He was a member of the State Police Street Gang Unit. He was working locally, but he was based out of north Jersey."

I was next up.

"Junkman will get taken out," Ranger said. "There are a lot of people looking for him. In the meantime, I want you to stay in the building. If I don't have to worry about you, I can have two extra men on the street tracking Junkman."

Fine by me. I wasn't anxious to be part of Junkman's coronation ceremony. And staying in Ranger's apartment wasn't a hardship.

I poured more coffee into my mug. "You have a lot of overhead here. How can you afford to have men following me around and looking for Junkman?"

"Junkman just killed a state cop. There's a big enough reward for Junkman to justify assigning some manpower to search for him. There's no monetary way to justify a security detail to watch over you. I bleed money every time you need protection."

I didn't know how to respond. I'd never really thought about Ranger as a businessman. He'd always seemed more like a superhero, recruiting men and cars from a parallel galaxy. Or at the very least, from the mob.

"Jeez," I said. "I'm sorry."

Ranger finished his coffee and stood. "I said there was no *monetary* way to justify your security. The truth is, you're a line item in my budget."

I followed him into the bedroom and watched while he got his gun, checked it out, and attached it to his belt.

"I have you listed under entertainment," Ranger said, sliding money and credit cards into his pants pocket. "This is a high-stress business, and you're comedy relief for my entire team. Plus, I get a tax break."

My eyes opened wide and my eyebrows shot up an inch into my forehead. This didn't sound flattering. "Comedy relief?"

Ranger gave me one of his rare full-on smiles. "I like you. We *all* like you." He grabbed me by the front of my shirt, lifted me two inches off the ground, and kissed me. "The truth is, I love you . . . in my own way." He set me back down and turned to go. "Have a nice day. And remember, you're on camera the instant you leave this apartment. I've given orders to stun-gun you if you try to leave the building."

And Ranger was gone.

I was totally flummoxed. I had no idea when Ranger was serious and when he was kidding. There was no doubt in my mind that I amused him. In the past, the amusement always felt affectionate, never malicious. Being a line item under entertainment was pushing it. And what the heck was I supposed to think about the *I love you* that was qualified by *in my own way*? I was supposed to think it was nice, I decided. I loved *him* in my own way, too.

The front bell chimed, and I opened the door to Ella. She had the basket of clean clothes I'd left in the fourth-floor room.

"Ranger asked me to bring these up to you," Ella said. "And your phone is in the basket, too. It was on the night table." She collected the breakfast tray and turned to leave. "When would be a good time for me to come in to clean?" she asked.

"Whenever it's convenient for you."

"I can tidy up right now," she said. "I

won't be long. There isn't much to do today."

Not counting my mother, no one had ever cleaned or cooked for me. I wasn't in the income bracket to have a housekeeper. I didn't know anyone, other than Ranger, who had help. It was a luxury I'd always wanted, but it was uncharted territory for me right now, and it felt weird. It was one thing for Ella to come in and make Ranger's life easier while he was out catching desperadoes. It was totally different to have her cleaning up my mess while I sat around watching television.

FIFTEEN

I SOLVED THE Ella problem by helping her make the bed and straighten the apartment. She wouldn't allow me to touch the laundry, not wanting to be held responsible should I mix Ranger's blacks with his whites. Although, from what I could see, he didn't have any whites, other than sheets. We'd moved from the bedroom to the bathroom. Ella was setting out fresh towels, and I was smelling the soap.

"I love this soap," I said.

"My sister works on the cosmetic floor of a department store, and she gave me a sample of the Bulgari. It's very expensive, but it suits Ranger. Not that Ranger would notice. All he thinks about is work. Such a nice handsome young man and no girlfriend. Until you."

"I'm not exactly a girlfriend."

Ella stood straight and did a sharp inhale, focusing her snapping bird eyes on me. "He isn't paying you, is he? Like the way Richard Gere was paying Julia Roberts in *Pretty Woman?*"

"No. Ranger and I work together. I'm a bounty hunter."

"Maybe you'll *become* a girlfriend," she said hopefully.

"Maybe." But doubtful. In this case, I didn't think love and sex equated to boyfriend. "Do you take care of all his properties?" I asked Ella.

"Just this building. I take care of the apartments on the fourth floor and Ranger. My husband, Louis, takes care of everything else."

Rats. I was hoping to get a lead on the Bat Cave.

Ella gathered the day's laundry and turned to go. "Would you like me to bring lunch?" she asked. "Ranger is never at home for lunch, but I'd be happy to make you a sandwich and a nice salad."

"Not necessary," I said. "I have some sandwich things here. But thank you for offering."

I let Ella out and my cell phone rang.

"Everybody's been trying to get you," Grandma said. "You haven't been answering your phone."

"I misplaced it."

"Your sister's driving us nuts. Ever since that fitting she's been impossible. I swear, I never saw anybody with such wedding jitters. I don't want to think what's going to happen if Valerie backs out. Your mother's hitting the sauce, as is. Not that I blame her. I take a nip now and then, too, what with all the googie bear and oogiewoogie snuggy sweetie stuff. Anyway, I just called to see if you wanted to go to the shower with Sally and me. Your mother's bringing Valerie."

"Thanks," I said, "but I'll get myself to the shower." Silent groan. The shower was Friday, and I didn't have a present. If Junkman was going to kill me, let it be today, I thought. At least I'd get out of the shower.

I disconnected and dialed Morelli.

"What?" he answered. Not happy.

"It's me," I said. "Have you been trying to call me?"

"Yeah. I worked a double shift yesterday, running down leads on Junkman. It was after eleven before I got home and checked my phone. Next time leave a message, so I know you're okay. Seeing your number pop up on my caller ID and then not being able to reach you doesn't do a lot for my acid reflux."

"Sorry. I wasn't calling for anything special. And then I misplaced my phone."

"Junkman got his cop."

"I just heard."

"I'd feel better if I knew where you were."

"No you wouldn't," I said. "But you'd worry less."

"I can read between the lines on that one," Morelli said. "Be careful."

No ranting and raving. No jealous accusations. Just an affectionate *be careful*.

"You trust me," I said.

"Yeah."

"That's really rotten."

"I know. Live with it."

I could sense the smile. I was entertainment for Morelli, too.

I disconnected and called Valerie.

"What's going on?" I asked her. "Grandma says you're having a meltdown."

"I saw myself in the gown, and I had a total panic attack. It wasn't just that I was fat, either. It was everything. All the fuss. I know it's my own fault. I wanted a wedding, but it's gotten really scary. And now I have to get through a shower! Seventy-eight women in the VFW hall. Good thing there isn't a gun in the house because I'd shoot myself."

"The shower is supposed to be a secret."

"*I planned it!* What was I thinking? And what if this marriage doesn't work out? I thought my first marriage was perfect. I was clueless!"

"Albert's a nice guy. You're not going to find him in the coat closet with the baby-sitter. You'll have a nice comfortable life with Albert."

And that couldn't be said for the two men in my life, I thought. They were volatile domineering alpha males. Life wouldn't be dull with either of them, but it also wouldn't be easy.

"Maybe you should elope," I told Valerie. "Just go off and quietly get married and get on with your life."

"I couldn't do that to Mom."

"She might be relieved."

Okay, I have to admit this was self-serving, because I really didn't want to wear the eggplant gown. Still, I thought it was decent advice.

"I'll think about it," Valerie said.

"Just don't tell anyone I gave you the idea."

I hung up and went into the kitchen to say hello to Rex. I dropped a couple Frosted Flakes into his cage; he rushed out of his soup can, whiskers twitching, shoved the cereal into his cheek, and rushed back to the soup can.

Okay, that was fun, but now what? What do people do all day when they have nothing to do?

I flipped the television on and surfed through about forty channels, finding nothing. How could there be so little on so many channels?

I called the office.

"What's going on?" I asked Connie.

"Ranger was in. He's looking for Junkman. He's got a lot of company. Every bounty hunter and every cop in the state is looking for Junkman. You heard about the latest killing?"

"I heard."

"Did you also hear about Pancek? He was shot in the head last night, at the corner of

Comstock and Seventh. Somehow he drove four more blocks before he lost consciousness and crashed his car. He's at St. Francis. It looks like he's going to make it."

"My fault," I said. "I chased him into Slayerland."

"Wrong," Connie said. "You followed him to Slayerland. Since you're not here, I'm assuming you're hiding?"

"That's the plan, but it's getting old."

"Yeah, you've been at it for what, three or four hours?"

I got off the phone with Connie and shuffled into the bedroom to take a nap. I stood at the edge of the bed and couldn't bring myself to get in and wrinkle the perfectly ironed sheets. I looked to the bathroom. I'd already taken a shower. I went back to the kitchen and shook Rex's aquarium.

"Get up, you stupid hamster," I said. "I'm bored."

There was a slight rustling in the soup can as Rex hunkered in deeper.

I could explore the building, but that would involve interaction with Ranger's men. I wasn't sure I was ready for that. Especially since they might be stun-gun ready should I make a break for freedom.

I called Ranger on his cell phone.

Ranger answered with a soft, "Yo."

"Yo, yourself," I said. "I'm going nuts here. What am I supposed to do? There's nothing good on television. There are no books or magazines. No cross-stitch, needlepoint, knitting. And don't suggest I go to the gym. It's not going to happen."

Ranger disconnected.

I punched his number in again. "What was that?" I said. "You disconnected me!"

"Babe," Ranger said.

I did a sigh and hung up.

RANGER WALKED THROUGH the door a few minutes after six. He tossed his keys into the dish and did a cursory shuffle of the mail Ella had brought up earlier. He looked up from the mail and locked eyes with me. "You're looking a little crazy, Babe."

I was coming off five hours of television and two hours of hall pacing. "I'm leaving now," I said. "I'm going to the mall, and I just waited around so I could say thank you. I appreciate the use of your apartment, and I'm going to miss the shower gel big-time, but I have to go. So it would be good if you made sure no one stun-gunned me."

Ranger returned the letters to the silver tray. "No."

"No?"

"Junkman is still out there."

"Have you made any progress?"

"We have a name," Ranger said. "Norman Carver."

"Norman's not going to be at the mall. And excuse me, you're blocking the door."

"Give it a rest," Ranger said.

"Give it a rest, yourself," I said, giving him a shot to the shoulder. "Get out of my way."

All day long the car keys had been sitting in the dish. And truth is, I didn't actually believe Ranger told his guys to stun-gun me. I'd stayed in the apartment because I didn't want to die. And I still didn't want to die, but I was resenting the passive role I was forced to play. I was antsy, and I was unhappy. I wanted my life to be different. I wanted to be Ranger. He was good at being a tough guy. I was crappy at it. I was also finding it ironic that I'd walked out on Morelli only to find myself in the same position with Ranger.

I gave Ranger another shove, and he shoved back, pinning me to the wall with his body.

"I've had a long, unsatisfying day," Ranger said. "I'm low on patience. Don't push me."

He was effortlessly leaning into me, holding me there with his weight, and I was immobilized. Not only was I immobilized, I was starting to get turned on.

"This really pisses me off," I said.

He'd been out all day, and he still smelled wonderful. His warmth was oozing into me, his cheek was resting against the side of my head, his hands were flat against the wall, framing my shoulders. Without thinking, I snuggled into him and brushed my lips across his neck in a light kiss.

"No fair," he said.

I shifted under him and felt him stir against me.

"I've got the weight and the muscle," he said. "But I'm starting to think you've got the power."

"Do I have enough power to persuade you to take me shopping?"

"God doesn't have that much power. Did Ella bring dinner up?"

"About ten minutes ago. It's in the kitchen."

He pushed away from me, ruffled my hair, and went to the kitchen in search of food. The door was left unattended. The car keys were in the dish.

"Arrogant bastard," I yelled after him.

He turned and flashed me the full-on smile.

I WAS STILL at the breakfast table when Ranger came out of the bedroom wearing a fully loaded utility belt and an unzipped flak jacket. "Try not to get too crazy to-day," he said, heading for the door.

"Yeah," I said. "And you should try not to get shot."

It was a disturbing good-bye because we both meant what we said.

AT FIVE O'CLOCK Lula called on my cell phone. "They got him," she said. "Connie and me have been listening to the police channel, and we just heard that they got Junkman."

"Any details?"

"Not much. It sounded to us like he got

stopped for running a red, and when they checked him out they got lucky."

"No one was hurt?"

"No call went out."

I felt weak with relief. It was over. "Thanks," I said. "I'll see you tomorrow."

"Have fun," Lula said.

If I hurried, I could pick something up for Valerie and make the shower. I left a note to Ranger, grabbed the keys to the Turbo, and took the elevator to the garage.

The elevator doors opened at garage level, and Hal burst out of the stair-well door. "Excuse me," he said, "Ranger would prefer that you stay in the building."

"It's okay," I told him. "Code red is over, and I'm going shopping."

"I'm afraid I can't let you do that."

So, Ranger hadn't been yanking my chain. He'd actually given orders to keep me here.

"Men!" I said. "You're all a bunch of chauvinist morons."

Hal didn't have anything to say to that.

"Get out of my way," I said to him.

"I can't let you leave the building," he said.

"And how are you going to stop me?"

He shifted uncomfortably from foot to
foot. He had a stun gun in his hand.

"Well?" I asked.

"I'm supposed to stun you, if I have to."

"Okay, let me get this straight. You're
going to stun-gun the woman who's been
living with Ranger?"

Hal's face was red, leaning toward purple. "Don't give me a hard time," he said.
"I like this job, and I'll lose it if I screw up
with you."

"You touch me with that stun gun and
I'll have you arrested for assault. You
won't have to worry about this job."

"Jeez," Hal said.

"Wait a minute," I said. "Let me see the
gun for just a second."

Hal held the stun gun out to me. I
took it, pressed it to his arm, and he went
down like a ton of bricks. Hal wasn't a
bad guy, but he was dumb as a box of
rocks.

I leaned over him to make sure he was
breathing, gave him his gun back, got
into the Turbo, and motored out of the
garage. I knew the control room would
see me on the screen, and someone
would check on Hal. I hated to stun him,

but I was a woman on a mission. I needed a shower gift.

Ordinarily I'd go to the mall off Route 1, but I didn't have a lot of time, and I was worried about traffic. So I stopped at an electronics store on the way across town and bought Valerie a picture cell phone and a year's service. It wasn't a real bridey present, but I knew she needed a phone and couldn't afford to buy one for herself. I swung into a pharmacy and got a card and a gift bag, and I was in business. I could have been a little more dressed. Sneakers and jeans, a white stretchy T-shirt, and denim jacket wasn't standard fare for a Burg shower, but it was the best I could do without making another stop.

The lot was filled when I got to the hall. The big yellow school bus was parked at the edge. My mother had hired Sally and his band to entertain. JoAnne Waleski was catering. When we did a shower in the Burg, we really did a shower.

I was in the lot when my cell phone rang.

"Babe," Ranger said. "What are you doing at the VFW?"

"Valerie's shower. Is Hal okay?"

"Yeah. You were caught on camera again. The men in the control room were laughing so hard when you stunned Hal they couldn't get down the stairs fast enough to stop you from leaving the garage."

"I heard they caught Junkman, so I thought it was okay to leave."

"I heard that, too, but I haven't been able to confirm the capture. I've got a man on you. Try not to destroy him."

Disconnect.

I went into the hall and looked for Grandma. Sally was on stage, doing rap in a red cocktail dress and red sequined heels. The rest of the band was in gargantuan T-shirts and baggy-ass pants.

It was too noisy to hear my phone ring, but I felt the vibration.

"Stephanie," my mother said, "is your sister with you? She was supposed to be here an hour ago."

"Did you call the apartment?"

"Yes. I talked to Albert. He said Valerie wasn't there. He said she took off in the Buick. I thought maybe she got confused and went to the shower without me. She's been getting confused a lot lately."

"Valerie doesn't have a Buick."

"She was having problems with her car, so she borrowed Uncle Sandor's Buick yesterday."

I got a sick feeling in my stomach. "I'll get back to you."

I located Grandma and asked if she'd seen Valerie.

"Nope," Grandma said. "But she better show up soon. The natives are restless."

I went out to the lot, got the gun Ranger always kept under the seat, and put it in my denim jacket pocket. Somewhere in the lot was a black SUV with Ranger's man in it. I thought that was a good thing. And my sister was somewhere in the powder blue Buick. That was a bad thing. I was associated with the powder blue Buick. That's why I wasn't driving it. I'd thought it was safely locked up in my parents' garage. Out of sight, out of the Slayers' minds. Not to panic, I told myself. Junkman was in jail, and probably Valerie was in a bar trying to get numb enough to survive the shower. I just hoped she didn't pass out before she got to the hall.

I called Morelli.

"You've got Junkman locked up in jail, right?" I asked him.

"We've got someone locked up in jail.

We're not sure who he is. He's telling us he's Junkman, but he's not checking out. He was driving a car with California plates belonging to Norman Carver, and Gang Intelligence tells us Junkman's name is Norman Carver."

"So, what's the problem?"

"He's too short. According to California DMV, Carver's a big guy. And we got a little guy."

"No ID on him?"

"None."

"Tattoos?"

"None."

"That's not good."

"Tell me about it," Morelli said. "Where are you?"

"Valerie's shower."

"I'm assuming Ranger's got a man on you?"

"That's what he tells me."

"Poor dumb bastard," Morelli said. And he hung up.

I wasn't sure what to do next. Part of me wanted to run back to the safety of Ranger's building. Part of me wanted to go inside the hall and fill my plate with meatballs. And part of me worried about Valerie. The worrying about Valerie part was at the front of the line. Problem was, I hadn't a clue where to look for Valerie.

I saw my mother pull into the lot and park. She hurried out of the car, and I met her before she got to the door.

"I left your father at home to wait for Valerie," she said. "I can't imagine what's happened to her. I hope she hasn't been in a car crash. Do you think I should call the hospital?"

I was mentally gnawing on my fingernails. I wasn't worried about a car crash. I was worried that Valerie had been spotted by a Slayer. I was worried that they sometimes staked out places I was known to frequent. Like my apartment. Not a thought I wanted to share with my mother. I had my phone in my hand, and I was about to call Morelli back when I heard a familiar rumble. It was the sound of gas getting sucked into an internal combustion engine at an astonishing rate. It was the Buick.

Valerie swung Big Blue into the lot and parked in handicapped parking a couple feet from my mother and me. Neither of us said anything because we both thought Val qualified.

"I got lost," she said. "I left the apartment, and I had so much on my mind I guess I was on autopilot. Anyway, next thing I knew I was on the other side of town by Helene Fuld Hospital."

I got a head-to-toe chill. She'd been way too close to Slayerland. In fact, she probably passed over Comstock. Thank goodness, luck had been with her, and she'd found her way to the VFW unharmed.

Grandma appeared at the front door to the hall.

"There you are!" she said. "Hurry up inside. The band ran out of steam and had to go outside to smoke some weed. I don't know why anybody'd want to smoke weeds, but that's what they said. And worse than that, we're gonna run out of food if we don't get this crowd to sit down soon."

I still didn't feel comfortable with the Buick being out on the streets. And I especially didn't want Valerie driving it home to my apartment. "Give me your key," I said to Valerie. "I'll move the car out of the handicapped spot." Way out. All the way to my parents' garage.

Val gave me the keys, and everyone went inside. I got into the Buick and started it up. I backed out of the parking slot, and I cruised the length of the lot to the exit. I'd spotted Ranger's man parked across the street. It was a smart spot that gave him full view of the entrance to the lot and the front door to the hall. Unfortunately, he didn't have a good view of the exit, so I made a left turn out of the lot to circle the block and come alongside him. He could follow me to my parents' house, and then he could give me a ride back to the hall. Val could go home with either my mother or me.

I'd barely made the turn out of the lot when the black Hummer came out of nowhere, swerved around me and pulled in front, forcing me into a parked car. I leaned on the horn and reached for Ranger's gun, but I had two guys on me before I got the gun in my hand. I did all the things I knew I was supposed to do. Put up a fight. Make noise. And it didn't matter. In a matter of seconds, I was yanked from behind the wheel and dragged around to the back of the Buick. The trunk was opened, and I was shoved in. The trunk slammed shut, and that was it. The world went black.

SIXTEEN

I REMEMBER SEEING a nature show on television where a ground squirrel was hiding in an underground den, and a wolverine reached in and grabbed the ground squirrel. It happened so fast it was a blur on the screen. That's the way it is with disaster. In an instant your future can disappear. And nothing can adequately prepare you for the moment. There's a millisecond of surprise and then a heaviness of heart when finality is recognized.

I didn't have the gun. It had fallen out of my pocket in the scramble. And I didn't have my cell phone. My phone was in my purse, and my purse was inside the car. I'd made some noise, so there was the possibility that Ranger's man might have heard me. I didn't think the possibility was good.

There might have been a way to open the trunk from the inside, but I was at a loss. It was an old car, designed before safety features like interior-opening trunk lids. I felt around the lock area, trying to pry the lid up with my nails, trying to trip a catch that I couldn't see.

I was twisted into a fetal position, wrapped around and on top of a spare tire. I knew there had to be a tire iron in the trunk. If I found the tire iron I might be able to force the trunk open. Or I might be able to do some damage when one of the Slayers opened the trunk. Enough to give me a chance to run.

The air was thick with the smell of tire, and the total blackness was smothering. Still, the smothering blackness was better than what awaited me when the trunk was opened. More irony, I thought. I drove Anton Ward to the shore like this. And here I am being driven to my fate under the same frightening, painful conditions. The Catholic in me rose to the surface. What goes around, comes around.

I gave up searching for the tire iron. Probably it was under the tire. And try as I might, I couldn't get myself into a position to get under the tire. So, I concentrated my energies on kicking at the trunk and yelling. The car was stopping for lights and pausing at intersections. Maybe someone would hear me.

I was so absorbed in kicking and yelling that I missed the moment when the engine cut off. I was in midscream when the trunk was opened, and I looked up into the faces of the men who'd abducted me. After all my recoveries, I was on the other side.

I'd always thought in a situation like this the major emotion I'd feel would be terror, but my major emotion was anger. I'd been taken away from my sister's shower. How freaking rude is that? And on top of it, I was still dieting, and I was cranky as hell. There'd been meatballs at the shower. And sheet cake. I'd been steadily working myself into a frenzy while I was in the trunk, thinking about the sheet cake. I glared out at the faces of the degenerate losers who'd kidnapped me, and I wanted to get close enough to them to sink my thumbs into their eye sockets. I wanted to draw blood with my nails.

I was hauled out of the trunk, in full rant, and dragged across the street to a bleak vest-pocket playground. The playground equipment was skeletal, covered with gang graffiti. The ground was littered with bottles and cans and fast food wrappers. The lighting was eerie. Dark shadows and an unearthly green wash from an overhead streetlight.

The playground was surrounded by four-story brick apartment buildings. Windows were tightly shut and shades drawn on the park exposure. No one wanted to see or hear what transpired here. This was the middle of the seven hundred block of Comstock Street. This was Slayerland.

Someone had painted a large white circle onto the cracked blacktop. I was shoved into the circle, and the members gathered around, careful not to step inside. Most of them were young. In their teens or early twenties. Hard to say how many there were. Could be ten. Could be fifty. I was still in a blind rage, too crazed to count.

A big guy stepped forward, his face lost in the shadow of his hooded sweatshirt. Junkman.

"This is the circle where we try the enemy," he said. "If you're not a member, you're the enemy. We already disposed of three of the enemy. This is your night. Are you the enemy?"

I didn't say anything. His fist swung out and caught me on the side of my face. The impact cracked like a rifle shot inside my head, my teeth cut into my bottom lip, and I staggered back. A roar went up from the group and hands grabbed at me, holding fast to my jacket, tearing my T-shirt. I lurched away, sacrificing the jacket to the grabbing men, going down to one knee.

This is the game, I thought, crawling to the relative safety of the center of the circle. They can't put a foot inside the ring. Only Junkman was inside the ring. And Junkman would continue to hit me until I was dragged out of the circle by the grabbing hands. And once I was out of the circle I guessed I was at the mercy of the gang, and they would do whatever it was that crazed depraved mobs did to women.

Junkman pulled me to my feet and hit me with another roundhouse swing, the force of the blow sending me to the circle's edge. I tried to escape to the center, but one of the men had a handful of T-shirt and another had me by the hair. I was yanked over the line and hand-passed deep into the mob. And brought face to face with Eugene Brown.

"Remember me?" Eugene asked. "You ran over me. Now I'm gonna be the first to run over you."

My nose was running, and my vision was blurred by tears. Hard to say if the tears were from fright or from roiling, flaming fury. I didn't think I had a lot to lose by getting in one last kick, so I swung from the knee with as much power as I could find, and I caught Brown square in the crotch with my toe. He doubled over and went to the ground. I'd probably get raped by every other member of the gang, but I had the satisfaction of depriving Eugene Brown of the honor. I'd shoved Brown's nuts halfway up his throat. Brown wasn't going to be raping anyone for a while.

A murmur rippled through the men behind me. I was ready to kick out again, but the mob's attention had shifted to the street. Several blocks south, a single set of headlights could be seen moving forward down Comstock. There'd been no traffic on the street prior to this. Probably there were Slayer sentries redirecting cars. Or maybe no one dared to travel the street after dark. I prayed that it was Joe or Ranger or Ranger's man in the SUV. No red light flashing. Hard to tell what sort of vehicle was attached to the headlights.

Everyone was watching the approaching vehicle. No one spoke. Guns were drawn.

The vehicle was a block away.

"What the . . ." one of the men said.

It was a big yellow school bus.

The disappointment was crushing. I knew who drove the bus, and it was unlikely he could pull off a rescue. His intentions were undoubtedly heroic, but I worried that not only couldn't he save me . . . he probably was rushing to his own death.

The bus was barreling down the street at an alarming speed, bouncing and swaying, barely under control. It was surreal. It was riveting. And the mob watched in stupefied silence.

The bus went into a skid as it came abreast of the playground. It jumped the curb and plowed into the stunned gang members, brakes squealing, gang members yelling and scrambling to get out of the way.

The bus lurched to a smoking stop in the middle of the circle. The door to the bus opened with a *whoosh*, and Sally wobbled out, all long, gangly, hairy legs and knobby knees, in his red chiffon cocktail dress and four-inch red sequined heels. His hair was Wild Man of Borneo. His eyes were dilated to the size of quarters.

I had a split second of mind-numbing terror for Sally. And then I saw that he was two-handing an Uzi.

"Rock and roll," Sally said.

A bullet zinged past him and bounced off the bus. I dropped flat to the ground, and Sally squeezed off what sounded to me like about seven hundred rounds. When the dust settled there were several bloody bodies writhing in pain on the blacktop. Some had been run over, and some had been shot. Fortunately, I wasn't one of them.

Junkman had been one of those run over, his feet sticking out from under the bus like the Wicked Witch in *The Wizard of Oz*. The rest of the Slayers had scattered like cockroaches when the light goes on.

"F-F-F-Fudge," Sally said. "Freaking fucking fudge."

"Guess you were scared, hunh?"

"Mother freaking fucking fudge," he said. "I almost pissed myself."

I was surprisingly calm. My life had taken on a feature film quality. I was living *Die Hard* in Trenton. And Bruce Willis was in drag. And I wasn't dead. I wasn't raped. I was almost completely dressed. I was beyond calm. I was euphoric. The anger was gone.

Sirens and lights were flashing in the distance. Lots of headlights. It looked like everything but the Marines were on their way to the playground.

There were a bunch of dropped guns on the blacktop. I kicked them around to make sure all of the guys Sally'd nailed had a gun by him, not within reach, but close enough to believe they'd first drawn on Sally.

Two heads popped out of the bus door. The rest of the band.

"Holy shit," one guy said. And they both retreated back into the bus and closed the door.

"We were taking a break out back, and I saw them grab you," Sally said. "I couldn't get across the parking lot fast enough to stop them, so I ran and got the bus. By the time I got it started up and out of the lot you were gone, but I got to thinking about this spot. I drive by here all the time on my route, and the kids talk about it, and how this is where the beatings and killings happen."

The first car to arrive was a Trenton PD blue-and-white. It slid to a stop behind the bus and Robin Russell got out, gun drawn, eyes wide. "Holy Toledo," she said.

"I called everyone I could think of while I was driving," Sally said. "Including the fire department."

No shit. I was going to have a seizure from the flashing lights.

Ranger pulled to a stop behind Russell's blue-and-white, and Morelli was behind Ranger. Morelli had his portable *Kojak* light, flashing red, stuck to the roof of his SUV. I knew he had to have flown through town to get here this fast.

Morelli and Ranger hit the ground running. They slowed when they saw Sally and me standing in the middle of the massacre, the Uzi dangling from Sally's trigger finger.

I smiled at Morelli and Ranger and gave them a small wave.

"My heroes," I said to Sally. "Upstaged by a guy in a red dress and heels."

"Freakin' humbling," Sally said.

Robin Russell was already securing the crime scene with tape. Ranger and Morelli slipped under the tape and picked their way around the bodies.

"Hi," I said to them. "What's up?"

"Not a lot," Morelli said. "What's up with you?"

"Same old, same old."

"Yeah, I can see that," Morelli said.

"You remember Sally Sweet," I said.

Ranger and Sally shook hands. And Joe and Sally shook hands.

"Sally mowed all these Slayers," I said.

"I made sort of a mess," Sally said. "I didn't mean to run over them like this. I tried to stop, but the brakes aren't what they used to be on old Betsy. And it's friggin' hard to, you know, brake in heels. But what the hell, it turned out okay, right? All's well that ends well."

Morelli and Ranger were both trying hard not to smile too wide.

"There's a nice reward being offered on Junkman," Morelli said to Sally. "Ten big ones."

Ranger looked at the gun Sally was holding. "Do you always carry an Uzi?"

"I keep it in the bus," Sally said. "Gotta

protect the little dudes. I tried an AK-47, but it wouldn't fit under my seat. I like the Uzi better, anyway. It looks better with the dress. The AK seems too casual to me."

"It's important to accessorize properly," I said.

"Fudgin' A," Sally said.

LIKE WHAT YOU'VE SEEN?

If you enjoyed this large print edition of
Ten Big Ones, look for other Random House Large
Print books available from Janet Evanovich.

To The Nines (hardcover)
0-375-43202-7 ($27.95/$41.95C)

Hard Eight (hardcover)
0-375-43170-5 ($25.95/$38.95C)

Seven Up (hardcover)
0-375-43111-X ($24.95/$34.95C)

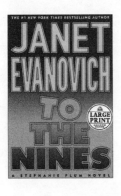  

Large print books are available wherever
books are sold and at many local libraries.

All prices are subject to change, check with your
local retailer for current pricing and availability.
For more information on these and other large print titles
visit www.randomhouse.com/large print.